TIME TO ACT

A Mercenary Tale

Anthony J Broughton

MINERVA PRESS

LONDON

MIAMI   RIO DE JANEIRO   DELHI

ISBN 0 75411 343 4

First Published 2000 by
MINERVA PRESS
315–317 Regent Street
London W1R 7YB

Printed in Great Britain for Minerva Press

TIME TO ACT
A Mercenary Tale

I would like to dedicate this book to three lovely ladies, Gracie, Doris and Iris.

Acknowledgement

I would like to thank my wife, Linda, and friends, Sal Derisi and Peter J Brown for their help and encouragement while I was preparing this book.

About the Author

Anthony J Broughton is the eldest of three boys and was born in Surrey where he lived and went to school. A keen photographer, he attended evening classes for advanced photography and was among those whose work was exhibited at Crawley public library. He enjoys comedy and is an ardent *Goon Show* fan. As a one time archivist for The Goon Show Preservation Society, he met both Michael Bentine and Spike Milligan, and was delighted to be invited to Spike's home as a dinner guest. A collector of local postcards, he also has a growing collection of old moneyboxes. Currently employed by British Aerospace as a Design Draughtsman, he has worked on Airbus, Harrier and Nimrod projects. *Time To Act* is his first published novel. With a recently completed sequel and a third book under way, he hopes to fulfil his ambition to become a full-time writer. Married, with two grown-up children, his wife is a nurse and they live in a small village in the Sussex countryside.

Foreword

In the year 2019, the nouveau 'Last of the Summer Wine' group strolled into their local watering hole and ordered three half-litres of synthetic real ale. 'Thirty Euros,' demanded the computerised drinks dispenser. 'Swipe now.' The group's 'Foggy' waves his hand in front of the machine's sensor and thirty Euros are deducted from his account at the Bill Gates Central Bank of the World. The drinks are then dispensed and the trio sit themselves down in a cosy corner and begin to reminisce. The tallest of the group asks, 'Did either of you ever read a book called *Time to Act* by Tony Broughton?' 'Tony who?' came the reply. 'Oh, never mind.' The topic of conversation changed to politics then sport, and Tony's name was never mentioned again.

I could be a member of this trio if I survive until then, and if I am, I will say that I knew Anthony J Broughton, a generally quiet man who goes about his everyday life in a businesslike manner.

Tony is interested in computers, photography and penning novels. He enjoys a fine malt whisky, a variety of musical compositions, the Goons, and he is happily married.

Tony is a decent man and good work colleague. Yes, I knew him. Hopefully, I will still know Tony in 2019.

Clive Bushrod
December 1999

Contents

List of Main Characters

Chapter I

The Mission

A woman crouched in the undergrowth. Her dark green eyes, peering from a blackened face, scanned the dimly lit area below searching for movement. The combat fatigues she wore couldn't disguise her shapely figure, but the man behind her, in similar attire, was oblivious to her femininity. He busied himself making his final checks, placing explosives and detonators in his backpack.

They were ready for the crucial part of their mission. In the clearing below, heavily camouflaged, were three wooden huts. Two housed the dozen or more rebel soldiers, who in turn guarded the important third hut: an ammunition store. The whole area was bathed in the fading incandescent glow of moonlight and all was quiet, with most of the soldiers still asleep, dreaming of the better life that their struggle against the western forces of evil might bring them one day.

'I've only seen a couple of guards wandering around,' declared Mike. 'This place is so inaccessible they're not expecting any visitors, and security's a bit lax. That's in our favour.'

It was 6 a.m. at the start of yet another warm, humid day in the African jungle, and the sun would rise within an hour. It was already hot and sticky, the quiet of the night beginning to fade, the jungle coming alive, heralding sounds of a new day.

'I guess it's nearly time?' asked Mike.

'It *is* time,' said Suzie, moving to his side and glancing at her wristwatch by the light of their torch. 'You're forever asking the time. Why don't you get yourself a watch?'

'What for? I know I can rely on you to let me know when the time's right.'

She breathed a sigh; would she ever persuade him to get a watch? She doubted it. 'Everything ready?' Suzie asked.

'I guess so.'

'Be careful,' she exhorted, helping him to strap his backpack on and picking up the Ingram sub-machine gun. She gave him a quick kiss on the cheek, and felt the roughness of his unshaven face on her lips.

He raised an eyebrow. 'I'll never wash there again.'

She playfully punched him. 'Just get in – do the job – and get your butt back here in one piece.'

Mike's face hardened. He liked to joke, but knew when it was time to be serious. 'Give me a minute to open the door. When I'm in, it should take only about three minutes to place enough timers, then I'll get out. If anything goes wrong and the alarm's raised, the floodlights will come on. Take 'em out. I'll ditch everything and make a break for it.'

Their eyes met. She nodded.

Mike took the torch from Suzie and slipped it in his pocket and, after watching the guard turn a corner, he slid down the stubble embankment where the trees and foliage had been cleared, making it more difficult to approach unseen. He crossed the dangerous, open ground to gain cover from an open-backed jeep parked outside the ammunition store.

The guard wandered back, smoking a cigarette. When he turned, Mike made his move, darting swiftly up behind him. Too late, he heard a rustle and twisted round. His eyes first showed surprise, then fear, when the commando knife plunged in, presenting the sudden knowledge that his life expectancy was nil. Mike's hand covered his mouth to muffle the anguished cries that swiftly faded to silence.

With the limp body slumped over his shoulder Mike darted to the jeep, dumping it in the back. Donning the guard's cap, he moved back to the ammunition store and examined the lock. It was secured by a crude bolt, screwed on the outside and fastened with a padlock.

'A schoolkid could get this off,' Mike mumbled, taking out his pocket knife. The screwdriver blade clicked open, and the screws were twisted out one by one.

Footsteps approached; the second guard was wandering back. Leaning on the door to hide the tampered lock, Mike bowed his head, pulled the cap down to mask his blackened face and waited, with knife at the ready.

Suzie watched; her finger tightened on the trigger, preparing for trouble.

The guard came close, holding a cigarette. 'Got a light?' he asked nonchalantly. His mouth opened in shock surprise at the unfamiliar features that looked up, and Mike's knife again found its mark, before the guard could utter a sound.

After hiding the body in the jeep, Mike glanced up at Suzie for a second, to confirm that everything was okay. He returned his attention to the lock, aware that his back was exposed to anyone unseen who unexpectedly approached. It should take only a few seconds to get into the store, but anxiety made it seem longer; feelings of almost nakedness were heightening the expectation of a bullet tearing into him at any moment. His partner, Suzie, was watching his back, and because his trust in her was total, it gave him the confidence to ignore his fears and get stuck in to the task.

From her vantage point she kept vigil, watching the seconds tick by with Mike struggling to remove the last screw. In final desperation he used his commando knife to prise the lock off slowly and gently. Suddenly the wood split and the lock came away with a crack. They both flinched and held their breaths. Mike dropped to his knees and checked that all was still quiet. It was, and he opened the door and slipped inside.

'Thank goodness for that,' sighed Suzie.

Entering the pitch-black, windowless store, Mike scanned the room with his torch. It was stacked to the roof with boxes of guns, ammunition and grenades, and was stiflingly hot. He shook off his backpack, took out the explosives and began to place them around the store, setting the timers for twenty minutes. With the back of his hand he wiped away beads of sweat that ran down his face, and scratched an irritating trickle that slid down his back.

'One blast should be enough to blow this whole lot sky high,' he said to himself. 'But I'm not taking any chances. I've got five charges. No sense in carrying any of them back. I'll prime the lot.'

Suzie pressed a button to illuminate the dial on her watch. 'Come on, Mike. For heaven's sake hurry up!'

Only two minutes had passed since he'd entered the store, but time for her ticked by slowly while she waited, crouched behind cover, watching for any sign of trouble.

Mike Randle and Suzie Drake were experienced mercenaries, though they were now known as 'Security Consultants'.

These days, the business had become legitimate and was striving hard to shake the image of white soldiers fighting on any side against black Africans solely for the money. Now it was run by businessmen like any other company, employing staff to do a job, and working only for governments or official agencies. Nevertheless, the name 'mercenaries' stuck, and still conjures up these images.

Few youngsters enjoyed their years attending school, and Mike had been no exception. Even so, he was a good scholar, always in the top five places in each of his classes, doing well at PT and sports. Nevertheless, when leaving school at sixteen, he found difficulty in securing a job that suited him. He was the outdoor type and refused to spend his working life in what he called 'a stuffy office'. After much searching, he joined the army.

By the time he fought in the battle for the Falklands, he'd risen to the rank of sergeant. As part of 2 Para he was among the first to land near San Carlos and was involved in the famous victory at Goose Green. But enjoyment at winning the battle was muted with the loss of seventeen men killed and thirty-five wounded. Mike's lack of discipline and flippant attitude towards dangerous situations and superior officers prevented him from further advancement, despite him being a resourceful soldier respected by the men.

When nearly fifteen years in the army came to an end he tried various jobs, but he lacked the skills and they lacked the excitement he was used to. Eventually, almost born of frustration, he settled on using his training another way, and became a mercenary.

The pay was much better, and if you survived – and he was a survivor – you need only soldier for half of each year to earn enough to live on comfortably. That appealed to him.

A six-feet-tall, rugged-looking man, his thick, dark hair was parted on the left and wavy at the back. Grey-green eyes, square jaw and aquiline nose gave him obvious good looks, despite his nose being broken in a barrack room brawl shortly after joining the army. He carried himself with an air of confidence, boosted by muscular features gained by years of tough army training. He was lean and exercised daily to stay that way. Being unfit and overweight was a sure way of getting into trouble in his type of work. In an emergency, speed was a top requirement. At thirty-eight, he'd yet to settle down with one woman and his relationship with Suzie was the closest he'd been to anyone.

Now, in the sweltering heat, infested with biting insects, he and Suzie carried out their mission. Much of the previous afternoon had been spent watching a helicopter ferrying arms and explosives in. Soldiers manhandled the crates carefully into the hut, unaware of the two pairs of eyes watching them.

Although the contents of the chopper was their target, Mike still admired the skill with which the pilot flew the craft. His guidance was precise, landing exactly on the spot each time, in a small space surrounded by dense jungle and trees. One wrong move would spell disaster and save them the bother of having to sneak in and blow up the arsenal. It would mean a wasted journey, but one they'd both happily settle for.

During the night, Mike and Suzie each grabbed a few hours' sleep, taking turns to watch. Now, in that time of restless slumber between sleep and waking just before dawn, they were making their move to destroy those arms.

A bank of floodlights covered the area, mounted high to give maximum coverage and ready to be illuminated at any hint of trouble.

The sky began to get lighter, turning from black to charcoal grey, as Suzie patiently waited at the edge of the clearing, where The General had his secret arms dump.

Finding it had been their first problem. Their base commander had obtained only sketchy information on the location and was relying on Mike and Suzie to track down the site. It was well hidden in the depths of the jungle, but both were experienced trackers and knew what signs to look for. They were far away from any established paths and hacked much of their way through dense terrain before locating the hideout.

Poised above that hideout, Suzie cradled the Ingram Model 10 sub-machine-gun in her arms and waited. The weapon was an old model, but its small size and light weight were a valuable asset, a major consideration when trekking any distance through difficult terrain. Few missions into enemy territory went without any hitches, and invariably someone spotted or questioned what you were doing and caused problems. But, along with Mike, she'd become tired of the killings and hoped she'd not have to use the gun – but if the situation demanded it, she would not hesitate.

Trouble was no stranger to her. As a teenager she ran away from school to travel the world, only to be brought back to Mildenhall, an approved school for girls. She hated it, with its strict rules and locked rooms. Soon after she got there, being the latest arrival, she was picked on by the school bully to make sure that she knew her place in the order of things. It was a miscalculation. Suzie refused to be bullied and she retaliated; a vicious scrap was inevitable. Both girls were bloody and bruised by the time the fight finished, but Suzie came out the winner. It was a tough lesson she learnt that day, but no one bothered her again. She was a loner, recognised the value of standing up for herself, and afterwards was always her own boss whenever she chose to be.

Escaping from the approved school, she hitchhiked to the continent, where she quickly discovered the need to be tough just to survive. Working her way around Europe and North Africa, doing any odd job she could find, led her to work as a courier for a wealthy industrialist, delivering packages locally. Her potential was recognised and gradually she became more trusted, the trips got longer and the goods more valuable. International travel with quantities of diamonds, smuggled into various countries, became her usual task. But her attractive face was becoming familiar to customs men who were asking more questions.

It was time to quit.

Her boss, unhappy about losing his courier, managed with some difficulty to persuade her to do one more trip. It was one job too many. She was stopped and searched. Customs men found stolen diamonds on her, and Suzie was sure she'd been set up. The large quantity she was supposed to be delivering wasn't there, but she held enough traceable stolen items to put her behind bars for a few years.

One day she vowed to find out the truth…

Prison was tough, but so was Suzie. Her reformatory school confrontations now demonstrated their importance. She bided her time until released on parole, pending her enforced return to England. But she wasn't about to let them dictate that to her, so she absconded and, through a chance meeting in a bar, came across a group of mercenaries who were about to go on a new venture. She joined them to elude the forces of law and order.

It was many years before she straightened things out with the English authorities over the problem of her jumping parole. Eventually, they decided that she was young, and the offence took place in another country, so she was allowed to return to England where she rented a flat in Tolworth, Surrey, less than five miles away from Mike's flat.

Suzie was a gutsy youngster with plenty of spunk, and only just into her twenties when she joined up. She was streetwise beyond her years, and that played a major part in helping her to be accepted into the dangerous job of becoming a mercenary.

She and Mike became friends on a mission that went badly wrong because of a traitor in their ranks, resulting in most of the men being killed. But they found their skills complemented each other, and their understanding helped them to be among the few who got out alive. They had remained close since that encounter, and in the following years went on missions together whenever it was possible. Suzie's mercenary exploits enabled her to hone the skills and talents she'd acquired, with Mike providing the benefits of his years of experience in the army.

At five feet nine inches she was tall for a woman, and possessed jet-black, shoulder-length hair, which she often wore tied back when on a mission. She was athletic, and her slim figure and long legs enabled her to outpace most men. Her eyes sparkled when she was happy. Her smooth skin, button nose and kissable lips made her a joy to watch. A smile transformed her face from statuesque good looks to a radiant glow of beauty and warmth that encompassed any fortunate onlooker.

Grit and determination accompanied her strong will to survive, added to good instincts and common sense that she had learnt the hard way during the difficult times in her already full life. This will to survive had helped her and Mike out of several difficult encounters, and gave them a good insight into each other's thinking. Now thirty-three years old, she'd had many admirers, but chose friends carefully. Experience had taught her to rely on only a few.

Suzie patiently watched the store and stiffened, seeing Mike leave the hut and scurry to the vehicle to gain cover; the timers were now ticking away the last minutes of The General's secret store. Mike's final and most dangerous dash, was to cross the twenty-five yards of open ground and up the sharp incline, to reach the relative safety of the undergrowth where Suzie hid. The sky was beginning to lighten, and the disappearing darkness took a lot of Mike's cover with it.

After a look revealed that all was quiet, he began his run and reached the steep incline. Scampering up the embankment, Mike had almost reached the top when two soldiers appeared by the store, spotting him. They shouted out a warning and the floodlights blazed on. Suzie broke cover and shots rang out, disturbing the quiet of the dawn. Mike fell to his face, clutching his leg as a bullet tore through it. Suzie's Ingram spat out a lethal burst, sending both rebels spinning to the ground in a hail of bullets, and the area plunged back into darkness when a second burst demolished the floodlights.

Grabbing Mike's hand, Suzie dragged him towards cover. The shots woke the camp, which came to life with shouts and movement. Soldiers emerged from their sleeping quarters and flashlights appeared.

Mike was struggling to reach the top of the bank when an almighty roar erupted. The storeroom exploded with such force that the blast threw Suzie onto her back and nearby emerging soldiers into the air.

'Shit! We've gotta get out of here,' she muttered, recovering and helping Mike to his feet. They scrambled away, amid shouts of confusion, with more explosions sending blasts of shockwaves through the air.

Mike, limping along, leant on Suzie for support as they fought their way through the tangled mass of jungle. After journeying for a couple of miles, they chanced a stop. A small clearing gave Mike the opportunity to rest for a few moments, while Suzie looked at his wound. She split open his blood-soaked trousers.

'The bullet seems to have gone through the edge of your leg and missed the bone. I don't think there's any real damage, even though it looks a bit of a mess.'

'Good. That's a relief.'

'You got your whisky flask on you?' she asked.

'I might have,' he replied defensively.

'I know you have, 'cos I've seen you taking surreptitious swigs. Come on, hand it over.'

'What for?'

'You'll find out,' said Suzie, taking the flask and pouring the contents over his wound.

'Christ! That stings. And it's a waste of good whisky. I knew you were going to do that!'

'I have to clean it to stop any infection.'

'I know. But it's still a waste of good whisky.'

Suzie ripped the arm from his shirt to bandage the wound.

'That was a good shirt,' he light-heartedly complained, watching her tear it off.

'I'll buy you another one when we get back,' she retorted. 'And I thought you were going to set the timers for twenty minutes to give us a chance to get away.'

'Yeah, I did. One must have gone off prematurely,' he suggested. 'Ouch! That's too tight. It hurts.'

'It's got to be tight to stop the bleeding. Stop being such a baby.'

Mike's pride was dented at that remark and he immediately shut up. Suzie looked at his pouting face and gave him a kiss on the forehead. 'There, there, it's all better now.'

'Gee, thanks,' Mike said sarcastically, taking a swig of what was left of his whisky and pointedly shaking the empty flask upside down for her to see. Suzie gave a gentle smile and shrugged.

The ammunition continued to ignite in the distance, sounding like a thousand firecrackers exploding, as they trekked back to their jeep. With nearly ten miles of jungle to negotiate, the going was slow because of Mike's wound. They followed their inward route but it was so dense that Suzie still had to carve through parts of it.

Reaching a high point they came across a clear patch of ground and rested. The sun had now poked its head above the horizon and shafts of light streamed through the trees. Suzie scanned the area behind them with binoculars.

'See anything?' asked Mike, spreading his jacket on the ground and sighing with relief at the opportunity to sit down and make himself comfortable.

'No, but unless they're going through one of the small clearings it's almost impossible to see anything but jungle.'

'Mmm. So why don't you sit down and rest for a while?'

'I just want to make sure there's nobody trying to track us.'

Suzie kept searching.

'Wait a minute. It's just as well I decided to take a look. We've got company. There's two men following the trail. They must be looking for us, there's nothing else around here for miles.'

Suzie lowered her binoculars and picked up the Ingram.

'We gonna wait for them here?' asked Mike, checking his pistol.

'No. I'll double back to the last clearing. I can get there first and catch them in the open.'

'Okay. Be careful,' he exhorted.

'Aren't I always?'

Mike nodded. He knew Suzie was capable and could take care of herself. She trekked back and waited.

The two unsuspecting rebel soldiers followed the trail across the clearing with little caution, and Suzie emerged behind them.

'That's far enough. Drop your guns and put up your hands,' she commanded.

After the initial surprise of discovering someone at their backs, they looked knowingly at each other and suddenly stepped apart, turning sharply with sub-machine-guns blazing. Anticipating this, Suzie had already moved aside and, with a short rapid burst, she dispatched them both.

'Why are men such idiots sometimes?' she thought. 'They hear a woman's voice and automatically think she's stupid. Well, these two won't need to worry about that any longer.'

Both wore scruffy combat gear, but one, wearing a flat cap, less so than the other, and looked more like an officer than one of the troops. Suzie searched them and found little of any value, but took their money, guns and a pocket watch from the officer.

Mike Randle heard the shots. From his hiding place in the bushes, he saw Suzie return and lowered his gun. She gave a nod and they both knew things were taken care of.

'It's unlikely there's anyone else following us so we can relax for a while. I've built up a lot of nervous energy and tension during this raid and I want to get rid of it,' explained Suzie. 'And I know just how to do that... Randy.'

She opened her jacket, revealing that she wore nothing underneath, and displayed firm pointed breasts with erect nipples. She threw the jacket on the ground next to Mike.

Stirred by this, Mike half-heartedly protested. 'You always call me Randy when you're after my body, but don't you think I should save my energy? We've a long way to go before we're out of this mess and my leg still hurts pretty bad.'

'Then we'll have to try and take your mind off it, won't we?' countered Suzie. She unbuckled both their belts and straddled him, laying the Ingram down beside them – just in case.

She bent and kissed him hard. Their tongues caressed each other and he fondled her breasts. They were both quickly aroused and spent little time in foreplay, before she mounted him and plunged enthusiastically into releasing her excess energy and tension. Making love in the open, and the possibility of danger, heightened their excitement, with the early morning sun intermittently beating down on them through the trees, swaying to and fro in the gentle breeze.

Suzie was rough in her lovemaking, ignoring Mike's injury and the hard ground they were on. All thoughts of the difficult journey ahead vanished from their minds as they moved rhythmically together in ever-increasing passion, rising to a crescendo. Suzie cried out in pleasure at the climax, sitting up and arching her back, projecting her breasts forward and enjoying the final ecstasy of feeling Mike cupping them in his hands. Slowly the passion then decreased.

They remained still for a while, basking in the glow of satisfaction and regaining their strength. Mike kissed her lovingly around the face, on her nose, eyes, chin and forehead, running his hands over her smooth body, caressing her buttocks and gently pulling her towards him, feeling greater penetration for a short time, before the excitement finally diminished in him.

When the energy subsided, Suzie rolled over and they lay for a while, feeling the warmth of the sun on their naked bodies. Mike was gratified to see that, even when lying on her back, Suzie's breasts were still firm and pointed, and he couldn't resist leaning over to kiss them, much to her delight. She caressed his face and they kissed passionately.

'I wish we could just stay here for ever,' she said.

'No chance,' he replied.

'Why not?'

'I've run out of whisky.'

Suzie chuckled. 'I wasn't really serious, but you might have found a better reason than that.'

Their short rest over, they were ready to continue the journey, with Suzie taking much of Mike's weight as he hobbled along. They rested frequently, checking for more pursuers, and several hours later were grateful to reach their jeep without any further encounters. Mike relaxed, and Suzie drove them back to their base: Camp Grey.

The route to the camp, on unmade dirt roads, was mainly through government-held territory. Even so, Suzie kept an eye out for a possible ambush, knowing that rebel troops made forays into other areas to intimidate villagers into joining them, or risk being massacred. Mike rested in the back of the jeep but kept his gun handy and his senses alert, despite looking half-asleep.

Among those greeting them on their return to the camp was a good-looking, coloured, American mercenary with a close-cropped hairstyle. He was stocky, brash and short tempered, often getting into a fight or 'barney'. It became his nickname and stuck. Barney had a chip on his shoulder. He was keen on Suzie and considered he was good enough to go out on some of the more dangerous missions with her. What he refused to accept was the good understanding that she had with Mike, which got them out of trouble on more than one occasion. Added to this, he was ten years her junior and she had no interest in him. Gently rejecting his continual advances with good humour became almost a daily ritual, but he never gave up trying.

Camp Grey was the largest of the government army camps and was the nerve centre from where the fight against The General and his rebel troops was controlled. Fighting had dragged on for several years and, in an effort to bring it to an end, both sides employed the use of experienced mercenaries, though the rebels had more difficulty in recruiting them. They could only hire them through unapproved agencies by paying large sums, stolen from the hard-working people they claimed to be fighting for.

Mike's wound proved to be not serious, but needed stitches, and the base doctor sewed him up and gave him a tetanus injection, much to his chagrin. The doctor praised Suzie for attending well to the wound in difficult conditions, and tried to persuade her to help him in the camp hospital. She declined the offer, firmly saying that she had no desire to be a Florence Nightingale.

When the doctor was through, Mike and Suzie's next stop was to make a report on the success of their mission to the camp commander.

'Well done, the pair of you! Destroying The General's arms dump should severely limit his ability to prolong this guerrilla war,' he exclaimed.

'I hope so,' said Mike. 'Too many people are getting killed.'

'Yes. But that's what it's all about. That's why we're here, to see that democracy is restored to this land. But now you both deserve a break for a while.'

'You did mention something about leave for us afterwards. I need a couple of weeks to let this leg heal properly, and our present contracts are nearly at an end.'

'Quite right. You should both take a holiday and recharge your batteries. I hope we'll see both of you back here after you've rested. We need good soldiers like you if we're going to stop The General and end this bloody war…'

Mike and Suzie listened in silence to the familiar lecture they'd heard the commander give to many recruits. Finally, he concluded, 'I'd like one of you to make a report on your mission for our files – before you leave.'

The weary pair looked at each other in exasperation. Writing a report was the last thing they wanted to do.

'My leg's hurting pretty bad. I think I should get some rest,' said Mike.

Suzie looked at him with half-closed eyes, knowing he was pulling a fast one.

'Okay, I'll do it. You'll have the report by morning,' she said.

Mike looked pleased with himself and grinned like a Cheshire cat.

After a bath and a good night's sleep, the change into civilian clothes felt good. They looked forward to relaxing for a while in a friendly atmosphere, where conflict and death didn't hang in the air like a mist surrounding them.

'I can't wait to get back to England to see Bonnie,' Mike said enthusiastically.

'I'm sure that's the main reason you're going there, really,' said Suzie, with a friendly dig.

'Bonnie is exciting... yet helps me to relax and wind down from the constant pressure in this place. Very therapeutic.'

'Stop it! You're making me jealous. I had hoped *I* might have become the most important thing in your life. Things between us have been very good lately.'

'Yes, that's true... it's a close thing... you know how I feel about you, but me and Bonnie go back a long way.'

'So you keep reminding me. Especially when I start getting close to you.'

Tickets were arranged for their flight, and Barney drove them the forty miles to the nearest airport at Roseburgh, just across the border in the nearby country of Karuna. Their car was searched thoroughly at the border checkpoint, to make sure that they weren't carrying any weapons, and their passports scrutinised before they were allowed to continue.

Posing as company representatives, to avoid the hostility that being mercenaries engendered, they caught a flight to Nairobi, where they said goodbye and parted.

Suzie went to Greece for a holiday and Mike flew home to England.

Chapter II

Zante

Following her flight from Nairobi to Athens, Suzie flew on to the Greek holiday island of Zante, where she knew Martin, the owner of a modern three-star hotel in Alykes. He was always pleased to see her and, even at the height of the holiday season, found a vacant room for Suzie to stay in.

Mike had promised to visit his Aunt Grace in Sussex and wanted to see Bonnie, but told Suzie that he might join her later if his leg healed quickly enough.

After his parents were killed in a tragic boating accident when he was five years old, their Aunt Grace adopted Mike and his younger sister, Tracy. Their father's elder sister was given custody of the children and raised them as her own.

She saw them through the school years and into their first jobs, devoting a great deal of her time to each. Despite being engaged when the tragedy occurred, she remained unmarried, and though never admitting it, suddenly having two children to look after was a big influence in this decision. Taking the place of both parents was a full-time job for many years, and she was determined that they would not miss out on the love and affection she knew her brother and his wife would have given them.

When Mike joined the army, she was a little hesitant about his decision, but realised that it could provide him with a career and was better than being unemployed.

Tracy worked in an insurance office after leaving school, and had several boyfriends before meeting Tony at a local dance club, after which they began dating. A year later they became engaged, and a further two years later were married. She was now a housewife with two children of her own and often complained to Mike that they rarely saw their uncle.

When he left the army, Mike tried to keep his new profession a secret from his Aunt Grace by telling her that he was a 'Security Consultant'. But she was too wily for him to fool for very long, and he knew she didn't approve of his new occupation. She constantly urged him to get a 'proper' job, and leave the dangers of fighting behind.

On his return to England, Mike stayed with his aunt at Silverdale Cottage, near Rye, the home he'd known for many years while growing up. Despite being isolated, Mike had enjoyed his childhood there and thrilled in playing 'cowboys and Indians' with his sister in the nearby woods. The only thing he would have liked to have changed was for his aunt to buy a television, but she didn't approve of them, and they had to make do with comics.

Grace delighted in taking regular walks with Mike through the woods whenever he stayed there. The exercise was good for both of them, and it helped to keep him fit while his leg healed. The rest of his time was taken up with Bonnie.

Grace didn't see him sometimes for hours on end. He'd disappear into the shed at the bottom of the garden to lovingly tend and service Bonnie – his Triumph Bonneville. Mike was proud of the 1977 744 cc OHV parallel twin Jubilee Special motorcycle. He rode it for relaxation, to unwind and dissipate the tension and excitement pent up in him after a tour of duty. The blue and silver, limited edition motorcycle purred through country lanes, the wind whistling past him, helping to blow away the nightmare memories of pain and death that he encountered all too frequently in his work.

Bonnie had been the biggest love of his life. But now he found that Suzie was more and more on his mind, convincing him that he was at a crossroads in his life. Firm decisions would have to be made soon – before it was too late.

On this occasion, when Mike stayed with Grace, she persuaded him to try for a job she'd seen advertised in the *Daily Telegraph*. To please her, he applied for the position of instructor at Tramer International, a private combat training school, and was surprised to be quickly accepted for a trial period. He telephoned Suzie to tell her about this new development and to say, reluctantly, that he would be unable to join her on holiday after all.

'I start the job next week, so I can't even be with you for a few days.'

'That's a shame, Mike. I was looking forward to us being together for a while and just relaxing, without having to worry about the next mission.'

'Yeah, me too. I thought we were due for some prime time together. We've got things we ought to talk about.'

'What things, Mike?'

'You know – things. We'll talk soon, and anyway it's about time I met Martin,' he said, changing the subject.

'Oh well, he's just an old school friend who's kind enough to let me stay here once in a while,' said Suzie, who was not sure that meeting him was a good idea.

'Right.'

'The weather here's scintillating,' she said, also changing the subject, 'and I'm getting a wonderful all-over tan.'

'Thanks. That helps,' sulked Mike with a touch of jealousy, picturing how gorgeous Suzie's body was, and knowing that all the men, especially Martin, would be lusting after her.

'Oh! But I envy you the chance to get away from the fighting and into a safe job. I'd like to do the same.'

'Yes, I know that, but life is going to be a bit dull… and I'll miss you,' Mike confessed, a little embarrassed.

'We'll see each other soon. You may be back quicker than you think. It may not work out.'

'That's true. I'm sure Martin will be pleased he's got you all to himself.'

'Yes, I expect so,' agreed Suzie, with a slightly embarrassed smile, wondering how much Mike had guessed about their arrangement. 'But I'd rather you were here.'

'Me too.'

'Are you going to ride to your new job on Bonnie?'

'No, I don't think so. I want to see what the place is like first. I'd hate to lose her. I'd rather leave the bike locked up, safe and sound, at Grace's. I'll probably go by train. Will you go back to Camp Grey?'

'Don't know. Not yet for a while anyway. Unlike you, I don't have anything else in the pipeline, so it may be a case of having to in the end. The money won't last for ever,' confessed Suzie.

'No, I guess not.'

'That is – when the agency finally gets round to paying us.'

'Yes, they're a bit slow, but it should arrive soon. Give me a ring before you return?' Mike asked.

'Of course. Let me know the phone number when you arrive. They don't want any female instructors at this place, do they?'

'I'll ask, but it's doubtful.'

Mike was aware that they had a good relationship without being tied to each other and knew he would see Suzie again. He still regretted being unable to join her, and considered ditching the new job and flying out to be with her. But that would upset Grace, and he didn't want that.

'What's the matter with me?' he asked himself, then answered his own question. 'I miss her, that's what's the matter with me!'

Meanwhile, Suzie went back to her sunbathing, stretched out by the bright, blue water in the hotel swimming pool, along with many other guests doing likewise. Martin made sure a lounger and sunshade was available for her every day. He spent much of the time finding excuses to speak to her, in order to drool over her shapely body, as she lay topless, soaking up the sun. Swimming was one of Suzie's loves, and she frequently took a dip in the pool, then let the sun dry her off. The rest of the time was whiled away reading a book and letting her body acquire a golden suntan. Working in the African jungle had given her and Mike suntanned faces and arms, but there was rarely any time available to relax and sunbathe. For the few women on the camp, sunbathing was frowned upon: the commander discouraged it, saying it was a distraction that the men could do without.

'Discipline is difficult enough to maintain as it is,' he told them. 'If women were allowed to run around half-naked there's no telling what problems it would cause.' If only he could see Suzie now, he'd really be shocked!

Martin knew Suzie at school before she was sent to borstal, and he had renewed their acquaintance a few years later when she stayed at the Sunshine Hotel while on a trip to Zante. His father had died suddenly, leaving him some money. He had used it wisely, and bought a rundown hotel and had it refurbished. It had cost all his inheritance, but the gamble had paid off with tourism becoming ever more popular on the island. The business had done so well that he was now expanding the hotel, having a third floor built. What he wanted most of all was a son to hand the business on to when he retired. But first he needed a regular girlfriend, a fact that had not eluded him – unlike the women in his life, who so far had.

At eleven stone and over six feet, Martin was tall and a little gangly. He considered himself a ladies' man, but never seemed to score the success that he felt he deserved. He was not unattractive, but his thin hair was beginning to recede and he was starting to get a bald patch, despite being only thirty-four years old. He dressed nattily, usually in slacks, a sports jacket, brogue shoes and a cravat tucked neatly into his crisp white shirt, which he changed at least once a day. Even in the heat of summer, he was rarely seen dressed more casually. He never sunbathed or went in the pool, saying that it was because he'd never learnt to swim, although others wondered if it wasn't that he was shy of his rather rake-like body. His character was not strong, but he was pleasant and enjoyed having Suzie stay at the hotel, parading her for the benefit of the guests as if they were a couple. She didn't object. It assured her a welcome there and a free room for a week or two, whenever she wanted. Even so, she felt obliged to spend the night with him once in a while to keep him sweet, though she omitted to tell Mike about this arrangement.

Martin was aware that Suzie saw Mike a lot, and although he wasn't sure what their work was or what relationship they had, he knew they were somehow connected to the military and were fond of each other. Though he and Mike had never met, they'd spoken once on the telephone when Martin had rung Silverdale Cottage to enquire after Suzie.

Martin frequently tried to encourage her to join him at the hotel and hinted several times that he'd like to make the arrangement permanent. While Suzie enjoyed her stays there occasionally to relax and get a suntan, it wasn't what she wanted for good at this stage in her life. She had to tread a fine line to keep Martin sweet on her without getting snared, upsetting him with an outright rejection, or spoiling her relationship with Mike. They'd been close friends for many years, but things had got more serious between them recently and she was a little worried what Mike might do or say if he ever found out that she paid Martin for her room in kind.

This time, she had a room at the rear of the hotel with a balcony overlooking the swimming pool and behind it the outdoor covered dining area. Beyond that was a panoramic view of the beach and sea, with a stone jetty pointing out towards the horizon like a long finger.

The main room had two single beds pushed together to make a double, a dressing table, chair and wardrobe, and an en-suite bathroom. Three pictures hung on the walls of the main room; one was modern, one Impressionist and one an English countryside landscape scene – all were copies. Two small rugs, to mask the cold tiled floor each morning when arising, were situated on either side of the bed, by a cabinet, with a reading lamp and a telephone.

It was October, close to the end of the season, and although there were still many guests, the hotel was not full.

A day of sunbathing and swimming over, Suzie rode the lift to the second floor and padded along to room 301. She turned the key and discovered that the door was unlocked. Martin had warned her that there'd been some thieving from hotel rooms recently, so Suzie was careful to lock it when she left. But then, the cleaner may have forgotten to lock the room, or more likely, Martin was probably waiting inside to 'try his luck' with her again.

'You here, Martin?' she called, entering the room, pulling off her sunhat and shaking the tangles out of her hair. All was quiet apart from the sounds of guests, still splashing and shouting in the swimming pool below, drifting through the air. The sliding glass balcony door was ajar with the curtains drawn to keep the room cool. Suzie threw her things on the bed and gazed around the room. It was clean and tidy, the bed had been made, and nothing looked out of place. She drew back the curtains, blinked at the bright low sun and stepped onto the balcony.

Suddenly her hair was grabbed, wrenching her head back, and an arm came round her throat. Suzie seized the arm; she tried to pull it away, but the grip was too strong. It was crushing her windpipe, making breathing impossible. She struggled to extricate herself and could feel the worsening pain in her throat, induced by the pressure relentlessly increased by the assailant, whom she could tell was a woman. Suzie thrust from side to side, trying to break the grip on her, but without success. The woman was strong and she was holding tightly on to Suzie's hair, pulling her head back and exposing her neck to the force she was applying.

Lack of air from the growing pressure on her windpipe became critical. Suzie began to feel light-headed and knew she had only a few seconds left to break the stranglehold on her before she would black out. A decisive move had to be made now, or all would be lost.

Jabbing her elbow back, she gave the woman a painful blow to the ribs and caused her to relax her grip momentarily. Grasping the opportunity, Suzie dropped suddenly to a crouching position, grasped the arm around her throat with both hands and flung the attacker over her shoulder. The move caught her by surprise and threw her off balance, but she clung on, the momentum catapulting them both forwards. They crashed into the balcony and toppled over the edge, causing the woman to relinquish her grip. Suzie snatched at the rail as they fell and grabbed the bottom of an upright with one hand. A piercing cry screamed out from the woman plunging towards the ground. She smashed through a sunshade into a table and splashed into the water.

Shrieks of horror from guests around the pool welled up in the late afternoon air. The body came floating to the surface, face down, with blood colouring the water. Looking up to see where she had fallen from, the guests saw a bikini-clad Suzie hanging from the second-floor balcony, and gasps echoed across the pool. Grabbing the rails with both hands, Suzie, close to blacking out, concentrated all her effort to pull herself back onto the balcony.

Martin heard the commotion, came rushing out and looked up.

'Oh Christ!' he exclaimed. 'Hang on, Suzie, I'll be there in a second,' he shouted, dashing back into the hotel and up the stairs three at a time.

He charged into her room, in time to see Suzie clamber over

the balcony and slump to the floor, gasping for air and holding her throat.

'Are you okay, Suzie? What on earth happened?' he asked, helping her to the bed.

'I'm not sure, Martin,' Suzie croaked. 'That woman was in my room and attacked me on the balcony. I don't know if she intended to kill me or not, but she certainly came close. God, my throat hurts. It feels like somebody's hit it with a sledgehammer.'

'You lie down. I'll get you a drink of water.'

Crowds gathered, taking a morbid interest in the tragedy. The woman's body was fished out of the pool and a blanket brought to cover it. This was the last thing any hotel owner wanted to happen, but Martin was more concerned about Suzie's well-being.

Police and ambulance were on the scene quickly. The doctor examined the body while the police inspector questioned Suzie in her room.

The fifty year old Greek policeman had granite features and, though not handsome, his bronze suntan, contrasted by a short-sleeved light shirt and muscular hairy arms, gave him an alluring appearance. He was assertive and made good use of his strong features to maximise his attractiveness.

The inspector informed Suzie and Martin that the woman was dead. Suzie explained about the sudden attack and confessed that she felt bad about her dying. The policeman was very casual about the whole incident, almost as if it were a daily occurrence.

After listening to Suzie's explanation of the incident, he questioned some of the guests before returning to her room. His easy manner and unflustered behaviour put Suzie at ease.

'I wouldn't worry too much about her death. It was clearly not your fault,' he remarked, in a deep, creamy voice. His almost perfect English, gained by years of interviewing tourists, was coloured by a pleasant, only slightly detectable Greek accent. 'I can see by the marks round your throat that you needed to defend yourself,' he said, caressing her neck.

His touch was gentle, and Suzie averted her eyes when they met. This was a man, she thought, who could charm almost any woman he took a fancy to.

'Yes, that's right,' chipped in Martin, anxious to clear her of any blame.

The inspector scribbled a few more lines in his notebook, then spoke to the doctor, who suggested that the woman was dead when she entered the water.

'She probably hit her head on the edge of the pool as she plunged in,' he surmised. 'We'll know more after the autopsy. The body's on its way to the mortuary now. From her skin colour, I would say that she was either Caribbean or African.'

The doctor, at the inspector's insistence, looked briefly at Suzie and checked the red marks around her throat, but concluded that she'd suffered no more than nasty bruising.

'That is good,' pronounced the inspector in a tactile manner which left Suzie in no doubt that he fancied her and would pursue things further, given the slightest hint of encouragement.

The dead woman was a guest at the hotel who, Martin confirmed, had arrived only the previous day.

'I think the woman was a thief,' declared the inspector. 'She may have panicked when you disturbed her searching your room, and hid. When you then went onto the balcony, she was certain to be discovered, and she attacked you to try and make a getaway without being recognised.'

Martin was happy to go along with the explanation and Suzie agreed, but privately, she doubted if it was the real reason. Nothing was missing from her room, and no other guests had reported anything stolen. The inspector, confident there was nothing more for him to do, left after asking Suzie for her home address. She gave Silverdale Cottage as her residence, an address which surprised Martin.

All traces of the incident were quickly cleared away and the pool area was soon crowded again, as if nothing had happened, much to the hotel owner's relief.

For the next few days, Martin kept an even closer eye on Suzie, saying that it was for her protection – just in case. But Suzie knew he liked to gaze at her topless figure whenever she sunbathed.

The incident worried her. Her instincts told her that there was something more to it than mere robbery. She had difficulty putting it out of her mind, and was glad of the company and attention Martin gave to her. She thought about phoning Mike to ask his opinion, but decided not to worry him.

The Sunshine Hotel, although containing sixty rooms, was still not big enough to cater for entertainment in the evenings. The nearby, much larger Brandon Hotel had eight floors, and did. Suzie spent many of her evenings there. For the price of a drink, she could watch the cabaret and see conjurers, impressionists or comedians. The hotel had a TV room where a major film was shown each evening from either satellite TV or video, and boasted a large ballroom with bar attached, where discos and the cabarets took place.

The room was usually full by the time the entertainment started, and that evening was no exception. All the tables and chairs were taken, and more guests stood around the bar and at the back of the room to watch.

Suzie wore a sleeveless halter-neck top, sandals and shorts for her evening out to see the show and have a drink. She arrived early and shared a table with an older couple who were staying at the hotel and enjoyed having facilities and entertainment laid on for them. They were friendly and chatty, telling Suzie they had stayed at the hotel every year for their last eight holidays.

It was the turn of a hypnotist that night. All watched enthralled by the performance, in the smoke-filled atmosphere, amidst the clink of glasses and bouts of laughter at the antics the volunteers performed.

While it was all good fun, Suzie wondered how many of the 'victims' from the audience really were hypnotised. She was a sceptic, and rarely took things on face value alone. Two men tried to chat her up during the evening, which was normal, but she was there only to relax and was not looking for any new involvements.

The show finished a little after ten, and Suzie wandered to the TV room and caught a film that was just starting. Randomly placed chairs were spread across the dimly lit room in front of the large projected TV screen. A spoof spy film was showing, and for the next two and a bit hours she forgot about all her problems and laughed along with a dozen or so other guests at the enjoyable fun.

Shortly before 1 a.m., with only the disco still going, she returned to her hotel. The night had become chilly and brought goose bumps to her bare arms and legs. She hurried back with arms tightly folded, and pushed through the revolving door into the lobby. Fresh from his evening rest, Martin was back on the midnight shift at the desk, still impeccably dressed.

'Hallo, Suzie. Had an enjoyable evening?'

'Yes, thanks. I saw a hypnotist and a film at the Brandon. Both were a good laugh. But it's late and time for my beauty sleep.'

'Want me to come with you and check everything's okay?' asked Martin hopefully.

'Thanks. But I'm sure I'll be all right. Goodnight, Martin.'

'Goodnight, Suzie. Sleep tight,' he replied, watching her push the lift button for the second floor.

Suzie entered her room, switched the light on and was grabbed by two men who bundled her onto the bed. A pillow was thrust against her face to mask any noise, and she thought they were going to kill her.

'Get that bloody needle into her quick, Chas. I can't hold the bitch much longer,' stated one man. Suzie struggled in vain to wrestle free from a knee digging into her back.

Chas thrust the hypodermic needle in her arm and injected the fluid.

'Okay, Ron, it's done. It's just a small dose and should calm her down but not knock her out. I'll give her a stronger one later, when we're on the plane.'

Suzie's head span round and round. She felt drunk, and could hardly sit upright on the bed when Ron released her.

'They're suntanned, but not Greek,' she thought, desperately trying to resist the drug which was rapidly taking hold of her. 'They look like tourists in their suits, but tourists don't break into your room at night and inject things into you. They remind me of Laurel and Hardy. And what's this about getting on a plane?'

Ron was thin, and his bony hands grabbed Suzie's arm. He pulled her to the dressing table and sat her on the chair, clearing a space and placing a piece of paper and a pen in front of her.

'Okay, Suzie, now I want you to be a good girl and write exactly what I tell you, slowly and carefully. Understand?'

'Yes, Ron,' replied Suzie in a flippant way, the drug taking full effect. She felt dizzy, as if she'd drunk about four strong whiskies very quickly, one after another.

'Chas, you finish packing her things and make sure you get everything,' Ron said to his partner, 'while I get silly Suzie here to write a note to keep Martin quiet.'

Chas puffed and wheezed, collecting Suzie's clothes from the wardrobe and bundling them into a suitcase, while Ron put the pen in her hand.

'Now, in your best handwriting, write: *Dear Martin, Got an urgent call and have to go. Thanks for everything. Love Suzie.*'

Grasping the pen tightly, Suzie pursed her lips and concentrated hard on her writing. When she finished, Ron picked up the sheet and scratched his head, perusing the squiggly writing, not sure whether she wrote normally that way, or not.

'I guess that'll have to do,' he said, sticking it to the mirror. 'Come on, get up,' he instructed, grabbing Suzie's arm.

'Where are we going?' she asked with a giggle, tottering against the bed.

'You're going on a jungle safari,' said Chas, grabbing the other arm and picking up her suitcase.

'Shut up, Chas. The less she knows, the better.'

He nodded. 'Okay.'

After a last look round, to make sure they hadn't missed anything, Suzie was led from the room. The empty corridor was quiet and in semi-darkness, with just a few lights glowing to show the way. Aware of the noise they were making, Chas and Ron tiptoed along, trying to keep a giggling Suzie silent and quietly march her into the lift.

'Let's hope the lobby's empty. If not, just keep moving towards the door. Don't stop for anything, and let me do the talking. Okay?' instructed Ron.

'Okay, Ron.'

'You can't be from the base. They'd just ask me to return, so you must be The General's men,' slurred Suzie, fighting the effects of the drug and trying hard to think clearly through the haze in her mind.

'Shut up, lady, or we'll be forced to carry you out,' snapped Ron.

They spilled from the lift, happy to see an empty lobby. But, hurrying across to the front door, Martin emerged from a back room behind the counter. He stepped forward. 'Hi Suzie. What's wrong?'

'She's just a bit drunk,' chipped in Ron, cursing under his breath at this unwanted intrusion. 'Had one too many. She got an urgent call and we've been sent to help her get to the airport on time. I think she's left you a note in her room.'

'I'm going on a jungle holiday,' mumbled Suzie.

They bundled into the revolving door and found that all three couldn't get through. Ron gave Chas a stare, pushed him away and went through with Suzie. Chas smiled at Martin and followed quickly. He stared after them, wondering what was going on.

A car drove up, and they shoved Suzie into the back seat and motored off. Martin stood outside and watched the lights disappear into the distance, bewildered at what he'd seen and certain something was not right.

Chapter III

Tramer International CTS

The man, dressed in combat gear, wore heavy boots, shouldered a heavy pack and carried a rifle. He sneaked through the undergrowth, treading carefully and quietly, then stepped on a twig. It snapped and he winced.

'Sod – didn't see that,' he mumbled under his breath. 'I hope nobody heard.'

He stood frozen to the spot for a full minute, his eyes eagerly scanning the dim, dank terrain, and only when satisfied that all was clear did he dare move forward again.

Then he saw him, about fifty yards away.

'There he is. I'm sure he hasn't seen me. I've got you this time,' he thought.

His target was ahead, moving surreptitiously from tree to tree for cover, before halting behind a large oak. He advanced towards him. His breathing became shallow; he was almost hardly daring to breathe at all, for fear of the noise it would make. He reached the tree without a sound, and quickly stepped round the side, dropping to one knee as he aimed his gun at... nobody – his quarry had vanished.

'Damn! Where's he gone?' he muttered.

Now he was worried. He glanced around, but his target was nowhere to be seen. What to do next? It was a question he had little time to think about. A noise behind prompted him to turn and see the man standing there, pointing a gun at him. He made a futile effort to get a shot off, but the instant he moved he heard the gun fire and felt a thud on his chest. He touched the spot with his fingers and saw they were covered in red.

'You're dead again, Jim,' pronounced the instructor, watching red paint run down Jim's jacket. 'That's the fourth time today, and you're not improving much. Perhaps you should think about skipping this part of the course. Not everyone's suited to this activity.'

'No, not yet, Mike,' he replied. 'I'm sure I can improve. I just need more time.'

'You're going to need more than that,' thought Mike. 'Some people are just not cut out to go sneaking around the undergrowth. It might help if he lost a bit of weight, but anyway he doesn't have the guile. He knows it's not for real; the adrenalin's not flowing. You need that to sharpen your reflexes.'

Mike Randle became friends with Jim Sterling when he took pity on him. He gave Jim extra help and encouragement, because of difficulties he was having with the combat training course.

'I think we'll call it a day,' suggested Mike. 'You look like you could do with a rest, and anyway it's getting late. You'll need to master the art of moving quietly through the undergrowth in daylight before you try it in the dark.'

'Maybe you're right,' Jim agreed.

It was murky, and the grey sky was gradually darkening, before finally turning black at the end of the day.

The ten acres of dense woodlands at the private combat training school where they were, served as part of the teaching course to imitate conditions of difficult jungle or heavily wooded terrain. The grounds contained an army camp for simulated attacks, a small stream across which temporary bridge-building techniques were learnt, and a firing range with bunkers where clients were taught to shoot a variety of weapons and handle explosives. Behind the wooded area was a skid track, which was available to teach driving skills in a variety of conditions, including 180-degree handbrake turns, for those whose protection included chauffeuring for their clientele. Added to the indoor gym, training of unarmed combat, lock-picking and teaching classes for arms and strategies – all was provided to give complete instructions to the clients of Tramer International Combat Training School.

'Okay,' Jim conceded. 'Let's get back. I'm starving anyway.'

'Me too,' echoed Mike, starting their return journey along the forest pathway.

Jim Sterling's uneventful career began in the Passport Office where he worked as a civil servant, a job he'd had since leaving school. Sitting at a desk all day gave him the excuse for being a little overweight, but despite this he was still quite sprightly. At thirty-nine, he'd kept his boyish good looks and, although a little below average height at five feet seven inches, he was still a ladies' man. His hair gradually darkened, from the blonde he had for the first few years, to the mousy colour it had now become. Staring at a VDU screen most of the day hadn't helped his eyesight, and for the last ten years he'd worn glasses, a feature which, with thoughtful consideration, enhanced rather than detracted from his looks.

He was clean-shaven with a round face and the beginnings of a double chin. A smile came easily to his lips, and his mischievous eyes and ready tongue were characteristics that endeared him to women. Some had tried, but none had yet convinced him of the benefits of getting married, and the relationships in his life had so far not lasted very long.

'How did you get this job, Mike?' asked Jim, the pair trundling along the pathway.

'I was soldiering in Africa, took a bullet on a mission, and flew home to recuperate. This job came along and it seemed like a good way to use my talents without getting shot at again – with real bullets anyway. I decided to give it a try. I've only been here just over a week and, to tell the truth, I haven't really taken to the job. My mind seems to be elsewhere a lot of the time.'

'Soldiering in Africa,' enthused Jim, picking up on the exciting piece of Mike's explanation. 'I bet that was great – apart from getting shot, of course. What happened?'

They left the dank smell of the wooded area behind and stepped onto the gravel pathway that led through the gardens towards the Tramer International headquarters. The building was edged by a border of flowers and bushes, and surrounded by lawns, all immaculately kept and in total contrast to the combat areas that were left to grow wild and kept boggy. This gave a good impression to clients when they first arrived, and created an understanding of why the course was so expensive.

It began to spit with rain as they approached the building, with Mike chatting about the mission, telling how his leg was injured and how he was helped back to base camp by his partner, Suzie.

'Suzie!' exclaimed Jim, with such surprise that he almost shouted the name.

'That's right, Suzie Drake. There are few women capable of taking care of themselves in such hostile conditions, but she's one of them.'

'And she practically carried you all the way back?'

'Not only that, but she dealt with two of the rebel guerrillas who were trailing us.'

'Wow! Sounds like quite a woman,' commented Jim, hurrying up the steps of the seventeenth-century stone house to avoid the rain now falling harder.

The large manor house was situated in the middle of the Hertfordshire countryside and provided lodgings and meals for clients during their training.

'What's she like, Mike?'

'Good looking, nice figure, black hair, a bit wild. She joined a band of mercenaries just to get away and do her own thing,' he said, pushing open the massive wooden front doors to the building.

Mike took a photograph from his wallet to show Jim. It was of himself and Suzie taken at Camp Grey. They wore combat clothing and each held a gun. His arm was around her waist, and he explained that the photo was taken shortly before their last mission together, when he was wounded.

Jim dumped his backpack and gun on the floor, and wiped the rain from his glasses. 'Mmm,' he exclaimed, adjusting them to feel comfortable. 'She's certainly a good looker. *I* wouldn't mind being lost in the jungle with her.'

Mike frowned at the remark but made no comment. Pictures of their rough lovemaking on that last mission flashed through his mind and brought a smile to his lips.

Jim bent to undo his bootlaces. 'Do you keep in touch with her?' he asked, with a quizzical look on his face at Mike's smile.

'I haven't seen her since that last op. She went on holiday afterwards to Zante, one of the Greek islands, to stay with an old school friend; at least that's what she says he is.'

Jim looked at Mike's expression and detected a note of uncertainty about the old school friend, and wondered what the relationship was between them all.

'When I rang her,' Mike continued, 'she was enjoying herself sunbathing topless and getting a great suntan.'

Jim gave a whistle, gazing appreciatively at the photo, trying to imagine her topless.

Snatching the picture back, Mike glanced at it once more and returned it to his wallet. 'She'd like to give up soldiering and settle down to a safer job, but I reckon she, too, would miss the excitement – just as I do. It's not easy to switch off. You get used to the challenge and the adrenalin flow.'

'Why didn't you go with her on holiday? It looks as if you're very fond of her.'

'I am. But it seemed more sensible to take this job. I'm beginning to wonder if I did the right thing. We enjoy each other's company, but like our freedom as well, though I have to confess to missing her more this time.'

Jim began to understand Mike's unease at knowing that Suzie was sunbathing topless on a holiday with an old friend. He too would be unhappy about it if it was his girlfriend there.

Pulling off their muddy boots, they placed them in the container supplied for all outdoor items, especially when they were wet or dirty, so that the immaculately kept house would remain that way.

Mike and Jim wandered across the tiled floor of the large entrance hall, beneath hanging chandeliers. They passed the entrance to the dining room and stepped up the wide carpeted stairs, enclosed by a delicately carved wooden balustrade. The portrait of the Ninth Earl of Darbie, whose family once owned the house, adorned the wall. At the top of the stairs, the Tramer International logo hung for all to see. The whole building echoed fine taste and good architecture, acknowledging that money was to be made in combat training, because enough people fancied themselves as a Rambo, or in exceptional cases a Mrs Rambo. They paid well for the privilege to play soldiers or secret agents and learn self-defence. Nearly one-third of those attending the school didn't have a genuine job requirement for the training.

At the top of the stairs, they turned left and sauntered along the central strip of carpet, covering the wooden floor of the long, oak-panelled passageway, to Jim's room. The smell of polished wood pervaded the air and reminded Mike of childhood aromas in his aunt's cottage, where she took pride in her antique furniture and polished it regularly.

'See you at dinner tonight?' questioned Jim, opening the solid wooden door to his quarters.

'Sure,' replied Mike, continuing along to his own room at the end of the passageway.

Rooms were all furnished much the same for clients. Each had a single bed, a wardrobe with a mirrored door, and a desk with a reading lamp and telephone. They were plain, furnished more for function than comfort or style. There was a bookshelf containing magazines and paperbacks, and the wooden floors were covered with hard-wearing industrial carpet tiles. The only concession to luxury was that they all had an en-suite bathroom.

Mike's room was a little more comfortable, with a double bed, a couple of rugs and a hi-fi unit. The room was bigger, to accommodate several filing cabinets for his notes and a PC.

Jim had a shower and scanned through his new clothes before deciding to wear grey flannel slacks, a cashmere sweater and a tweed sports jacket. After coarse combat fatigues and boots, it was nice to wear something comfortable with shoes that were light. He eyed his reflection in the mirror, happy with his choice. Other clients sported a variety of styles ranging from a very casual check shirt and jeans, to a smartness which seemed out of place in a combat training school, even considering the high cost involved in taking the two-weeks' course.

Tripping lightly down the stairs with a spring in his step, Jim heard the murmuring of voices and clattering of plates and cutlery from the dining room. Twenty tables were available that sat two, three, four or six, and clients grouped them together as they wished; it was where friendships were made during their stay. There were no women on the course this time, and Jim, who looked and felt a little out of place among the mainly younger and more muscular men, ended up on a table for two by himself in the corner. Mike joined him to keep him company.

Most clients were already seated and waiting for their meals when Jim entered, nodding his good evenings and making his way to the table. Mike arrived soon after, wearing corduroy slacks and a polo neck sweater.

'You're looking very smart tonight,' commented Jim.

'Why, thank you, sir. It's nice to get out of those rough clothes at the end of the day – a luxury I'm not used to,' explained Mike.

'It's steak and salad tonight.'

'Great. I'm hungry enough to eat a horse.'

Unlike breakfast, which was self-service, waiters served the evening meals. The cuisine was designed to be healthy; part of the encouragement for everyone to keep fit. The high-fibre, low-fat food that was served was not Jim's idea of tasty food. He liked pork, chips, hamburgers and other fried foods, but would have to wait until the course was finished before returning to this luxury. He always maintained that most women liked a man who was not all skin and bone, partly to ease his conscience about being a little overweight, though genuinely believing it to be true.

'I'm not the muscular type, and that's that,' he told Mike.

During dinner, Jim steered the conversation around to Mike's career in the army, and his exploits as a mercenary, enquiring about Suzie a great deal.

Mike told him numerous stories of daring deeds and near misses, many from his time in the Falklands, which got more outrageous as the evening wore on.

It continued to rain heavily outside, and the wind became stronger, lashing rain and bushes against the windows in a staccato rhythmic beat. Inside, things were snug and warm, with the gentle murmur of conversation and laughter filling the air, along with the smell of coffee wafting through the room. Few clients left, preferring instead to sit and chat together about the triumphs and failures on the course that day. Mike sat with his back to most of them and enjoyed listening in on their conversations, and smiled at the exaggerated claims of success made by some.

Jim commented on the weather, saying that he was glad to be in the dry. 'I imagine you've had to be out in all sorts of weather?'

'Yes. Including monsoon rain. That really got you wet.'

'These tales of daring exploits are fascinating, Mike. You're obviously a very versatile man, but you say you're still not sure about this job, so I'd like to put a proposition to you.'

'Go ahead.'

'I've got a problem that someone with your skills and experience may be able to help me with.'

'Go on. I'm listening.'

Jim explained that he'd recently won a lot of money on the National Lottery. With his winnings he'd bought a nice house, a comfortable car and had come on the course to give himself breathing space and learn how to handle unwanted guests. He needed to decide what direction his life would now take, which had dramatically changed since his win. It had been a rollover jackpot with him holding the only winning ticket. He was almost apologetic about scooping such a large amount and remarked that possessing it had brought problems he hadn't counted on.

'That's the sort of problem I wouldn't mind having,' declared Mike. 'Suzie and I could start a business of our own, and forget about security consultants and fighting, and the like.'

Jim sighed, 'That all sounds very well, but do you realise all the trouble it's caused me?' he said, ignoring Mike's plight. 'The begging letters I expected. I just throw all of them away because I don't know which are genuine and which are trying to con me. It's the threats I hadn't anticipated.'

'Threats?' replied Mike, disbelievingly.

'Yes. Somehow people find out where I'm living, and come knocking on the door. They think I've got more money than I need and should give them some. They get quite nasty when I tell them I can't give money to everyone who asks. They all seem to think that *they* should be the exception. I don't want to live in a fortress behind closed doors all the time, so that's why I moved to a new home in a quiet cul-de-sac in a private road in Weybridge. But some of them still find me.'

'Want another coffee?' Mike asked.

'Thanks,' replied Jim.

Mike called over the waiter and their cups were refilled. 'So you have a few nuts who want to try and squeeze some money out of you. Big deal! What do you want me to do about it – shoot them?' he said sarcastically with a chuckle.

'No, I've already done that – I want you to get rid of the bodies.'

'What!' said Mike, in a muffled cry, trying hard not to be heard, and glancing round to see if anyone was looking his way.

'Only kidding, Mike! But there have been threats to me, personally, and I've had my car damaged because I said no. It's expensive getting a Rolls Royce repaired. Not that I can't afford it you understand, it's all the hassle involved. What I really need is a chauffeur, who can also be a bodyguard.'

'Chauffeur! Bodyguard! Me?' Mike said incredulously, almost choking on his drink. 'I thought this job was bad enough. With that, I'd be bored stiff in no time at all.'

'I'd pay you well, and of course you could continue to teach me about self-defence and so forth. I've got a fully equipped gym at the house.'

'I don't know. It's not the sort of job I see myself doing for very long.'

'You could have your own rent-free apartment, and occasional use of the Rolls when off duty,' Jim said, trying to make the job sound inviting.

'I'll think about it,' conceded Mike, 'and let you know.'

'Okay. That's fair enough.'

Clients began to drift away and return to their rooms at the end of the evening.

'Time I hit the sack, Jim,' said Mike. 'I've got work to do in the morning.'

They bade each other goodnight and Mike retired for the night.

The wind abated and the rain was easing. Jim stared through the window at the gardens and illuminated pathway, lost in thought, and was brought back to reality by the smart bow-tied waiter clearing the table. Jim said goodnight and trundled up the stairs to his room, wondering what Mike would eventually say to his offer, but not holding out much hope that he would accept.

Chapter IV

Capture

Suzie opened her eyes and blinked repeatedly. She was still disorientated and unable to focus properly or distinguish what she saw. And what was that terrible noise droning away in her head? Her body ached and felt heavy, as if its weight were holding her down, preventing her from moving.

Gradually, her thoughts came together, and she began to remember the last few events before she had blacked out completely. She recalled two men waiting in her room to grab her, then injecting her with something that made her dizzy, and the room seem distant and dreamlike. Vaguely, she remembered being pushed into a car, whisked to an airport and hustled aboard a small aeroplane. Aeroplane – that's what it was! It was the roof of an aeroplane she was staring at, and the droning was the jet engines.

Suzie was slumped in a seat, reclined back almost to a lying position, and strapped in with a belt, but not tied down.

'That was careless of them. They must be expecting the drug to last longer than this,' she surmised.

With great effort, she lifted her head and looked around the cabin. It was small, with seats for only six people. Curtains were pulled across every window, but she knew it was still dark outside. Unbuckling the belt, she sat up. Her head started to swim, forcing her to wait for a few seconds, until it began to clear. Then she realised that her halter-neck top was not on properly.

'They've been groping me while I was out, the bastards! I'll get even with them for this,' she angrily determined, straightening her top.

A door at the rear of the cabin opened and Suzie lay down, pretending still to be dreaming. Chas Jones came to check and bent over her. He looked to see if she was still unconscious, when her eyes opened. It stopped him in his tracks for a second, long enough for Suzie to hit him with a right hook.

'Take that, you pervert!' she said with satisfaction.

The force of the blow, coupled with the momentum of his weight, sent him reeling across the cabin, crashing into the seats, sprawling over them and ending in a crumpled heap on the floor.

Searching him, Suzie found a gun and staggered towards the cockpit. A myriad of dials and controls came into view when she opened the door and confronted the pilot. He turned, and his face was transformed to horror, looking at the gun she waved at him while steadying herself in the doorway.

Suzie motioned him to take off his headphones. 'Turn the plane round and go back,' she demanded.

'I can't. We haven't enough fuel to get back to Zante,' the pilot advised.

'So where are we headed for?'

Before he could answer, her gunhand was grabbed from behind and bony fingers clasped her mouth. The weapon swung back and forth as both fought for its possession. Suzie was dragged backwards through the doorway but held on to the gun and drove her way forwards again, attempting to wrench the weapon away. She was fighting to prevent possibly the only chance she had to escape from being plucked out of her grasp. The pilot stared wide-eyed and terrified when they staggered back into the cockpit with the weapon swinging round in front of him. Suzie pushed wildly backwards, crashing them both into the door, slamming it shut. In the struggle the gun went off, close to Suzie's head, momentarily stunning her. The bullet drove into the pilot's chest, knocking him half off his seat with only the belt preventing him from hitting the floor.

Ron Willard snatched the gun away. 'Stupid bitch. Now look what you've done.'

The door opened and Jones stumbled in, looking a little the worse for wear, holding a handkerchief to stem the blood running from his nose. 'What's happened? I thought I heard a gun go off.'

'You did. Silly Suzie here's shot Philip. Watch her for a moment,' Willard said, feeling in vain for a pulse in the pilot's neck. 'He's dead.'

'Christ! Who's flying the plane then?' Jones exhorted.

'It's on autopilot. Give her another bloody jab and put her out. She's messed things up enough already, I don't want her interfering any more,' Willard said, holding Suzie tightly by her arm.

Jones returned with the syringe and jabbed it into Suzie's backside. She was not expecting it and jumped at the surprise it gave her, then came over dizzy and passed out. Jones carted her back to the seat.

'And tie her down, just in case, so she can't cause us any more trouble,' he was instructed.

He strapped the seat belt on and tied Suzie's wrists to the arms of the seat, then returned to the cockpit. Willard, meanwhile, had moved the pilot's body into one of the vacant seats in the cabin.

'Sit down!' he ordered, pointing to the co-pilot's seat.

'What me? Look at all these ruddy knobs and dials. I can't fly a bloody plane. Can you?' Jones said nervously.

'I have flown, but a long time ago and nothing as sophisticated as this.'

'Can you get us down okay?'

'I don't know. I've been with Philip on many of these trips and watched him land dozens of times.'

'That's good,' Jones sighed with relief.

'But, knowing what to do and actually doing it are two different things. I want you to put on the headset and talk to the control tower when we come in to land. I need to concentrate on what I'm doing and not be distracted. Got that?'

'Sure, Ron. Anything you say. Just get us down in one piece.'

'It'll be light by the time we get there, so at least I'll be able to see the runway.'

'Thank God for that.' Jones was highly nervous with beads of sweat glistening on his forehead.

'Is silly Suzie tied up okay?'

'She's strapped in tightly. Even Houdini couldn't get out of that seat. She won't bother us any more on this trip,' he asserted.

'Good. I don't want any more slip-ups,' Willard instructed.

'She certainly packs a punch for a woman,' Jones said, fingering his swollen nose. 'Nice pair of tits, though.'

'Forget about her tits. Let's concentrate on what we've got to do.'

Willard instructed Jones on how to use the radio, when the time came. It was a simple task, but in his highly nervous state he took time to master it.

'Okay,' explained Willard. 'Now I'm going to take the autopilot off to get a feel of how the plane responds.'

'Hell! Don't do that. It's dark. You won't be able to see where you're flying.'

'I don't need to see. The instruments show me height, direction and speed,' he stated, pointing to the dials in front of him. 'Now, hold tight, because the plane may veer a little until I get the hang of it.'

Willard flipped the autopilot switch off and the plane immediately nosedived.

'Christ! What's happening?' screamed Jones, gripping the arms of his seat so tight that his knuckles went white.

'It's okay,' assured Willard, pulling the steering column towards him and stabilising the plane, which returned to a level flight and all went smooth again. 'This is a nice plane to fly. Very responsive to the controls,' he announced to his nervous associate.

'I'm pleased to hear it. So there's no problem in landing?' he asked, eager for a positive response to quell his fears.

'I wouldn't go so far as to say that,' teased Willard, beginning to delight in the challenge. 'But I think we've got a fighting chance, so just relax for a while.'

Flying the Hawker Siddeley HS125 business jet was an enjoyable experience for Willard, so much so that he left the autopilot off to completely familiarise himself with the controls. To him the next two hours passed quickly. Not so for Jones, who thought that this was his worst nightmare.

They approached the airfield as dawn broke, illuminating the land in a cascade of sunlight. Long shadows moved swiftly across the earth, decreasing with each passing minute of sunrise.

Jones tried to contact the tower on the radio. 'It's no use, Ron, I've tried several times, but can't get a reply. Are you sure this is the right way?'

'It's right, and the frequency's right. But that's okay. It's not unusual to get no reply this early in the morning. Philip often couldn't get through to anyone. They're probably all still in bed. I just wanted to make sure that the runway's clear when we come in to land. If they're all asleep, it should be fine, so here goes.'

The aeroplane made a gradual descent and Jones looked in horror at the treetops getting closer. 'Where's the airfield? All I can see is trees and jungle,' he said nervously.

'Relax. It'll all come into view in a moment. The runway's quite short, so we have to put down quickly right at one end. That much I remember Philip saying.'

'What's that noise?' said Jones in a panic.

'Stop worrying, will you? You're beginning to make me nervous. That's the landing gear going down.'

'Landing gear?'

'Wheels to you.'

Then almost out of nowhere the clearing and airstrip was directly in front of them. They approached the single runway and continued to descend, when to their horror they saw a Cessna 150 light aircraft taking off towards them.

'Oh shit!' cried Willard, pulling the control column back. The plane levelled out and began to climb as the Cessna got nearer and nearer. Jones stared, wide-eyed, watching it get closer and closer, and when it looked as if a crash was inevitable, he shut his eyes and yelled. Willard banked the jet hard over and the two aircraft shot past each other with only a few feet between them.

'You can open your eyes now. We've missed him,' Willard announced, bringing the aircraft back onto an even keel.

'I thought my number was up, that time,' Jones replied shakily, 'and we still haven't tried to land yet!'

'I forgot that you come in to land against the wind, and that's in the opposite direction. I'll make an approach from the other end. You get on the radio and try to contact them again and make sure nobody else is about to take off.'

Willard brought the aircraft round in a wide circle. Jones tried once more to make contact, but without any success.

'Still no response, Ron.'

'Okay. Keep your eyes peeled, and we'll try again.'

This time the runway was clear and Willard made a safe, if

slightly bumpy, landing. Jones looked petrified, staring at the end of the runway hurtling towards them. He was sure the plane wasn't going to stop in time, but it did – just. Willard could feel the relief emanating from him when the aircraft finally came to a standstill and was taxied off the runway.

Suzie was still knocked out and oblivious to all this high drama. Willard and Jones sat for a few minutes in the cockpit and savoured the good feeling of still being alive.

'Well done, Ron! You were fabulous,' enthused a grateful Chas Jones.

'Nothing to it really,' he bragged. 'Now let's get our meddling passenger to The General, before she does any more damage. She's been nothing but trouble from the start, I'll be glad to get rid of her.'

Suzie staggered off the private jet at the flying club. The General had overrun the surrounding area, in his bid to overthrow the government and take control of the country.

Several light aircraft and a helicopter were parked on the tarmac next to a small, wooden building that sported a washed-out sign declaring it to be 'The Jetuloo Flying Club', confirming to Suzie that it was The General who'd orchestrated her abduction.

She recalled the briefing that she and Mike were given at Camp Grey before their last mission, when the commander had told them that arms were being flown in and transferred to a secret stockpile deep in the jungle. The map they were shown included the airstrip, Camp West, which was now in The General's control, and mainly uncharted jungle, where the arms were thought to be stored. This was where the helicopter, which they'd watched unloading, had brought its deadly cargo from. Suzie wondered if it had been piloted by the man that she shot.

'Well, he won't be ferrying any more arms in now! The General must have found out who destroyed his precious stockpile,' Suzie thought, 'and now he wants his revenge on me and Mike.'

This small private airstrip was used by The General to bring arms, drugs and people into the country, and was one of the major reasons both sides wanted to control the area.

Still apparently feeling the effects of the drug she was given,

Suzie almost fell down the aircraft steps and had to be supported by Willard and Jones. Stepping onto the tarmac after a five-hour journey, she felt the impact of the already humid atmosphere.

During touchdown on their eventful landing, Suzie had woken up with a head that thumped, and she was dizzy again. The few minutes that it took them to get her off the plane had allowed her head to almost clear, but she continued the pretence of being drugged when they woke her to disembark, and she staggered from the plane, looking for a way to escape.

An older, but well-kept, chauffeur-driven Mercedes came towards the jet and parked nearby. Suzie's two inattentive chaperons casually helped her towards the vehicle while the driver got out and stood by his open door.

It was now or never.

Flanked by the guards, each holding her upper arm, Suzie suddenly lifted her arms up and broke free of their grip. She grabbed their lapels and stepped back, pulling the men together with force.

The speed of the move took them by surprise and their heads cracked, dropping them to the ground like a brick. The driver was slow to react and, by the time he did, Suzie was upon him and kicked him in the crotch, just in time to stop him from reaching the gun in his jacket.

'Shit – that hurt,' she swore, wishing she had boots on instead of sandals. The chauffeur doubled up in pain and was shoved aside. The two guards staggered to their feet in a daze, unable to prevent Suzie from jumping into the car before they could reach her.

'Thank goodness for central locking!' she murmured, as they frantically tried to open each of the doors and banged on the windows.

The key was still in the ignition, tyres squealed and the car sped off with spinning wheels burning rubber on the tarmac, leaving a trail of smoke drifting in the air. The driver and guards chased after her, with guns blazing away. But this was The General's car, and it was built with bulletproof glass and panels. Following two attempts on his life, he was worried that someone might succeed one day, so had the vehicle specially customised and imported for his personal protection.

Charging across the tarmac towards the building, Suzie searched for the exit and was dismayed to see the barrier down. She prepared to crash through, and accelerated when, because it was The General's car approaching, the guard lifted the barrier. His jaw dropped when Suzie waved to him as she sped out of the flying club and away.

Recalling the map they had been shown at the briefing, Suzie turned south towards the border. The narrow, badly made road, through mainly uninhabited jungle, was rutted with holes. The steering wheel was violently twisting back and forth, with Suzie clutching on hard. Glancing in the mirror, she expected to see them chasing her, but when nobody appeared, she gradually relaxed and slowed down, to avoid shaking herself and the car to pieces.

Heading towards Kitsulana, Suzie was elated at the good progress she was making – when it suddenly changed. A large army lorry, with spinning wheels throwing clouds of dust into the air, appeared from nowhere to block her path. She slammed on the brakes and the Merc skidded to a halt. Rebel soldiers emerged through the clouds of dust and charged towards her, shouting and waving their guns. Suzie thrust the car into reverse and screamed back down the road only to see another army lorry pull out behind her, blocking her retreat.

'Oh hell!' she cried, jamming the car back into forward drive and accelerating at the oncoming soldiers, scattering them in all directions.

With her foot to the floor, the car crashed up and down the ruts and hammered towards the lorry. Suzie aimed between the big wheels, but as the vehicle loomed larger, the gap looked too small, and too late she realised that the car wouldn't go through. Screaming, she ducked. The bonnet disappeared under the lorry and everything went black. Her ears filled with a terrible graunching sound of metal tearing and windscreen shattering. Pieces of glass sprayed in all directions and the top of the car ripped off, grinding it to a halt.

But daylight shone on her. Suzie sat up with a broad smile across her face, when she realised that the car had burst its way through to the other side and she was still alive. Twisting the key, the Merc sprang into life and she stamped on the pedal, accelerating away. Soldiers, emerging from the bush, fired at her motoring down the track. With the top gone, so had her protection, and bullets whistled past her. The jubilation she felt quickly turned to disappointment when two tyres were hit and burst. The car vibrated ferociously and Suzie couldn't hold on to the violently twisting steering wheel, forcing her to slow to a crawl.

'I've gotta ditch this and make my way on foot,' she told herself.

Soon the soldiers were out of vision, so she jumped from the car and let it run into the undergrowth to hide it. The almost unrecognisable vehicle lurched into the bushes, became entangled and stuck, with the boot still visible.

'Oh bugger!' Suzie cursed, diving into cover of the trees to elude the soldiers who were fast catching her up.

Still wearing her holiday gear of sandals and shorts, the undergrowth tore at her limbs as she scurried through the jungle. Soldiers would comb the area and Suzie knew she had to keep going if she wanted to elude them.

Suddenly a figure stepped out in front, startling her. She froze for a second, then recognised him.

'Barney! What the hell are you doing here?'

'Suzie,' he hesitated. '…Didn't expect to see you in this neck of the woods. I'm scouting for the commander to get information about The General's headquarters. It's quite near here.'

Suzie breathed a sigh of relief. 'Thank goodness I bumped into you. The General's soldiers are chasing me. They can't be very far behind.'

'Right. This way. Follow me.'

Suzie stayed close to Barney, forging his way along, until they came to a well-trodden path where they stopped.

'I thought I heard someone behind us,' he warned. 'Keep to this path. It'll lead you towards the border. I'll take a look and see if we're being followed, then I'll catch you up. If I get delayed, you'll have to find your own way back as best you can. Sorry I can't spare the gun.'

'That's okay, you may need it. Thanks, Barney. I'll see you shortly,' said Suzie. He nodded and she pressed on.

Only a short distance away she heard a rustle behind her and stopped. She was about to turn round when a searing pain erupted in her head, exploding in a bright flash for an instant then rapidly disappearing to a black emptiness. Suzie had the distant, dreamlike sensation of being carried, as she drifted in and out of consciousness. She thought she heard voices echoing in the distance, but then they too disappeared.

When she eventually opened her eyes, she gazed at a dark, grimy ceiling. Her head was now thumping again.

'What happened? The escape, the chase, Barney. Somebody carrying me,' she said to herself. With consciousness returning, Suzie tried to unscramble her thoughts through the haze in her mind.

The ceiling she stared at was wood, as were the walls. The room was sparsely furnished, and the only window covered by a faded, threadbare curtain. Dimly lit by a single, bare lightbulb hanging from the ceiling, the room contained a sweet, fragrant smell hanging in the air, that Suzie couldn't place. The sound of men marching to shouting of orders drifted through in the background. This was a hut on a military camp, and she could guess which one.

'Christ, my head is thumping again. It feels like I've been hit with a sledgehammer.' She tried to lift her hand to feel the spot, and found that her wrists and ankles were shackled to a bed. Suzie had no clothes on and was covered by a rough horsehair blanket.

'What the hell is going on here? I wonder what happened to Barney. I hope he got away and is bringing the troops back.'

She jumped when the door suddenly opened and a stocky, fifty-two year old African man in a military uniform entered.

'Good afternoon, Miss Drake,' he said, in a deep gruff voice in good English. 'I am, The General.'

He had a chubby face and was clean shaven, with dark, straight hair cut very short and receding at the front. Below average height and overweight, he wore a tatty general's uniform that had seen better days. His eyes were small and beady and, despite first impressions of him looking friendly, Suzie soon realised that they bore into you, and it made her aware that he was cunning and deadly. Not a man to be messed about or crossed.

'How did I get here? Why haven't I got any clothes on? Get these shackles off me,' ordered Suzie.

'So many questions and demands. Have I not had the cuts and scratches on your arms and legs attended to? And do you not smell the lovely flowers in here?'

'So that's what the sickly pong is. Don't expect me to thank you.'

'I didn't, but I have tried to make it more comfortable for you and had hoped that you might co-operate.'

'No chance, but you can get me a pill for this blinding headache.'

'Alas, those are the sort of comforts we have to do without when we are fighting a jungle war.'

'So why am I here?'

'You will no doubt find out the answers to all your questions in due course, Miss Drake. However, in the meantime, *I* am the one who will ask, and you will give me the answers.'

'I don't know what you want but you can go boil your head in oil,' Suzie defiantly spat. 'Perhaps this fat bozo doesn't know about Mike,' she thought. 'If I delay, it might give him time to learn what's happened, and do something to get me out, especially if Barney's got back.'

'You would not like it in the prison hut,' The General warned. 'The guards there do what they like with the prisoners, and they all enjoy having a woman… if you understand my meaning.'

Suzie understood.

'Don't force me to lock you in there.'

'You don't frighten me. You can still get lost. I've got nothing to say,' announced Suzie.

'What anger and aggression from such a lovely-looking lady! But then I should have expected that after seeing how you not only escaped from my two bungling guards, but killed my pilot and the woman I sent to search your apartment.'

'So it wasn't a simple burglary! But, anyway, she tried to kill me and fell over the balcony in the struggle. It was an accident.'

'An accident! I suppose what you did to my beautiful

Mercedes was also an accident?' he said, caressing the word 'beautiful'.

'Scratched the paintwork, did I?'

'We'll soon knock that cockiness out of you, and your friend.'

'Friend? What friend?' Suzie asked, perturbed by the comment.

'Why, your friend Barney, of course.'

'What's happened to Barney? Is he all right?'

'Worried about him, are you?'

'Concerned. He tried to help me. Where is he?'

'Then I shall let you see him.'

The General left. The room fell silent and Suzie looked around, making a mental note of her surroundings. If an opportunity to escape came, any knowledge she had could be of use; a lesson Mike had emphasised.

A few minutes later The General returned with Barney. His hands were tied behind his back.

'Hallo, Suzie. How are you?' he asked.

'I'm okay. And you?'

'Okay. Sorry about all this. They jumped us from behind.'

'Enough of this silly talk,' interrupted The General, putting a gun to Barney's temple. He looked at Suzie. 'I want some answers, and right now or I'll blow his head off.'

'You wouldn't.'

He cocked the gun.

'No don't,' shouted Suzie. 'All right. What do you want to know?'

'That's much better,' he crowed, lowering his pistol.

The guards took Barney away, and The General pulled up a chair and sat beside the bed.

'Now, Miss Drake, let's have a cosy chat. There are a few things that I would like some information about…'

Chapter V
Hear and Prepare

Jim ate the last spoonful of breakfast porridge, in the training school dining room, and downed his carrot juice, neither of which he liked very much. The previous evening's rain had stopped, replaced by a brighter start to the morning with raindrops glistening in the sun and pathways rapidly drying. The dining room was buzzing, with guests chattering and china clinking, but there was no sign of Mike. Jim was wondering why he'd not appeared for breakfast as usual, when into the room he dashed, anxiously striding towards him.

He stood and leant on the table, towering over Jim. 'That offer you made me last night. Were you serious?' he enquired with some urgency, then plonked himself down in the chair.

Jim was taken aback by this sudden strong interest. 'Of course, I'm serious. Why, what's happened?'

Mike explained, 'I've just had a panicky phone call from Martin in Zante, who runs the hotel where Suzie's been staying. He thinks she was abducted by two unsavoury-looking blokes in the early hours of this morning. She was wobbly on her feet when they left, and they told Martin she was drunk. Yet he'd seen her only fifteen minutes earlier and she was sober then. A note left for him in her room was scrawled, and not in her usual neat handwriting, and the whole thing looked rushed. Before she was bundled into a car, apparently making for the airport, she mumbled something about going on a… jungle holiday.'

'Jungle holiday?' questioned Jim.

'Yes. I reckon that probably means The General's men have snatched her and taken her back to his headquarters. I can't think of any other explanation for it.'

'Oh no! Could he have found out who blew up his ammo dump?'

'Possibly, but why abduct her? If he wants to get even he could've had her killed there and then.'

'Maybe he only knows about her and wants to find out if anyone else was involved.'

'Mmm, perhaps,' Mike thoughtfully replied. 'Martin also said there was an incident a few days ago when a woman intruder in Suzie's room scuffled with her and fell from the balcony. She plummeted to her death, while Suzie was left hanging by her fingertips and had to scramble back to safety.'

'Wow! Sounds like a hairy incident. Too much of a coincidence?'

'I reckon so, especially as the woman may have been African.'

'They might torture Suzie to make her talk. She could be in real trouble. What can we do?'

'What *you* can do,' Mike emphasised, 'is give me that job you spoke about and allow me to have six months' advance and some time off so I can sort this thing out.'

'Time off? Advance? You haven't even agreed to start yet.' Jim sounded incredulous.

'I know, but I don't have enough ready cash at the moment. There's the air fare, the jeep and lots of equipment I need funds for.'

Mike had already made up his mind to help Suzie and was determined to get the money somehow.

'Lovely Suzie's in trouble. You wouldn't want me to turn my back on her, now would you?' said Mike, playing on Jim's obvious enchantment for her.

'No. Of course not. You know I wouldn't. You can have the money, I've got plenty.'

'We'll call it a loan. I'll pay you back when my money comes through from the agency,' promised Mike.

'When will you need it?'

'Soon as possible. I'll book a flight out from Heathrow tomorrow if there is one.'

'Okay. I'll have the money ready by then.'

'In dollars?'

'If that's what you need.'

'It is.'

'Okay. Dollars it'll be.'

Jim's readiness to advance the cash was a much needed boost and saved Mike valuable time. He helped himself to a bowlful of porridge and began making a list as he ate. Apart from the plane ticket, all the equipment would be needed when he arrived in Africa. He counted his good fortune in having soldiered in the area and acquired knowledge of the topography, which helped him to assess the equipment he needed. Working on a rough plan of attack enabled him to draw up the list. It was long, would be difficult to obtain and costly to fill.

'Is this all?' said Jim sarcastically, scanning the catalogue of equipment. 'You're not going to start a war, are you?'

'The war's already started. I'm joining in – with my own rules.'

'It won't be easy to get Suzie out, if this General's snatched her, and could be very dangerous. Suppose he's found out you were together when you blew up his ammo dump? He might be holding her as bait to trap you.'

'Yes, I've thought of that. It just means I'll have to be extra careful,' Mike said, squashing any argument before it started. 'I'd like to find out where they're holding her before I leave, but that's easier said than done. The General tends to move about to avoid getting caught by government troops, but he recently overran one of their army camps and may still be there,' he said, dropping the spoon into his half-eaten bowl of porridge. 'I've lost my appetite.'

'Would your old commander know where he is?'

'He might. I could contact him and try finding out, but I need to do it without arousing his suspicions. It would save a lot of time and be much safer than asking questions when I get there. Trouble is, I don't want him to know about Suzie.'

'Why not? Couldn't he give you some help?'

'If he knew, he might go charging in and get her killed. I'd rather handle it myself.'

'Perhaps I could help you there,' Jim said, anxious to assist. 'My father's a ministerial bigwig in Whitehall. He may be able to use his influence to find out.'

Mike almost spat the words out: 'Minister! Whitehall! Thanks, but you've done enough already. I don't think we ought to involve anyone who's a Whitehall official... even if he is your father. In my experience they don't usually approve of mercenaries. If he goes asking a lot of questions and stirring things up, it might make what I'm planning a lot more difficult.'

'I'm sure it'd be okay,' Jim insisted. 'I'll be very diplomatic about it, and I won't mention your name.'

Mike reluctantly agreed to let him try, but only because he was desperate for the information.

Jim sipped his carrot juice and pulled a face. 'How're you going to arrange for the things you'll need when you get there?'

'I've got an old army buddy who runs a bar just across the border in neighbouring Roseburgh. I'll get in touch with him. I'm sure old Paul O'Conner can get the equipment I need – with the right sort of persuasion.'

'Persuasion?' echoed Jim, putting his half-empty glass down.

'Yes, persuasion. Money,' Mike said, rubbing his fingers together in the time-honoured gesture. 'That's partly why I need the advance.'

Mike swallowed his glass of carrot juice in one go and screwed up his face. 'God, this stuff's awful.'

The waiter collected Jim's empty cereal bowl, balancing it expertly on top of the others on his arm. After thanking him and waiting until he'd gone, Jim cleared his throat then enquired gingerly, 'Need any help when you're over there?'

'Ah! That's very thoughtful of you, but I really need someone here near a telephone, just in case I want to call for back-up,' Mike said unconvincingly. 'Is that the time?' he asked, glancing at Jim's watch. 'I've got a lot to do. I'll see you later.' Then he swiftly departed to make his telephone calls before Jim could challenge him again.

Still hungry, and looking at the half-eaten plate of porridge Mike had left behind, Jim thought that perhaps porridge was not so bad after all. He went to the breakfast bar and spooned out a second helping, but passed on the carrot juice.

Between the training sessions he took that morning, Mike tried to ring Paul in Roseburgh and was frustrated by the difficulty in getting through. He had a free period after lunch, and used the time to sort out the rest of the details and eventually managed to contact Paul.

Jim continued his instructions with more enthusiasm than before. Visions of the impending task Mike would undertake, spurred him to improve his performance. Fantasising his role on the mission to rescue Suzie, he was more aggressive and his actions more positive. This change in attitude surprised his tutor as he practically ripped the entire dummy to shreds during bayonet practice. The instructor began to wonder if he'd overdone things and cracked. Training that afternoon on the shooting range also went well. His aim was much better with both rifle and hand gun. He shot every guerrilla who held Suzie and ended the day feeling rather pleased with himself, if exhausted by the extra energy his enthusiasm had generated.

Before dinner, Mike showered and changed, deep in thoughts about Suzie, wondering how she was coping. Since receiving the telephone call from Martin, he'd been too busy to stop and think clearly about the implications of what he was about to attempt. During this quiet time alone in the shower, he again reflected on the way they made love in the jungle and, although there were no ties between them, he began to realise that he'd be devastated if anything happened to her. Wandering back into his room with a towel tied around his waist, he told himself to listen to his own advice and think positively: 'Suzie is resilient, she will be okay. She is still alive, and I can and will get her out,' he told himself.

Surveying his clothes in the oak wardrobe, Mike chose to wear light slacks and a T-shirt. Donning fresh garments felt good and lifted his spirits. It was past 8 p.m. and he snapped himself out of his maudlin mood and marched down to dinner, feeling refreshed and confident of his ability to handle any problems that stood in his way.

Entering the already full dining room, Mike smiled and politely nodded to those seated at their tables. He sidled over to Jim, who was waiting for him.

'Hi, Mike. How'd you get on?'

'Okay, thanks, Jim,' he replied, dragging out the chair to sit down.

'Good. Tell me about it.'

The waiter hovered, ready to take their orders. Soup of the day was vegetable, and it was served quickly.

They talked in low tones, careful not to be overheard, and started their evening meal.

'I had quite a job getting through to Paul, but eventually managed it. The phone lines out there are a bit hit-and-miss. Anyway, he said he could get most of the things I want, and it would only take him a couple of days,' stated Mike.

'Excellent. At least, the first hurdle's over,' remarked Jim.

'That's right. I booked a ticket to Roseburgh via Nairobi for tomorrow evening. I fly from Heathrow at 5 p.m. on a British Airways flight. Paul said he'd meet me at the other end.'

'Good! The cash will be ready for you to collect in the morning from the airport branch of my bank.'

'Thanks, Jim. I hope it didn't cause you too many problems.'

'None at all. It's amazing how co-operative bank managers can be when you've won a fortune.'

'I'll bet.'

'Before I won the money, he hardly knew I existed. Now he calls me Jim and can't do enough for me.'

'Money certainly talks.'

Jim boasted to Mike how much better he'd done that day in his lessons, and Mike was genuinely pleased. Although Jim didn't tell him what spurred him on, Mike could guess and thought to himself, Now the adrenalin's flowing.

The main course that evening was chicken, one of Jim's favourites, and, having expended so much energy that day, he was hungry and tucked into it with relish.

The evening passed quickly. Mike and Jim chatted about strategies, oblivious of the hubbub from other guests' gossip and laughter. They discussed possible obstacles that Mike might encounter, and he used Jim as a sounding board, to bounce ideas back and straighten things in his mind.

They continued to talk until nearly midnight.

'Talk is okay,' expounded Mike, 'but action's the only way to get anything done, and no amount of talking can prepare you for all that may happen. So now, it's… time to act.'

'Right,' replied Jim. 'That's why I'd like to come with you.'

'Thanks. I know you want to help, but you don't have the

experience for this sort of operation. Playing make-believe at a training school is okay, but it's no substitute for the real thing, and I don't have time to watch out for both of us. I've got my work cut out looking after me. Out there, you could get seriously killed.'

Jim smiled at the joke, but understood what Mike meant.

'You really will be more useful staying here next to a phone.'

'Yes, I understand that, Mike. It's just that I want to do something more positive.'

'Well, if it does turn out to be The General who's snatched her, and we don't yet know that for sure, you might get that chance more quickly than you imagine,' Mike said, rather mysteriously.

'Why's that?'

'How about driving me to the airport tomorrow?' Mike asked, avoiding Jim's question.

'Sure. But aren't you the one who's supposed to be thinking about becoming a chauffeur?'

'True,' Mike smiled. 'But not yet. I'll talk to you about the job when I get back. After all, I've got to pay you back somehow.'

'When you get back? Don't you mean *if* you get back? From what you've said this evening, it's likely to be dangerous. I hate to think of you getting hurt, and I want my advance back, so you make sure you return!' Jim said in a cheeky tone, trying to disguise his anxiety.

'I'll be back. And thanks for the loan,' Mike said, slapping Jim on the shoulder. 'The stuff was very expensive, as I expected, especially as I need it so quickly. Paul knows that, and he was always ready to make a quick buck – even if it was from an old pal.'

'That's okay. I'm pleased I could do something to help,' Jim said dryly. 'And by the way, I rang my father. He told me he'd see what he could do to trace Suzie's whereabouts without stirring things up. He was quite okay about the whole thing and didn't ask too many awkward questions.'

Mike raised his eyebrows suspiciously, then said, 'Okay. That's good.' He was somewhat wary of this 'ministerial' help, but resisted the temptation to say so. 'Didn't he ask you who wanted the information... and why?'

'Sure. But I just said it was for a friend. No names, no explanations, like I told you.'

'Okay. Thanks. I phoned my old commander and tried to find The General's whereabouts without arousing his suspicions. I told him I was thinking of rejoining him soon, and he was very pleased. I didn't like deceiving him that way, but I did find out that The General's still holding Camp West, so that has to be my starting point.'

With the talk all finished and the evening gone, Mike rose from the table. 'It's late and I've still got my packing to do. I'll see you at breakfast. If we leave here about one o'clock that'll give us plenty of time to get to the airport. Check-in time is 3 p.m.'

'Okay. I'll see you tomorrow. Goodnight.'

He left Jim sitting at the table with a half-empty glass of carrot juice, visualising the mission and wondering if he would get the opportunity to meet the lovely Suzie Drake. He didn't want to consider the consequences for either of them if things went wrong. Suddenly aware all was quiet, he looked up to find he was the last one left in the dining room. All the other clients had retired for the night, or gone to the TV room for a chat. Finishing most of his carrot juice with a grimace, like nearly everyone did, Jim slowly trudged back to his room. Yawning as he wearily climbed the staircase, he suddenly felt very tired, the activities of the day beginning to catch up with him.

Mike was also preoccupied with thoughts about the days ahead when he entered his room and turned the light switch on.

Nothing happened.

He tried the switch several times, but the room remained dark. His senses rang alarm bells and he was suddenly aware that something was wrong, and he instinctively knew there was someone in the room. Realising he was outlined against the corridor lights he stepped inside the door, closed it and dropped to one knee. A knife whistled past his head and splintered the heavy wooden door with a thud as it drove its way in.

Chapter VI

Two's a Crowd

Mike crouched behind a chair in his room and waited silently while his eyes adjusted to the darkness and he listened for movement to pinpoint his attacker. If only he had a gun with him. He cursed not having the foresight to hide one in the room, but then if he had, the intruder may have found it. Dodging bullets was an altogether different proposition to tackling a man with a knife.

Moving forward, he kept low, gliding across the floor, cat-like on all fours, and caught a glimpse of the shadowy outline of a man passing the window. He inched his way carefully through the mess littering the room and noted that the attacker was still armed with a knife. Moonlight glistened on the blade as he swept it before him, probing the air for his victim.

Poised like a runner in the starting blocks, Mike leaped forward and grabbed at the knife with one hand and the man's throat with the other. They crashed into the furniture, pitting their strengths against each other, twisting round in their battle and falling to the floor. Mike pinned the man down with a strong grip on his throat, choking and sapping his strength and at the same time bending his assailant's wrist back, almost to breaking point, in an effort to wrestle the knife from him. The man gripped Mike's hand on his throat and tried to pull it away to relieve the pressure on his windpipe. Pain and fear drove him to make a great effort, and with a surge of energy he forced Mike off and they rolled over, locked together. The knife plunged into the intruder as he fell on top of Mike. With a grunt of surprise his grip relaxed, his eyes opened wide showing the fear that encompassed him, and the full weight of his body slumped onto his intended victim.

Pushing him aside, Mike stood up but, before he could check the man, his head exploded with bright lights. He lost reality, the

71

room drifted into the distance, disappearing into blackness as unconsciousness overtook him. His legs buckled and he collapsed to the floor.

Traipsing down the long corridor, Jim heard a crash from Mike's room and smiled at thoughts of him being a great jungle fighter, but struggling to get his suitcase packed.

He stood and listened for a few seconds, heard nothing more and, with a shrug, opened his door. He was tired and wanted to get to bed, but changed his mind and thought that it might be amusing to see what sort of mess this great fighting hero was getting into with his packing. Closing his door, he carried on towards Mike's room.

Flickering his eyes open, Mike gathered his scrambled thoughts and lifted his face from the carpet. He rose gingerly to his feet, felt the lump on the back of his head and grimaced at the pain oscillating through his brain.

'There must have been two of the buggers. Well, one of them's not so chirpy now,' he mumbled to himself.

Feeling his way to the desk he found the upturned lamp and switched it on. The room was a shambles. They'd searched everything. All the desk and cabinet drawers were pulled out, books and files littered the floor, and his once neat pile of clothes were strewn everywhere.

The intruders had vanished. There was blood on Mike's T-shirt and a trail on the carpet led to an open window, indicating that one man was either dead or badly injured.

A knock on the door interrupted his thoughts. Mike tottered forwards and bumped into his desk.

'Come in,' he yelled, unwilling to stagger any further.

Jim opened the door and sauntered in. His expression rapidly changed to a look of horror. 'What on earth's happened to you, and the state of this place? It looks like a hurricane has hit it.'

'Tell me about it,' retorted Mike. 'Somebody was very anxious to search my room.'

Jim glanced at the knife buried in the door. 'There's blood on your shirt. Are you hurt?'

'No, fortunately. We did a tango round the room and dropped to the floor. He wasn't so lucky and fell on his knife. I was about to check him when my skull caved in,' he moaned, clasping the back of his head.

'There were two of them?'

'That's right! I didn't expect that. The window's open, so I guess that's how they got in and out. The climb's not difficult, but must have been hard with an injured man.'

'You'd think this sort of place would be secure.'

'Yeah. Wouldn't do for it to be known that a school, training security and bodyguards, was broken into. I'll have a word with them about it when this is all over.'

'You not going to report it then?' Jim asked.

'No, I don't think so. Not at the moment. Let's just keep it as our secret for the time being. Okay?'

'Sure. Whatever you say.'

Mike sat down. 'I could do with a drink,' he said. 'Got any Scotch in your room?'

'You know alcohol isn't allowed. But as it so happens, I have a small flask – for medicinal purposes only, you understand.'

'I understand. I've got one as well, but it may take a while to find it in this mess – assuming it's still here, of course.'

Back in Jim's room, Mike related the encounter in graphic detail while he sipped a Scotch, and Jim bathed the cut on his head.

Mike grumbled, 'I wonder what they wanted. Unlike you, I don't have a lot of money, so that can't be the reason.'

'Something in your murky past, no doubt. You didn't leave anyone at the altar, did you?' Jim asked, trying to make light of the situation.

All he got for his troubles was a glare… again.

After putting his room straight, with Jim's help, replacing the light bulb and removing what they could of the blood from the carpet, Mike packed his suitcase.

Earlier that day, he'd spoken to the MD of Tramer, in his plush first floor office, sitting behind a large imitation antique desk. Mike explained about the predicament Suzie was in, and said he was leaving to fly out there to help her. Although sorry to lose him so soon, the MD was understanding and wished him good luck.

'If everything goes okay, you can resume the job when it's all over, if you're still interested,' he said helpfully.

'Thanks,' said Mike, who now had the offer of two jobs on his return. 'Wonders will never cease,' he muttered quietly.

'Pardon?'

'Just thinking aloud,' explained Mike. 'Okay if I borrow one of the specialist lock picks we use here?'

'Of course. Please have it as a gift from me.'

Now, with his head throbbing but his packing done, Mike carefully made a slit on the inside of his belt and hid the lock pick. He took a shower and went to bed, grateful to sink his bruised body into the soft sheets. His mind was still active and he stayed awake until the early hours, mulling over thoughts about the break-in. One explanation returned to him again and again when he considered the motives.

'If my guess is right, there'll be more trouble. The stakes could be high, so I'll have to take more care from now on,' he decided.

Tiredness gradually overtook him and his eyelids became heavy. He settled down to sleep, with the comforting lump of a gun he'd collected from the armoury under his pillow for company.

The following morning at breakfast, Mike briefly discussed with Jim the previous night's incident, which by then seemed a long way off. The most tangible thing was the lump on the back of his skull.

'What with the crack on my head, a lumpy pillow and a million thoughts racing through my mind, I didn't get much sleep last night.'

'Lumpy pillow?' questioned Jim.

'I had a gun underneath it – just in case they returned.'

'Oh, I see. I also had a job getting to sleep. I couldn't stop thinking about the dangerous task ahead, or your uninvited guests.'

The day was bright but overcast: ideal conditions for Mike, who spent most of the morning on a ten mile run with a heavy back pack, to ensure he was close to full fitness. The route took him, and two other clients who regularly jogged, on a trip around the local countryside, along public footpaths, through woods and ospffields and across the occasional lane. They passed through local beauty spots, but concentration on their task meant they saw little of them. By the time the training school was in sight again, they were all beginning to flag a little. Perspiration poured from them, and they were glad to get their sweaty things off and take a refreshing hot shower. Mike's leg stood up to the run well, with only the slightest twinge of discomfort.

'I reckon I'm as fit as I'll ever be,' he told himself, 'but fit or not – I go!'

During the long run, his determination and resolve increased with every stride he took. He and Suzie had always looked out for each other, and nobody was going to spoil the good relationship they had – certainly not a tinpot general who wanted to rule by force. Mike was raring to go, and he reckoned The General had better watch out!

Along with seven others, Jim spent the morning in a large, ground-floor room that was once the library and still contained shelves on three walls from floor to the high ceiling. The original books had been removed when the house was sold, and many of the shelves were still bare and collecting dust. Some were refilled with books on combat, war strategy and weapons, but most of this information was fast becoming available on CD-ROM, and four computers and a printer now occupied one corner.

The remainder looked more like a school classroom. Desks faced the teacher's table and chair, where he sat in front of tall windows which had plain frames of squared timber set into the walls and hand-wrought iron casements – a typical feature of this period of building.

The class this morning was learning how to pick locks with both specialist lock picks and makeshift ones. Mike, who found the delicate art not to his liking, had recently completed the course.

'Give me a gun or a stick of dynamite any day. At least I don't feel like I've got two thumbs on each hand with them,' he protested. 'Fiddling with locks is for cissies,' he continued, a remark that he regretted almost before the words were out of his mouth when the rest of the group stared at him, giving him a feeling of discomfort, a thing he was not used to.

75

The culmination of each lesson was for pupils to be handcuffed and given a hairgrip to pick the lock. Four managed the task, and Jim was first, pleased with himself that at last he'd done something better than the others had.

After his shower and a rest, Mike said his farewells to staff and clients, and he and Jim set off. By 1 p.m., their adventurous journey had begun, with London Heathrow Airport the first stop.

Jim's gleaming Rolls Royce Silver Cloud was a car he'd dreamt of owning most of his adult life. Now, at the age of nearly forty, he'd been able at last to realise that dream. The car crunched down the gravel driveway, out through the large wrought-iron gateway that was the exit to the impressive grounds of Tramer International, and on to a quiet country road.

It wasn't long before Mike had the uneasy feeling that they were not alone. 'I think we're being tailed, Jim. We'll have to make a few unorthodox moves to check.'

'Really? Wow! Do you think it's the same lot that visited you last night?'

'Maybe.'

'What do you suggest?'

'We'll reach the motorway shortly. That should give us the opportunity to find out.'

They moved on to the M25, which was crowded as usual, and Jim moved into the outside lane and accelerated. Almost immediately, a dark green Range Rover from four cars back did the same, and when the Rolls slowed down and moved back to the nearside lane, they followed suit.

'The Range Rover is following us all right,' warned Mike. 'We'll have to try and lose it.'

'I didn't get to do the driving section on the course,' informed Jim, 'but I'm a pretty good driver and this is a very quick motor.'

'I wouldn't worry about that,' Mike countered. 'We just want to lose them, not enter a Grand Prix.'

A slow-moving car pulling a horsebox held up the Range Rover as they went into a lane restriction at some roadworks. When they emerged, Jim sped up to 75 mph and put distance between them. He turned off at the next junction, at Mike's suggestion, and parked in a side road.

'If they were following us, we've lost them now,' Jim said gleefully.

'I hope so, but we'll still need to keep a lookout. It won't take them long to figure out we pulled off at that junction. Fortunately, they can't just turn round on the motorway. We'll wait for ten minutes then move on.'

While they waited, Mike was busy writing. 'Take this. It's the address of my flat in Surbiton, and my Aunt Grace's cottage near Rye. I'd like you to check the flat, if you will,' he requested.

'Sure – be glad to,' Jim replied.

'Here's the key,' Mike said, slapping it into Jim's hand. 'Those guys I bumped into last night are looking for something they think I've got. I'd feel a lot better if you'd also call on my aunt to see that she's okay and gently warn her to be on the lookout for strangers, without alarming her,' he emphasised.

'Okay – consider it done. You don't think they'd turn up at her place, do you?'

'I hope not, especially after visiting me and getting more than they bargained for. But I don't want to take any chances, just in case.'

'Right.'

'And if *anyone* asks you if you know where I am, Jim – say no.'

'Right.'

'And would you lend me your watch, please?'

'My watch?' questioned Jim.

'Yes, your watch!'

'Haven't you got one?'

'No, I haven't.'

'Why don't you get yourself one?'

'Don't *you* start!'

Jim looked bemused at the remark, but just shrugged and handed his watch over.

'Thanks. Does it have an alarm?'

'Yes. I'll show you how it works.'

'That's okay. I'll figure it out on the plane. It'll give me something to do on the long journey.'

Jim slipped the Rolls into gear and they quietly moved back onto the motorway. The car telephone buzzed. It was Sir Joseph

Sterling, Jim's father, and his enquiries had revealed that The General was holding Suzie Drake at Camp West. Jim thanked him and passed the information to Mike.

'That's great news. Suzie's still alive and it confirms what I suspected. I don't know how he got the information, but do thank your father for me.'

'Sure,' chirped Jim, feeling rather pleased with himself.

The remainder of the journey was uneventful, with no sign of the Range Rover. The never-ending stream of traffic increased dramatically when they neared the airport, making it impossible to see if anyone was following.

Jim brought the Rolls to a gliding halt at the entrance to Terminal 4 and handed Mike his case.

'Take care of yourself, Mike. I still want my loan back.'

'Yes, of course. I'll ring Gracie tomorrow evening. If you can be there, I'll let you know how I'm progressing.'

'Okay,' said Jim, extending his hand.

They shook hands warmly. Jim handed him a cheque for the cash he needed and Mike thanked him, picked up his case and disappeared through the automatic doors, joining the throng of late holidaymakers.

The terminal was buzzing with activity as lines of people queued to book in, and others stared at flight information boards or pushed trolleys, piled high with luggage. Those about to leave were mainly white-faced, while the returning tourists from abroad sported glorious suntans. It prompted Mike, queuing for his flight, to recall his conversation with Suzie, telling him about her all-over tan. Gradually he moved forward until he reached the desk, checked in, then made his way to the bank to collect the money.

Locking himself in a cubicle in the men's washroom, Mike stashed the dollars in a moneybelt and strapped it round his waist. Satisfied that it didn't show beneath his loose fitting shirt, he tapped it for good luck, then went looking for a telephone to ring his aunt.

'Hallo, Gracie, it's Mike.'

'Mike. How are you? How's your new job going?'

'I'm at London Airport. I have to make a trip back to Africa.'

'Why, what's happened? Are you giving up the job?'

Mike avoided the questions. 'I've got some business to take care of. I shan't be long.'

'An old army friend rang, asking where you were, so I told him about your new job.'

'Oh! What was his name?'

'He didn't say. Just that he needed to get in touch with you on an urgent matter.'

'Okay, Gracie. I think he found me last night. Listen, a friend of mine, Jim Sterling, will be dropping in to see you some time tomorrow.'

'All right, Mike, but why?'

'You can't miss him, he drives a Rolls Royce. Make him welcome, will you?'

'But...'

'Got to go now, Gracie, they've called my flight. I'll ring tomorrow night. Bye,' he finished, and was gone.

Grace gave a puzzled look at the receiver still in her hand, almost as if she expected it to give her an answer. She was used to her nephew rushing off at a minute's notice. 'Nothing unusual in that,' she told herself.

Mike sat in the restaurant drinking coffee and waiting for his flight to be called. He now knew that they were aware of his aunt's address. He didn't like that and had to rely on Jim's warning to convince her of the possible dangers.

Jim drove home to his new detached house in Weybridge, one of the early purchases he made after his win. It was situated in a quiet cul-de-sac by the river Wey, close to a weir from which it got the name of Weir House. A three-storey open plan dwelling, it boasted all the modern conveniences and luxuries Jim could never afford before. The garage, utility, games and spare rooms were on the ground floor along with the gym. A spacious, carpeted living room with central open fireplace, dining room, large kitchen/breakfast room, cloakroom and study occupied the first floor. A second-floor balcony was reached by a winding open stairway, leading to the two bathrooms and five bedrooms. The house was furnished throughout with good quality Parker Knoll furniture, but Jim spent most of his time in the study with his books, records and computer. Financial help was offered when he won his millions, and on their advice he had invested most of the money and now lived comfortably on the interest.

Percy, the old gardener, looked after the half acre of rear gardens. He delighted in pottering around, pulling up weeds, pruning trees and shrubs, and having a big bonfire as often as he could, despite it being a smoke-free zone. Employed by the previous owner of the house, he was inherited by Jim, who was happy to keep him on. Gardening was not one of his loves, though he wanted the pleasures of strolling through and enjoying a well-kept garden that would impress his friends and guests.

Gladys did cleaning and housekeeping. Getting on in years, she could only manage one day a week, and then struggled to cope with such a large house and many stairs at her age. She wanted to give up the job and only stayed on as a favour to Jim, and because she'd spent many happy years in employment there and had a great affection for the house. Jim was advertising for someone to work three or four days each week, but so far without success.

Opening a window to let in some fresh air, Jim saw a Range Rover turning the corner to leave the street, and wondered... but then dismissed the idea. He sorted through a stack of letters, left neatly in a pile on the sideboard by Gladys, and threw half of them away. The few that remained were mostly bills.

Jim exercised in the gym for twenty minutes, took a shower, then ordered a takeaway meal by telephone from the local pizza parlour. It was delivered half an hour later and he settled down to read his letters and watch satellite television. An action film was showing, one of his favourites, but he found his mind wandering to thoughts about Mike and Suzie. Unable to concentrate on the film he turned the TV off, and after setting the burglar alarm, went to bed.

The following morning, he enjoyed a fried breakfast with toast and black coffee, but no carrot juice. Though still a bachelor, he rarely cooked anything for himself other than a fried breakfast, instead relying on pre-cooked meals and the more than occasional pizza or takeaway.

He had a chat with Percy about things that needed to be done in the garden. But when it came to it, he left him to make most of the decisions, while giving the impression that he was still in charge.

Jim filled the Rolls with petrol at a local garage, then set off for Mike's flat after first letting the rush hour traffic fight along to their destinations. The leisurely drive to Surbiton took less than an hour.

The address he sought was in a suburban avenue with a mixture of houses. Most were Victorian and converted into flats, including the one he was looking for. Flat four, number twenty, turned out to be on the first floor. The sound of his footsteps echoed emptily around him as he climbed the concrete stairs and crossed the bare wooden floorboards to the old-fashioned, windowless front door with a number four painted on it.

Jim rummaged through his pockets, found the key and let himself into the hall. His heart quickened, when he gazed through the open living-room doorway and saw the state of the room.

It had been ransacked and was in the same dishevelled state that Mike's quarters at Tramer had been the previous evening. Jim stood in the centre of the room and could feel the anger welling up inside at the senseless damage surrounding him.

The flat had typical Victorian high ceilings. The large living room, tastefully decorated with warm pastel shades, had plain but functional furniture. A four-seater settee and two armchairs surrounded a gas fire fitted into an original Victorian fireplace. A dining table and four chairs by the front window overlooked the street below. Mementoes from Mike's travels once graced the mantel and shelves, but were now scattered and broken on the floor along with his books. The homely look of the room had been wrecked.

The dining room led to a small bedroom above the main entrance used as a guest room. Off the hallway was the master bedroom, bathroom, and tiny kitchen which had a rear entrance to an open metal fire escape that criss-crossed the back of the building. This was where the intruder had gained entrance. A pane of glass in the back door was broken, making it an easy task to reach in and unbolt the door.

Jim explored the flat and went into the main bedroom. It too was wrecked, and he was stopped in his tracks, seeing a body on the bed with a pillow on top of the victim's head. Black powder burns surrounded a hole in the pillow, used to muffle the sound of the gunshot. With his heart pounding Jim lifted it to take a look, immediately regretting it. He rushed to the bathroom and was sick. The colour gradually came back to his face and his pulse rate steadied only to climb once again at a sharp knock on the front door.

'Oh no,' he groaned, closing the bedroom door. 'Now what?'

Two men stood at the front door.

'Good morning – Mr Randle?' enquired the first man. 'I'm Inspector Davidson and this is Sergeant White.' He took a wallet from his pocket and produced an identity card. 'We're from Surbiton Police Station. May we come in?'

Chapter VII

Rye

Inspector Davidson was a stocky man of average height aged around forty, with a balding head and a bushy moustache. Sergeant White was a little younger and over six feet. He was clean-shaven and had short hair, almost a crew cut, giving him a hard look. He nodded curtly and said nothing.

'Good morning, Inspector. I'm James Sterling, a friend of Mr Randle. He's away at the moment and I'm looking after the flat for him.'

'I see,' retorted the inspector, staring over Jim's shoulder. 'Looking at the mess I can see in the living room, you don't seem to be doing a very good job of it, if I may say so, sir.'

Jim felt peeved at the remark, but realised that he was in an awkward situation. He was unsure whether to tell the policemen about the body. But after the trouble at Tramer, Suzie's abduction, and Mike telling him not to let *anyone* know where he'd gone, he decided not to say anything to avoid any difficult explanations.

'I only arrived myself in the last few minutes. This is how I found the place. It's obviously been burgled.'

'In that case it's very fortunate we should call now. We can take details of the offence.'

'Why are you here, anyway?'

'A neighbour telephoned the station last night to complain about noise coming from this flat, which he said he thought was empty. That must have been when the place was being ransacked. Our constable on the beat investigated straight away but got no reply, and all was quiet when he called. A report of the incident was left on my desk and we're following it up.'

'I see. You'd better come in then.'

They entered the living room. The inspector glanced round,

made a few notes in his book and asked questions for the next ten minutes, mainly about Mike Randle.

'Right, Mr Sterling. I think I've got all the details. Perhaps I should take a look in the other rooms?'

'No,' countered Jim a little anxiously. 'As I've said, this is the only room that's in a mess. The rest of the flat seems to be untouched.'

'Very well. It's a pity you can't say if anything is missing, but I'm sure Mr Randle will get in touch with us as soon as he returns from – where did you say he went on holiday?'

'I didn't. I don't know where he's gone, Inspector. He simply said that he was going on holiday and would I keep an eye on the place for him.'

'I see. In that case we'll get the local bobby to stop by on his patrol and see Mr Randle when he returns.'

At last the inspector seemed satisfied with the information he'd received and they both left. Once more the sergeant just nodded and departed without having said a word.

Closing the door, Jim leant on it and gave a sigh of relief, thankful that they hadn't insisted on looking in the other rooms. Now he had a decision to make about the body in the bedroom.

'What the hell am I going to do? I can't leave it there, and there's no way of contacting Mike... dad, I'll have to ring dad. He'll know what to do.'

His father was surprisingly unperturbed when Jim rang to tell him about the body and how he'd found it, for even his son was unaware that Sir Joseph Sterling had connections with British Intelligence. This was by no means the first time he'd had to deal with this type of situation.

Mr Joseph Sterling began his working career as a young man carrying out Foreign Office duties, before going into the navy near the end of the Second World War. After leaving the services, he picked up his career and landed a job as a foreign attaché, gradually working his way up the ministerial ladder until he finally became a foreign diplomat. He was rewarded with a knighthood for his services on his sixtieth birthday. His wife died two years later and he transferred to a desk job in Whitehall as a troubleshooter, to oversee police and intelligence matters.

With an eye to retiring soon to a cottage in the countryside, his knowledge and renowned diplomacy made a successor difficult to find. Much of this was due to his charming manner, which projected a gentleness that disguised his skilful and cunning mind, along with a knack of asking the right questions without seeming to be intrusive. Still an active man, the years had been kind to him and although his hair was greying now, it was still thick and gave him the appearance of being younger than his sixty-four years. His small moustache, once black, had, with time, turned grey and was now almost white. His eyesight was still good but he occasionally wore glasses, mainly for reading and driving. He walked with a straight back and still reached his full height of five feet eleven inches, confirming the impression that he was once in the services.

Jim explained about the visit by two local police officers and remarked how pleased he was that they had left without checking the rest of the flat.

'Really,' said Sir Joseph. 'That was careless of them, and rather fortunate for you, son. You might have been ringing me under totally different circumstances if they'd been more thorough. Which station did they come from?'

Jim gave his father details about the policemen and what was said, along with the address of the flat, deliberately leaving out who the owner was.

'Okay, Jim. I've got all that. I imagine the flat belongs to Mr Michael Randle?'

'How do you know that?' Jim sounded surprised.

'His name came up when I made enquiries about Miss Suzie Drake for you.'

'Oh, I see.'

'I'll get Sandy to come round straight away. You let him in, then depart immediately. He'll tidy things up and leave the place secure.' Almost as an afterthought he added, 'By the way, this military camp where your friend's pal Suzie Drake is being held. My sources tell me the place is apparently quite well defended, so I hope he knows what he's doing.'

Jim realised that his father had a good idea what Mike was attempting. 'He's a very capable man and aware of the difficulties,' he said.

'Well, I hope you're right.'

'I'm expecting to get a call from him this evening, so I'll pass your concerns on. Oh, and by the way, he asked me to thank you for the information about Suzie Drake.'

'I only hope it doesn't get him killed.'

'He daren't. He owes me money.'

'Pardon?'

'Just a private joke.'

'Oh, I see. What are your plans now? Going home?'

'No, not yet. I promised Mike that I'd visit his aunt in Rye to...' he hesitated, 'to give her something from him, and I want to see how he's progressing. That's where he's going to ring this evening. I'll grab a spot of lunch first then take a leisurely drive down there. When your blokes arrive, I'll be on my way.'

After about half an hour, two men in boiler suits arrived. The tall redhead introduced himself as Sandy, and Jim was pleased to get out of the flat and leave them to it. He took a quick look at a map to check the route and began the journey to Sussex.

An hour or so later, Jim stopped at The Bondsman, a seventeenth-century pub near Reigate, for one of his favourite lunches, a ploughman's and a pint. Sitting in the garden on a wooden picnic bench, he enjoyed his meal in the sunshine, while gazing over the North Downs towards the coast. He took in deep gulps of fresh air, which had a slight bite to it, to cleanse himself mentally of the image and smell of the body that had unnerved him a little – though not enough to spoil his appetite.

When his meal was finished, Jim downed the last drops of his pint and continued the journey, occasionally remembering to check if he was being followed. Each time he looked, he was sure someone was trailing him, but then they turned off. Eventually, he decided that he was being paranoid about the whole thing, and settled back to enjoy the journey along the A21 through lovely Sussex countryside on this slightly chilly but sunny autumn afternoon, in his warm, comfortable car.

The signpost read three miles to Rye. Jim stopped to ask directions from a postman who was only too pleased to help the man in the Rolls Royce. Following the instructions given, he soon found Silverdale Cottage, reflecting that driving a Rolls was still regarded as something special and impressed many people.

The cottage was situated in a small country lane bordered by great oak trees, with shrubs hiding the wide expanse of rolling hills and fields behind. The end of the lane, alongside the cottage, disappeared into a wooded area beyond a five bar wooden gate and a stile. A green and white sign pronouncing a public footpath, arrowing the way into the woods, stood at a slight angle to the gate. Few other homes were in sight of the cottage, a seventeenth-century long-span house, converted at one time into three cottages and now converted back to a single dwelling. It had a great Elizabethan chimney, relic of a now vanished farmhouse kitchen.

It was nearly 5 p.m. by the time Jim reached the cottage. The sky had darkened, covered by a layer of black clouds that gave a depressing atmosphere and felt like a prelude to a gathering storm. It was in stark contrast to the feeling of tranquillity and peace that enveloped him when he opened the wrought-iron gate and walked up the curved pathway to the covered cottage doorway. It crossed his mind that such a property would be good to own as a country retreat, and might help him to elude his unwanted visitors.

Before reaching the front door it opened, and a woman stepped out to greet him, bathed in the warm glow of the doorway lantern. In her mid-sixties with grey-blonde shoulder-length hair, she was quite tall and had sharp, well-defined features with a strong jawline and straight nose.

'You must be Jim,' she stated, extending her hand. 'Mike telephoned from the airport and said you'd be coming. I recognised the car.'

'Hallo, er, Aunt Grace?' Jim said, uncertain how to address her, while shaking her hand, which had a firm grip.

'Call me Gracie,' she said. 'Do come in.'

She walked erect and looked intelligent and efficient, was attractive, but had, nevertheless, remained a spinster. Dressed smartly and younger than her years, this gave her an appearance which belied her age.

Through the now only remaining original cottage doorway,

embellished with every device known to the rustic carpenter, they passed into a small entrance lobby that led into the living room. There, a log fire was burning to counter the chill of the evening, now approaching fast. The fireplace had jambs of stone and a massive oaken chimney with an elaborately carved overmantel and ornamental iron plates at the back. A bunch of rusty old keys hung over the fireplace. The room contained many antique plates, both on the walls and on a magnificent late Victorian sideboard, and the subdued light of a corner lampstand illuminated the room.

Jim sat in a comfortable armchair, warming himself by the fire, and a beautiful longhaired tortoise-shell cat jumped onto his lap. She had a cheeky face and began to purr when he stroked her.

'Oh, that's Emmy. You're not allergic to cats or anything, are you?' Grace asked.

'No. I love cats. She's gorgeous, isn't she?'

'Yes. Emmy and I go back a long way. I've had her for more than twelve years now.'

Emmy continued to purr loudly. She rose, circled Jim's lap and sat down again, making herself more comfortable.

'I'm afraid she's a bit of a flirt and can't resist sitting on an empty lap, especially if it's a man's.'

'So I see.'

Grace invited Jim to stay for dinner and went into the kitchen at the rear of the cottage to prepare it, leaving the door ajar, allowing them to talk. She was anxious to know why Mike had returned to Africa so soon and what had happened to his new job.

Jim agonised over how much to tell her and mentioned that Mike would be phoning later that evening, though she already knew. He soon found that she was sharp, asking probing questions, and could tell when she was being fobbed off with half-truths. Mike hadn't said that he was to keep things from her, so in the end he decided that it might be better simply to tell her everything. Before he could do so there was a knock at the door, which Grace answered.

'Good evening. I'm Inspector Davidson and this is Sergeant White. And you are?'

'I'm Grace Randle.'

'Ah! Good, then we have the right address. We'd like you to

help us with our inquiries regarding a break-in at Mr Mike Randle's flat in Surbiton. May we come in?'

'It's a bit late to be calling and I'm in the middle of preparing dinner. Can't it wait until tomorrow?'

'We've had a long journey and would like to get this sorted out now. We won't take up much of your time,' promised the inspector.

'You'd better come in,' said Grace, stepping aside and beckoning them into the living room.

'Good evening, Mr Sterling. We meet again.'

'You're a long way from Surbiton, Inspector,' said Jim suspiciously. 'What brings you two here?'

'This is now a murder inquiry and we'd like to ask you and Mrs Randle some questions about her son.'

'Mrs Randle!' exclaimed Grace with surprise. 'I'm *Miss* Randle, and Mike is my nephew, not my son.'

'Oh, I see. I'm sorry about that. Umm… our computer must have the details wrong,' he countered hurriedly. 'I'll see the information is corrected.'

The inspector seemed unsure about things and Jim began to sense something was wrong. 'You said murder?' he queried.

'Yes. We returned to the flat to ask you some more questions and take another look, but you'd gone. The door was unlocked so we went in, and what should we find but a body in one of the bedrooms.'

'A body!' exclaimed Jim. 'You can't have. They'd have taken him away by then.'

'Ah!' said the inspector, realising he'd made an error. 'I see. In that case,' he said, taking a gun from his pocket, 'we'll have to get our questions answered some other way, won't we?'

Grace was shocked when the weapon was produced, but kept her composure, the action eliciting an expression of indignation across her face.

'Perhaps you'd both like to sit down?' said the inspector, pointing to the chairs with his gun to reinforce the implied request. The sergeant, seeing him produce the weapon, followed his lead and did likewise.

'So… you're not policemen,' Jim stated.

'How observant of you,' the inspector said sarcastically. 'No. My name is Douglas Payne, and my associate is Dan Warren, affectionately known as Bunny to his friends.' He continued, 'Has Mike Randle visited here recently?' Then, turning to Grace, he asked, 'And where is he now?'

Grace looked at Jim, who frowned a little and shook his head slightly. She understood what he meant.

'I told you at the flat, he's on holiday but didn't say where he was going,' Jim stated.

'I asked the woman, not you, so button up,' Payne threatened, pointing a crooked finger at him.

'I don't know where he's gone. He often goes abroad at a moment's notice for work or holidays,' Grace confirmed.

'No matter. We're pretty sure he's gone to Roseburgh. We reckon you took him to the airport yesterday, after you gave us the slip on the motorway.'

Jim said nothing. Grace was concerned but determined not to let it show.

'I asked if he's visited here recently.'

'You seem to know everything else,' sneered Jim. 'How come you don't know that as well?'

'Don't get clever with me or you'll regret it,' Payne snapped, pushing the gun into Jim's face. 'I'll ask just once more.'

'Yes. He stayed here for a short time a couple of weeks ago while a wound in his leg healed,' offered Grace. 'Why?'

'Ah!' said Payne, ignoring her question. 'And are any of his things still here?'

'One of the bedrooms is his. He uses it whenever he stays here. All the things in there are his.'

'And where is this room?'

Grace told them, and they listened in horror at things being smashed as Payne searched the room.

He returned with a smirk on his face. 'Bring the car round to the front of the cottage, Bunny.'

'Right-o,' Bunny replied.

'So he does speak,' observed Jim. 'I was beginning to think his throat might have been hurt recently, or perhaps he had a stab wound.'

Bunny gave him a contemptuous look. 'You're a bit too clever for your boots. It could have been you who stabbed Jack.'

'Get going,' Payne told him. 'I'll take care of things here.'

Jim and Grace gave each other a worried glance.

'Like you took care of the man in Mike's flat, I suppose,' suggested Jim.

'No, that was Bunny's handiwork. He got a bit angry after Jack was stabbed and lost his head a little, but that doesn't matter now.'

Bunny opened the front door and stepped outside. There was shouting and several shots rang out. He came crashing back through the door, falling to the floor, with blood oozing from two bullet wounds in his chest.

The shock caused Grace to draw breath sharply. She rose, and Payne put his arm around her throat. He turned to Jim and shot him at point blank range in the chest. The force of the bullet knocked him into the armchair, which toppled over backwards, sending him in a complete somersault crashing face down on the floor. He remained still.

Grace screamed and Emmy scrambled away from the noise and hid in the corner.

'Shut up or you're next,' shouted Payne angrily.

Putting his gun to Grace's head, he marched her through the front door, glancing at Bunny as he stepped over him.

By light from the doorway, two men were visible along the pathway. One was lying on the ground with a bullet wound bleeding in his left side, while the other bent over him. He had a gun in his hand.

'Toss that gun into the bushes, or else…' threatened Payne, with his gun at Grace's temple, emphasising his unfinished sentence.

The man looked scornfully at him, but obeyed, and Grace was dragged towards the Range Rover hidden by the side of the cottage. Payne was forced to relax his grip a little when opening the car door and Grace snatched the opportunity to break free. She gave him a hefty kick in the shins before spinning on her heels to run back to the safety of her cottage.

The stranger near the doorway saw this, and he dashed to the bushes to look for his gun. Retrieving the weapon, he raced towards the Range Rover as it burst into life and tore down the side of the cottage, crashing into the rear garden and demolishing everything in its way. The man followed, firing after him as he ran. Payne's vehicle charged across the large expanse of lawn and ploughed through the back hedge into a field, just missing the shed with Bonnie in. Once across the field it crashed through a gate into a side road and was accelerated away.

Chapter VIII
Africa

Mike Randle gazed from the aircraft window at twinkling lights below, getting ever larger as the Boeing 747 came in to land at Nairobi airport. The four thousand mile journey had taken nearly nine hours, and he was tired.

It was 4.30 a.m. local time, and sleep had eluded him on the plane. At Nairobi, he sat in the airport holding lounge for almost an hour, drinking coffee and waiting, unable to relax, eager to complete the journey. This time in limbo frustrated him; he was anxious to begin the search for Suzie. Eventually the connecting flight was called, and he boarded the Airbus A320 to complete the last six hundred miles of his long journey.

Through the cabin window, he watched a spectacular sun peer over the horizon to send shafts of yellow light beaming across the sky, illuminating the contours of the earth. By the time the aircraft came in to land at Roseburgh Airport, the sun had risen in the sky and the temperature was already starting to climb.

Filing along the gangway with the other one hundred and fifty or so passengers, Mike stepped through the door and inhaled a lungful of air that had a familiar smell. A wall of heat slapped him in the face, bringing memories of the country flooding back. The temperature was almost 30°C, and the tarmac shimmered with the rising heat. He thought about Suzie, wondering how she was coping, or even if she was still alive, and he got a sick feeling in his stomach whenever he thought she might not be. He'd no real plan on how to get her out after locating her, and he was relying on experience to enable him to handle each situation as it unfolded. At least he was familiar with the surrounding area and the camp she was in. A previous important mission there a few years ago was now taking on a new significance.

Unaware of binoculars trained on him by a figure in the

visitor's viewing gallery, he descended the aircraft steps and joined the throng of passengers being ushered towards the terminal. While Mike was crossing the tarmac, so two local men approached the passport control officer. They'd all met before and knew the drill. After exchanging a few hushed words, the men discreetly handed an envelope to the officer, then retired to a nearby room to wait.

The terminal was bustling with people. Most were there to greet friends and relatives from the incoming flight. The arrival and departure building was modern, having been erected for only a few short years, but was already too small for the ever-expanding number of visitors who passed through it. The increasingly common practice of charging a tax to all visitors using the airport was introduced to pay for an extension, the plans of which were well under way.

Mike jostled with the other passengers to collect his suitcase from the one and only carousel provided for incoming luggage, then proceeded to passport control. The queue moved slowly forward until he reached the front and presented his papers.

Opening the passport, a man in a grey uniform and flat cap thumbed through the pages. 'I see you left our country only a short while ago. What brings you back so soon, Mr Randle?' he asked, in a strong African accent.

'Business,' replied Mike. 'Unfinished business. I was unable to complete an important deal on my last visit, but I'm hoping to do so this time. I'm a sales rep.'

'I see. Perhaps you would be kind enough to go with this gentleman,' he said, closing the passport and handing it to a nearby man in a similar uniform. 'He'll take you to a room while we make a few checks.'

'What's this all about?'

'Just go with the officer, please. We won't keep you very long.'

Mike was shown to a nearby room, which was windowless and contained only a table, a telephone and four chairs. The two men, already sat in the room, said that they were customs officers and this was just a routine random check they often made; though Mike noted neither wore a uniform and made no attempt to provide proof of their claims. Instructed to empty out his pockets and open his suitcase, he complied and wondered if they would subject him to a body search and find the money belt around his waist. It would be difficult to explain why he was carrying so much cash, and he couldn't afford to lose it. He was already forming a plan of attack and bracing himself for a fight, if it became necessary.

'What is your destination, Mr Randle?' the first man asked, flicking through the pages of his passport.

'Roseburgh. I'm staying with a friend.'

'Exactly where?'

'At his pub, Paul's Bar. It's on the far side of the city, situ—'

'Yes. I know where it is, thank you,' he interrupted.

The other man, searching through Mike's belongings and suitcase, looked up and shook his head.

'Everything seems to be in order,' the first man said, closing the passport and tossing it onto the table in front of Mike. His clothes were bundled back in the suitcase. 'Thank you for your co-operation. You may proceed with your journey. I hope you have an enjoyable stay in our country.'

Mike said nothing, picked up his passport and pocketed his personal things, then collected his now bulging suitcase and walked out leaving the door open.

Closing it after him, one of the men picked up the telephone and dialled. When the call was answered he reported, 'Mike Randle has arrived. We searched him but found nothing. He's staying with a friend in Roseburgh at Paul's Bar. We let him continue on his way.'

The airport terminal had all but emptied by the time Mike emerged from the interrogation room. His footsteps echoed across the main hall as he walked towards Paul, standing in the middle with hands on hips, looking lost. When he saw Mike, a big grin crossed his face, and they greeted each other with smiles and handshakes before making their way to the car park.

'I'm sorry I kept you waiting, Paul. Customs men searched me. At least, that's what they said they were.'

'That's a bit unusual. I've never known them to bother with people coming in from England before.'

'That's true. I've never been searched before, and it didn't feel right somehow. It almost seemed like they were expecting me.'

'Could that be?'

'Maybe – but I wouldn't have thought so. Not yet anyway. Still, they didn't find everything,' he said, quietly fingering the money belt.

Paul was a stockily built, five feet six inches tall, forty year old diminutive Irishman. He had a round, slightly plump face with staring eyes, thinning hair and a small moustache. Answering to the nickname Paddy, he was also known affectionately as Adolf, due to the 'resemblance', mainly because of the moustache. Despite living in the area for many years, he'd not lost his Irish accent and even exaggerated it on occasions for more important visitors.

He led Mike to an ex-British armed forces, open-topped Land Rover from the early sixties and threw the ignition key to him.

'You drive. This "Jeep" is the vehicle you'll be using, so you might as well get used to it. The tank's full.'

Mike slung his suitcase in the back and they set off on the ten-mile journey to the pub.

'Did you manage to get all the equipment I asked for?' enquired Mike, accelerating out of the airport complex.

'Yes, most of it. Some of it's not exactly what you requested, but I think you'll be happy with what I've got. It wasn't easy at such short notice.'

'You're being well paid,' Mike reminded him.

'That's true, but it's not why I made a special effort to get everything you asked for.'

Mike looked at him and nodded his appreciation. 'Thanks,' he said.

Following a brand new road sign, he turned along the main carriageway towards the city of Roseburgh. The area was barren, with only a few trees and isolated shacks dotting the landscape. They'd journeyed less than a mile when, from a side track, an old Austin A50 saloon car swung in behind them containing three shabbily dressed locals. Two back-seat passengers leaned through the windows brandishing guns and began firing. Bullets ricocheted off the jeep, and Mike jammed his foot down hard and accelerated the old vehicle to its maximum speed.

'You got a gun on you?' he asked.

'No, not me,' said Paul, half-turning to look at their pursuers. 'I don't carry one in case I get stopped by the police. Since this country became democratic they're not keen on civilians arming themselves, especially foreigners. I'd be deported if they caught me with one in the street.'

'Great! So now what?'

Bullets continued to whistle past them as they hurtled along the road, overtaking an old, ramshackle airport bus.

'We can't outrun them on this road. They're gonna catch us before we hit town,' warned Paul. 'We'll have to take avoiding action. There's a side road on the right just around the next bend – take it. It's a small bumpy dirt track and this jeep should have the advantage over a saloon car.'

Mike wrenched the steering wheel round, and the jeep skidded sideways into the corner and up the bumpy road. With the accelerator pressed to the floor, he charged along the rough, winding track edged with a few bare bushes. For a short while they gained an advantage, but the track smoothed out, the saloon car gained on them, and the shooting began again. Clouds of dust billowed out behind the jeep as they tore along the narrow road, with Mike fighting to keep control, weaving from side to side to avoid the bullets whizzing their way. The dustcloud made it impossible for the pursuers to see clearly and aim with any accuracy. The chase continued for several miles. Mike gained distance around bends and up inclines, only to lose it again on the straight. He and Paul clung on tightly to the jeep, bouncing over ruts, shaking them so violently that they were almost thrown out.

Then near disaster struck.

A bullet nicked Mike's left arm. He instinctively grasped at the wound with his other hand and the jeep swerved out of control, compelling him to wrestle with the steering wheel to avoid ploughing into the scrub. The vehicle slewed sideways, but he kept going with his foot firmly to the floor on the accelerator pedal. Mike swore profusely, seeing blood soak through the arm of his shirt.

'Another shirt ruined,' he joked. 'We've gotta do something about this lot. I didn't come all the way out here just to get shot in the back by a bunch of banana lovers in a beat-up old saloon.'

They approached a crossroads and screeched to a halt. The road opposite was a rough, winding track flanked by bare trees and the occasional scrubby bush. Mike crunched the jeep into gear, tore across the road and along the track. The saloon car followed, crashing up and down the rough terrain in an attempt to keep up.

Features of the land began to change with more trees and bushes starting to appear, giving better cover on the winding road. Rounding a bend, Mike saw that the track led to a narrow wooden bridge over a river, thirty yards ahead. Stamping on the brakes, he swung the jeep into the bushes. The saloon car came blindly tearing round the bend amid clouds of dirt and dust. Mike reversed the jeep and rammed the pursuing car, throwing it off course and sending it careering towards the edge of the bridge. All four wheels on the Austin locked up when the driver jammed the brakes hard on in an effort to stop the vehicle skidding on the loose surface. But its momentum carried it unerringly forward, bursting through the wooden railings, and plunging over the edge.

The car soared through the air. Terrified screams rang out above the roar of the racing engine, and the vehicle nosedived into the murky water, fifty feet below. It somersaulted onto its roof and splashed into the river, sending a great jet of water skywards, soaking the bridge and bank. The river rushed in, filling the car, and it quickly sank.

Mike drove onto the bridge. They peered over the edge and saw the wheels disappearing under the water. A large pocket of air bubbled to the surface and was the only sound to break the unfamiliar silence that now filled the gentle breeze as it wafted in from the river.

Nobody got out of the car.

Mike and Paul looked at each other, and then Mike drove on without speaking.

Paul said, 'That was a close shave. I wonder why they were firing at us? How's your arm?'

'Okay. It's only a scratch.'

'I've a gorgeous young lady named Jenny working for me at the pub. I'm sure she'll be only too happy to take a look and bandage it for you. She's a very versatile female with lots of talent, which, if you're lucky enough, you may find out about,' he said, rather mysteriously.

'Look,' began Mike. 'I'm sorry about all this trouble. I honestly never dreamt they'd be on to me so quickly over here.'

'What do you mean?' enquired Paul, a little startled at the comment.

He listened attentively. Mike told him about the break-in at Tramer, how he narrowly missed getting a knife stuck in him, and that he had to lose a tail on his way to the airport. Paul asked if he knew any reason for this, but got no answer, only a shrug of the shoulders.

Directing Mike back to the main road, they continued their journey to the pub, with little more said between them.

Roseburgh, the capital of Karuna, was fast becoming a large modern city, attracting many people. This was mainly due to the existence of the nearby airport, which started life as a military base with a small landing strip and a few wooden huts. When the country stabilised and elections overtook dictatorship, the new government commercialised the airport, and made rebuilding and expanding it a priority, although it could still only boast one runway. With continued incidents of fighting between government and rebel forces in the neighbouring country of Kitsulana, further expansion this close to the border was slow to develop for fear of the trouble spreading.

Mike and Paul reached the city outskirts, where mainly wooden or corrugated iron shacks appeared. These gave way to rough-built breeze-block buildings and, finally, to modern high-rise structures in the heart of Roseburgh. The hustle and bustle of cars, buses and taxis took people about their daily business in this expanding, busy metropolis.

The city had attracted many large institutes and banks, and was fast becoming the business and banking centre for the region. Tourism was not yet a thriving industry but, with government finance and encouragement, was steadily growing. An uphill struggle faced them in their attempts to distance themselves from the troubles across the border.

Mike drove through the city centre and towards the outskirts on the far side, where Paul's British-style pub was located. A two-storey wooden structure painted green, it had a ground-floor verandah and first-floor balcony at the front with a yard at the back. A typically British weather-beaten pub sign hung from the balcony proclaiming that this was Paul's Bar with the P and B in large fancy letters linked together.

The pub opened from 3 p.m. to 3 a.m., and was situated less than ten miles from the border, attracting soldiers from neighbouring Kitsulana, where alcohol was in short supply because of the fighting. It was understood by the customers, that Paul's Bar was for drinking and meeting women. Rarely was there any trouble, and then it was generally over one of the many hookers who frequented the pub. They were encouraged to do business there because it was good for trade, and because Paul made money from three upstairs rooms he rented to the girls, to engage in their evening activities.

By the time he and Mike arrived, it was nearly noon. Entering the bar, Mike was introduced to the attractive, coloured female, Jenny, who was busy wiping and stacking glasses, and to Manny, a local man who helped in the bar.

After the heat and bright sun outside, the pub in subdued light with the blinds pulled, was cool, and smelt of beer and stale cigarettes. It seemed strangely quiet with the fruit machine and jukebox standing silently in one corner, waiting for a coin to drop in the slot before erupting into action.

Jenny gave a warm smile when introduced to Mike. A thirty-four year old former beauty queen, she had close-cropped dark hair and piercing black eyes. Her smooth features and wide mouth combined to give her an attractiveness that was highly photogenic. The tight jeans she wore exaggerated her long legs, and a full, curvy figure was apparent under her thin chiffon top, which was tantalisingly close to see-through and rippled up and down in waves with her every movement.

'I'm pleased to meet you,' she said in a quiet voice, extending her hand, only to withdraw it quickly with a gasp. 'You've been hurt. There's blood on your shirt.'

'It's nothing. Just a scratch,' explained Mike, in his best macho style, trying to impress.

'You must let me clean it for you.'

'Why don't you show Mike to his room and attend to him there?' suggested Paul.

Jenny glided towards the stairs with Mike following closely, surveying her figure from the rear and giving a quiet whistle of appreciation at the delightful sight.

'Don't forget we open at 3 p.m.,' yelled Paul.

'Yes, I know,' she replied with a pout. 'That gives me plenty of time.'

Mike wondered why she wanted plenty of time and, after Paul's comment, he was intrigued to find out.

Upstairs, Jenny led him along a dimly lit passageway accommodating doors to six bedrooms, an office and a bathroom with a shower. The curtains were drawn in his room, keeping it cool. Jenny pulled them open and Mike gave a gratified nod to himself, seeing her full beauty silhouetted against the light. She pushed open the balcony doors to let fresh air in.

Outside, the traffic sped past, with the pop-pop sound of small motorcycles creating clouds of dust, drifting in. The room was small and sparsely furnished with only a double bed, and a wardrobe pushed into an alcove. The walls were painted light green, but the sun had bleached most of the colour out of them. It smelled fresh, without any mustiness, so Mike guessed it had probably been used and cleaned quite recently.

He dumped his suitcase on the floor and glanced in the wardrobe. Paul had filled it with the combat fatigues and boots he'd asked for, along with some of the equipment he needed, but not any weapons. They must be hidden somewhere safe.

'Take your shirt off. I'll get the first aid box,' Jenny purred.

Mike took off his shirt and flexed his muscles for effect. She bathed and bandaged his wound.

'You're right, it's not much more than a scratch I'm pleased to say,' she remarked.

'Me too,' he said, enjoying her gentle touch.

'You've a good physique, Mike, and plenty of muscles, but they're tense and tight,' she explained, feeling his biceps. 'What you need is a massage to relax you and get rid of all that tension.'

'You can tell that just by feeling?'

'Of course. I'm a trained masseuse. It's one of my many

talents. Would you like me to do you now?'

Many possible answers flashed through Mike's mind, but he restrained himself and simply answered, 'Yes, please, if it's not too much bother.'

'It's no bother at all. I enjoy it.'

Mike stripped to his shorts and lay on the bed while Jenny prepared the oils.

'I don't want to splash any of these on my top, so if you don't mind I'll take it off,' she said, slowly removing it, well aware of the effect it was having on him.

'Umm… no. You go right ahead,' Mike effused, trying not to sound too enthusiastic. He gazed at her smooth skin and full breasts, realising how sexy she looked dressed only in jeans, and knowing she was giving him the come-on.

She sat astride him, her supple fingers working the oils into his back and legs. He felt warm, relaxed and at ease, and nearly went to sleep. When his back was done, she turned him over and worked on his torso from above his head. He watched her full bosom gently moving just inches from his face. She firmly stroked away all the tension in him.

It became obvious that this was having an effect on him as the bulge in his shorts grew.

'That's better. Your muscles are much more relaxed now – well, most of them, anyway! I reckon you're about done,' she pronounced, wiping her hands on a towel.

Mike pulled her down onto the bed and rolled over on top. 'Now I reckon it's about time you were done,' he said.

She put the palms of her hands against his shoulders and pushed hard, but he was too strong for her and easily held her down. Despite the struggle she put up, a smile played across her lips and her nostrils twitched, giving a signal that she was only waging a token resistance. Mike pressed down harder and brought his face closer to hers. She relaxed, allowing him to kiss her gently on the lips, then smiled and put her arms around his neck. Their open mouths met with a force that made their lips burn, while their tongues fought each other.

Mike undid the zip on her jeans carefully, as she asked, and saw that she wore no underwear. She deliberately, slowly and tantalisingly removed them, making him wait. He cupped her breasts, kissing and sucking her nipples, teasing them until they were firm and erect, heightening their expectations. He explored her body with his lips, the aromatic fragrance of the oils lingering in the room, mixing with the taste of her skin. He kissed her all over, her breathing became deeper and the excitement grew until she could stand it no longer. She wanted him inside her now and tried to help him enter. Mike held back and now made her wait, moving slowly, teasing her, making her desperate for that moment of satisfaction when he finally penetrated her.

The initial pleasure of entering brought renewed intensity and the strong desire for movement, which Mike resisted when they were joined together. Quietly they lay with him inside her, kissing and petting, waiting for the excitement and thrill to build up again until they could no longer remain still but began a gentle rhythm. Gradually the pace began to get faster, then Jenny squeezed her thighs together, restricting the movement and slowing their lovemaking down almost to a stop. Now she made him wait until she was ready to continue. Mike wriggled back and forth, but could gain little movement, and the expectation of pleasure grew within him. Finally she relaxed, opened her legs and clasped him around his buttocks. She was wide open, inviting him to take her now with all his energy. He was more than ready, and their rhythm became faster and faster, rising to a crescendo, with both reaching a climax and uttering long groans of ecstasy at the delight and pleasure throbbing between them.

The passion slowly diminished, and they relaxed, embraced and kissed once again, but more gently this time. Jenny cried out in disappointment when he withdrew, and left her with an empty feeling inside.

They lay beside each other, drained but satisfied, and rested. She asked Mike about his visit, but he was reluctant to say too much after the ambush, and Jenny asked a lot of questions.

Mike thought about Suzie while he lay there, feeling a tinge of guilt over the pleasure that he'd enjoyed, while she might be languishing in a cell or, even worse, be suffering torture or humiliation at the hands of her captors.

'Penny for your thoughts,' interrupted Jenny.

'Oh, just thinking about an old friend.'

'Hmm… female no doubt. Care to tell me about it?'

'Not right now. Some other time maybe.'

It was approaching pub opening time. Jenny dressed and gave Mike a kiss, leaving him there, glowing, contented and sleepy, while she returned to the bar to begin work.

After several hours of much needed rest, Mike took a shower, dressed in jeans, light T-shirt and trainers, and went down to the bar. Jenny was the star attraction, with customers swarming round her like bees to a honey pot, even this early in the evening. She saw Mike and gave him a smile and a wave, much to the chagrin of many of the hopeful punters who cast an envious look in his direction. He felt special and enjoyed it. Pub customers were arriving all the time, and the place was beginning to buzz.

At the bar, Mike beckoned Paul, who was serving, and in a low voice asked, 'Where have you put the weapons? I'd like to take a look at them.'

'They're in the back of the stock room down in the cellar,' he replied, wiping his hands on a cloth and returning it to a rail. 'I'll show you the way.'

He led Mike downstairs to a stock room and tossed over the key, then left him alone to check the items.

Carefully inspecting the guns, Mike took them apart and reassembled them to make sure they were in good working order. There'd be enough to think about when the time came, without having to wonder whether his gun would jam. Mike checked the ammunition, selecting a few cartridges at random and taking them apart. They were all good. The four hand grenades, he had to trust were in working order. They, too, looked okay.

The sub-machine-gun was a Heckler & Koch MP5, instead of the Ingram M10 he'd asked for. Still, it was an excellent weapon and he was pleased to get it. The handgun was a Browning high-powered GP-35 9 mm pistol he'd requested, along with a Heckler & Koch P7 in a shoulder holster, and plenty of ammunition.

When satisfied that he'd done all he could to ensure everything was in order, Mike placed all the equipment in a holdall and took it to his room. He looked for somewhere to hide it for the night. Not many places. The wardrobe pulled away from the alcove and had an upright jutting out at the top. Among the gear was a rope. Mike grabbed it, looped a length through the handles and tied it to the upright. He swung the wardrobe back into the alcove until the holdall touched the wall, and he knew it was the best he could do under the circumstances.

'Should be fine for the short time they'll be there,' he declared. He locked the door on his way out and pocketed the key.

The jeep was parked in the backyard, and Mike checked the essentials, making sure the spare cans of petrol were full and no damage had been done during the fracas from the airport. One of the cans had a bullet nick in the handle.

'Good job it didn't go into the can. It's full of petrol. No telling what might have happened,' he thought.

Mike returned to the bar, which was now nearly full of customers and smoke, and had a sixties hit song blaring out from the jukebox.

'I'm very pleased with the equipment, Paul,' he shouted above the music. 'I assume you could only get four "pineapples".'

'That's right. I was lucky to get those at such short notice.'

'No matter, you've done well. I won't ask where you got it all from.'

'Good,' he replied, 'because I wouldn't tell you anyway. And I won't ask what you want it for, or where you're going, though I'm sure you've a particular destination in mind. I could probably take an educated guess and not be far wrong, considering the type of equipment you've asked for.'

Mike ignored the implied question and shook hands with him.

'Thanks for all you've done ol' buddy,' he said, handing him an envelope with the payment in it.

'That's okay. I'm pleased to take your money any time,' Paul retorted, stuffing the envelope in his inside pocket. 'If you manage to survive your excursion and bring any of it back, I might even consider giving you a small refund,' he said, emphasising the word 'small'.

Mike smiled and said, 'Just a couple more things, Paul. Do you know if that rough track through the jungle that bypasses the border checkpoint is still there, and passable?'

'Yes, I thought you might be wondering about that. I'm sure it is. It's been a while since we last used it, but I reckon some of the soldiers we get here, still come by that route. Next?'

'I'd like some provisions for the trip.'

'That's already taken care of. There's a supply pack in the fridge, enough for one week, and on the floor next to it there's a large can for water and a smaller flask to keep on you.'

'Great. One last thing. I'd like to make a telephone call to England.'

'Follow me, I'll show you where there's a telephone you can use in private,' he offered, taking Mike up to his office. 'The lines aren't very good, that you already know, so you may have to keep trying,' he warned, unlocking the door. 'I'll leave you to it.'

'Okay, Paul, thanks.'

Mike picked up the telephone and inserted his finger, spinning the dial.

Chapter IX
Who's Who?

In the rear garden of Silverdale Cottage in Sussex, the man stood and watched the Range Rover's lights disappear into the distance. He holstered his gun and ran back to his injured colleague, lying on the ground, bathed in light from the open cottage front door. Grace was standing by him.

'Hang on, Bill, I'll get the medics here in a hurry,' he said reassuringly, then turned to Grace. 'Where's Jim Sterling? Is he all right?'

'I think he's dead. The one who got away shot him,' she replied in a quivering voice.

'Oh Christ, no! His dad'll have me court martialled. We came here to guard the pair of you.'

He ran to his car, grabbed a mobile phone and punched out the numbers. When the call was answered he spoke anxiously.

'It's Brooke. We need the paramedics here at Silverdale Cottage fast. I've got three men with gunshot wounds and possibly two are fatal. Bill's got a nasty hole in his side and he's losing a lot of blood.'

'Okay,' said a dispassionate voice, which could be heard in the background relaying the message. 'They're on the way now.'

'Get the patrol cars to watch out for a dark-coloured Range Rover which could have some damage to the front…' He went on to give a description of the driver and the direction he took. 'I'm going to check the other two men.'

'Right. Do you want me to tell Sir Joseph?'

'No. Not yet,' he answered quickly. 'I want to see his son first to find out how he is. I'll contact you again in a few minutes.'

'Okay, Colin. His son isn't one of those injured, is he?'

'I'll talk to you again in a minute,' was the evasive reply. He threw his mobile onto the car seat and dashed back to his injured colleague. 'The medics are on the way, Bill. Just hold on for a bit longer.'

Bill smiled but said nothing. He was white with shock and wondered if this was the way that he was meant to end his life, shot on a seemingly innocent task of checking on someone in a tranquil country cottage, with Colin, his young DI partner.

Turning to Grace Randle, the DI spoke in a warm, gentle voice, the anxiety now diminished from its tone. 'I'm Detective Inspector Colin Brooke. My partner here is Detective Sergeant Bill Harding. We're from Special Branch.'

Brooke was a tough-looking man of thirty-two, just over six feet tall with dark, slightly wavy, combed-back hair. Despite being clean-shaven, he always seemed to have stubble around his strong jawline. Friendly, grey eyes, a cleft chin and dark complexion together created a handsome face that women found attractive. He liked to keep fit and was muscular and lean.

Brooke took off his jacket and folded it to make a pillow for Harding's head. 'Take it easy, Bill, they'll be here soon,' he said reassuringly.

The man he had shot lay in the living room doorway. Only a quick check was needed to confirm that he was dead. Two patches of blood stained his shirt red where the bullets from Brooke's H&K M7 had gone right through him, giving him no chance to retaliate.

Grace went into the living room and gasped at seeing Jim get to his feet, blood running from a gash on his forehead.

'I thought you were dead,' she said, with relief in her voice. 'Why aren't you?' she asked quizzically.

Jim opened his shirt to reveal a bulletproof vest, saying, 'Mike told me to wear this if things started to look dangerous. He kept it at his flat. After finding a dead man there, it seemed like a good idea, so I put it on while waiting for the men to arrive.'

Brooke was relieved. 'Thank goodness you did,' he said. 'Now I can ring in with some good news.' He left, to stay and comfort his partner.

'Who was this dead man?' Grace quizzed. 'And waiting for what men to arrive?'

'The men who took the body away,' Jim exclaimed.

Grace looked puzzled and said, 'It sounds as if we've got a bit to talk about.'

Brooke remained with Harding until the paramedics arrived, then phoned in. Sir Joseph Sterling came on the line, eager for news of his son. Brooke was pleased to tell him that, despite a few bruises and a gash on his forehead, he was okay.

'I'll get the medics to check him over and take him for a precautionary X-ray if necessary.'

'Good. I'll want a full report when you get back, but give me the gist of it now.'

'Certainly, sir. We had a bit of difficulty finding Silverdale Cottage and it was dark by the time we arrived. There were no vehicles parked outside except the Rolls. As we approached the front door, it opened and a man came out acting suspiciously. I challenged him, said that we were policemen and he drew a gun. He shot Bill before I could respond. I fired back, hitting him twice and killing him. While I was checking Bill, another shot came from inside the cottage and I was about to investigate when a man came out, holding Grace Randle hostage with a gun to her head.'

Brooke described how the second man fled, after the resilient Miss Randle, who was not afraid to tackle the man, got away from him. He emphasised that she was shaken by the experience but not hurt, reiterating that so was his son, saved by a body protector he'd collected from the flat in Surbiton.

An ambulance and several police cars arrived on the scene. Harding was quickly attended to and sped away to hospital. The body was removed, and Jim was checked over by one of the medics. Apart from his cut forehead, which only required a sticky plaster, all he suffered was bruising, with no other apparent ill effects. Jim refused the advice to go to hospital for a full check-up.

'I'm fine,' he told Brooke. 'I was just working out a strategy to take care of them when you two arrived. I've had instruction at the Tramer International Combat Training School, you know.'

'Oh really!' was Brooke's surprised comment.

'Yes. He only shot me because he panicked when you arrived and started shooting.'

'When *I* started shooting?' Brooke questioned, hardly believing what he heard.

Grace smiled at Jim, who gave her a wink without letting Brooke see. Brooke was not sure if Jim was serious or not. To Jim, who was still shaking inwardly at the horror of the past few minutes, his joking was a self-defence mechanism to mask the fear he felt at his brush with death.

Things returned to normal and most of the vehicles left. A hot, sweet cup of tea was Grace's answer to the shocks they'd received. Detective Inspector Brooke joined them, though he declined the sugar. All thoughts of the evening meal were forgotten for the moment, with neither Grace nor Jim having an appetite for food.

Between them, they gave Brooke a brief account of what happened before he arrived. He was curious to know why Payne had searched Mike's room. Grace said that she would check to see if anything was missing and let him know.

'I've instructed a constable to stay on duty outside tonight,' Brooke explained, 'though I'm not expecting any further trouble. It's unlikely they'll be back.'

Grace looked pleased at his concern. 'Thank you, Inspector. That's very good of you.'

'Not at all. But I'll need to get a full account about tonight from both of you.'

'I'm expecting a long distance call from my nephew soon. Can it wait until tomorrow?' Grace asked.

'Yes, of course. I'll come back in the morning if that's convenient. Shall we say about ten o'clock?'

'That's fine, Inspector. We'll expect you then. Goodbye.'

She closed the door behind him and stared at the blood on the hall carpet. It sent a shiver through her.

'How on earth does Mike cope with such things?' she asked herself. 'I'll arrange to get the carpet cleaned tomorrow.'

The detective inspector returned to his office in London. His work now began, to find out all he could about the dead man and try to establish a motive for the crime.

Sir Joseph Sterling took a keen interest in the case. Although it was getting late, he went to the incident room to see for himself what progress was made and to speak to Brooke.

'There's something strange about this incident, Colin. I haven't worked out what it is yet,' he said.

'Yes, sir. We don't know what they were after. They were looking for something that's tied in with Mike Randle somehow. That also means it's probably linked to the murder of Jack Carson in his flat.'

'Yes, I'm sure you're right.'

'Jack was just a small-time crook who worked for anyone who'd pay him, so that doesn't give us any leads. Perhaps we'll have a better idea what's going on when records send the information through, on both our victims.'

'I hope so. I'm worried that my son's mixed up in something a lot more dangerous than he's aware of. He was lucky tonight, but his luck may not last.'

Meanwhile, Jim had accepted Grace's invitation to stay the night, and they now sat in the light of a roaring log fire, discussing the evening's dramatic events and sipping a Pimms. The drink was new to Jim. It was stronger than he thought at first taste, and after downing it in a couple of gulps on an empty stomach, a mellow feeling overtook him.

'This is a nice drink, Gracie,' he said, sucking the fruit out of the slice of orange from his glass. 'And a bit stronger than I realised. I'm feeling a bit squiffy.'

'Yes,' she grinned. 'Perhaps it'll help you sleep tonight.' She looked at his slightly glazed eyes, and Emmy took advantage of his comfortable lap to sit on.

He smiled to himself, stroking the cat's soft, long, shiny coat. 'Ironic isn't it?' he said. 'Mike particularly emphasised that I wasn't to alarm you. He'll probably have a fit when he finds out what's happened.'

'Yes,' she agreed. 'Probably. I do wish he'd ring.'

For the umpteenth time that evening, they both looked at the turn-of-the-century marble chiming clock over the fireplace. While they waited, Jim told Grace about the telephone call Mike had received from Martin, saying that Suzie was in trouble.

Grace said she understood why Mike wanted to help. 'He's very fond of her and spoke a lot about her during his stay. He even brought her here to meet me on one occasion.'

'Really! What's she like?' Jim enthusiastically asked.

'I found her to be very refreshing. She was apparently a bit wild in her younger days, but she's matured into a lovely girl. She has a strong sense of loyalty and is purposeful and forthright. She's the sort of person you can rely on and who won't let you down. I think she'd like to change jobs to something more civilised and leave the problems of soldiering behind.'

'Yes, she does. Mike told me so.'

'I'd like to think they'd both find something else, and maybe, just maybe find something together. Mike's not getting any younger and I keep hoping he'll settle down and start a family, before it's too late.'

Jim recognised the mothering instinct in Grace. He'd been under much the same sort of pressure from his own mother, before she died. And lately, his father had taken up the mantle, but in a quieter way.

The telephone rang and they both jumped. Grace answered it and smiled at the sound of Mike's voice. After confirming that Jim was there, she explained about her other visitors that evening, but played down the seriousness, in a vain attempt not to alarm him. Mike was shocked at what he heard and had mixed feelings about Special Branch being involved, but at least Jim and Grace should be safe. He asked her to check on something in his bedroom, and meanwhile he spoke to Jim.

Mike asked Jim to do him a favour. Jim listened closely and confirmed that he could manage the task without any problems.

'Be careful,' pleaded Mike. 'I don't want you getting into any bother, especially after what's happened today. I'm not sure I should ask you to take the risk.'

'I'll be all right. Don't worry!' insisted Jim. 'You said I could help, and you've got enough to think about already.'

Grace returned and spoke to Mike again. 'Yes. You're right, it seems to be missing. I can't find it anywhere among the mess. It looks as if that's what they were after. It was definitely there yesterday when I dusted,' she said.

'Okay, Gracie. It just confirms what I already suspected. Please don't tell anyone else what's missing.'

'If you say so. But I don't like fibbing, as you well know. Jim has told me why you've gone back. Be careful. This man, The General, sounds like a nasty individual.'

'Yes. I rather thought you might extract things from him. This is my type of territory. It's what I'm good at, so don't worry.'

'All right. I never could get you to pursue mundane things, you've always got to have some excitement in your life.'

'That's what life's for.'

'When will you ring next?' she asked.

'I'm not sure. So don't fret if you don't hear from me for a few days.'

Mike said nothing about the trouble on the way from the airport. Enough problems had surfaced without alarming Grace any further.

The line crackled a few times, then went dead. Losing a connection was considered quite usual in that part of the country, where the telephone system was still primitive compared to western standards. Mike had about finished his conversation and decided to leave it at that.

He returned the telephone to its cradle and pondered for a long time over what he'd heard, staring blankly out of the window at the stars twinkling in the clear night sky. The situation at home was looking more dangerous that he'd anticipated. Things were starting to get out of hand. Two, possibly three, men were now dead, and only the protective vest had saved Jim from being the next. He wanted to deal with the problem himself, but he couldn't be in two places at once, and only he could free Suzie. He had to trust Jim and hope he could avoid getting into more difficulties. On reflection, he wondered whether it had been a good idea asking him to get involved at all. If things went wrong and he was hurt... 'That's the wrong attitude – think positive!' he encouraged himself.

Mike returned to his room for a rest. With noise from the bar, the girls using nearby rooms, and his mind turning over the problems, it took a while before sleep encompassed him. Gradually, he drifted off and became oblivious to the thumping of the jukebox blasting out pop music.

The night wore on, and the music stopped in the early hours.

The punters all drifted away, apart from a couple who were still with the girls for a while. All fell silent for a few hours until the whole cycle could begin again.

The alarm on Jim's watch woke Mike at 5 a.m. He was still feeling dozy but a cold shower, a legacy of army days, freshened him up. He dressed in T-shirt, camouflage jacket and trousers, heavy boots and a peak cap. Quietly pulling the wardrobe out, he collected the holdall, checked the contents and crept along the dim passageway to the stairs. One of the bedroom doors opened and Jenny stood there, naked.

'Good luck, Mike. I know you don't want to talk about why you're here, so I guess it could be dangerous. Look after yourself.'

He wanted to explain what he was doing and why, but contented himself with giving her a kiss.

'See you soon,' he said, with a smile and a wink, before walking on down the stairs.

The aroma of stale cigarettes and beer pervaded the air in the bar, where a few empty glasses were scattered around. Much of the clearing up was left until late morning, after Paul and Jenny had got some much needed sleep. Despite being a daily occurrence, when bar closing time arrived, both were tired and pleased to lay their heads on a pillow. Only Manny remained in the bar until the last customers had left. He was busy emptying ashtrays and wiping the tables.

Mike collected the provisions and loaded up the jeep in the backyard. He felt a prickle in the back of his neck, as if someone was watching him. He turned and stared at the windows, but it was too dark to see if anybody was there. When everything was loaded, he set off for Camp West. A pair of eyes behind the curtains watched him leave.

Motoring towards the border in the quiet early morning, the jeep's throbbing engine was the only sound to be heard. A clear morning gave the promise of another hot day, with a jet black sky full of a million twinkling stars his sole company along a route lit only by starlight and the jeep's headlights.

Gradually, he left the town behind. The number of buildings thinned out and eventually disappeared altogether with each mile that he put behind him.

The sky was getting lighter by the time Mike reached the turn-off he sought. Everything looked much the same as it was when he had last seen it.

A stop for a few moments enabled him to get the weapons from the holdall and buckle them on. The sub-machine-gun lay on the seat beside him, and the jeep slipped without effort into four-wheel drive and moved into the jungle. Deeper in, the track became rougher, bouncing Mike up and down. But the jeep, though it had seen much service, still handled the difficult terrain with ease. The ground remained boggy in places, and the vehicle rocked through water-filled ruts. Despite his slow progress, Mike noted fresh tyre tracks with satisfaction, confirming that the path continued to be used.

The sun rose slowly, great shafts of light penetrating the trees, enough to blind for a moment, then slipping back into darkness again, the process repeating itself over and over. Sounds of the morning coming to life with the rising sun mingled with a fresh, clean smell that accompanied the start of each new day for a short time.

A small gully clearing with steep sides, densely covered with trees and bushes at the top, lay before him. A fallen tree blocked the track.

Mike stopped the jeep immediately, switched off the engine and pocketed the key. He took off his sunglasses, threw them on the seat beside him and clicked off the safety catch on the sub-machine-gun. He sat quietly for a few moments, listening and searching for movement, but saw nothing.

'After those problems at the airport, I'm certain The General knows I'm on the way. This is the perfect spot for an ambush and I'm a sitting duck at the moment,' he told himself.

Grabbing the gun, he vaulted from the jeep and crouched down against the rear wheel, his back covered for the moment. With the gun cradled in his arms and his finger on the trigger he carefully checked one side.

Remaining motionless, Mike scanned the area above, looking for anything that stirred. Jungle noises seemed to increase in volume and the gentle breeze swayed trees back and forth, making it difficult to detect movement.

Perspiration trickled down Mike's face. He sat rock-like and watched, for what seemed like ages, instinctively knowing that something was amiss. Years of fighting had given him a sort of sixth sense. He knew someone was watching him; he could feel their eyes on him.

Then he saw it. A slight movement high up and to his right.

'Okay. So it is an ambush. Mustn't let on I've spotted them,' he thought.

Mike watched from the corner of his eye. Again he saw something, more clearly this time.

'Looks like a rebel soldier, hiding, just waiting. Why, when he's got an almost clear shot? There'll be more of them,' he reasoned. 'Perhaps they've been told to take me alive if possible. He could be waiting for others to close in – probably from the far side of the gully – behind me.'

Mike listened attentively. His experience of fighting in the jungle had taught him that it was almost impossible to move through this terrain without making some noise. Sure enough he heard movement behind him. Certainly one, more likely two, inching their way closer to his back.

'Got to catch them quickly and hope they're together. If they separate, makes it much more risky.'

In one quick movement Mike dropped to the ground and rolled under the jeep to the far side with his gun ready. Two soldiers, stealthily creeping forward were alarmed to see him suddenly appear below the jeep. The quiet of the jungle was shattered. Birds spread their wings and flapped disapprovingly as Mike's sub-machine-gun sprayed out a burst of bullets. Neither rebel reacted quickly enough to fire, and both were dead by the time they hit the ground.

Rolling back to the other side, Mike looked for the first soldier. Despite a careful search he saw nothing and knew that, after seeing his two comrades die, he'd be more cautious now.

Quiet calm returned to the jungle in this game of cat and mouse. The birds settled. Minutes ticked by with no sign of the first man. Mike was well aware of the benefits of patience in such a situation, and he knew his task was to wait for his attacker to make the first move.

He considered the soldier's options. 'I haven't seen anyone else – so if there were three of them, he's the only one left, and he's not likely to risk trying to take me alive any more. He needs a clear shot at me under here. That means he'll have to be at ground level. With the tree trunk in front making the perfect cover, *that's* the spot I reckon he'll choose.'

Trusting his logic and instinct, Mike crawled to the front of the jeep and trained his gun at the top edge of the tree trunk. A boggy patch lay beneath his vehicle, and Mike was compelled to lay in it while he waited, cursing at the increasing number of flies he had to flick away from his face. Minutes trickled by, but he remained constantly alert and searching ceaselessly in case he was wrong. After what seemed almost an eternity, but was in reality only a few minutes, he detected a slight movement near one end of the tree trunk and gave himself a wry smile.

'Looks like I guessed right – won't be much longer now.'

He steadied himself, licked his dry lips and prepared for what he now knew was inevitable.

The soldier rose quickly from behind the tree with his gun poised for the kill. He was met by a volley of bullets, which splattered across his chest and spread-eagled him to the ground before he had a chance to realise what hit him.

The rattle of sub-machine-gun fire died away, and again the quietness of the jungle returned to normal. Mike waited ten minutes before venturing out from beneath the jeep. He approached the tree quietly and cautiously peered over the top.

The soldier was dead. It was all over.

He relaxed and let the tension in his body ease, lowering his arms and straightening his back. Mike brushed away the damp leaves stuck to the front of his jacket...

Suddenly, a searing pain in his shoulder made him drop his gun. A shot rang out which he barely heard, and a bullet knocked him sideways to his knees, crashing him against the tree trunk. He hunched his left shoulder and put his right hand inside his jacket to cradle the injured arm.

A soldier stepped from behind a tree, high above the gully, and descended towards him. He had a Mediterranean look and wore a big grin on his face. With a sub-machine-gun held steadily in his hands, he trod carefully, moving closer to Mike, not taking his eyes off him once, and slowly picked his way down.

'You must be one of The General's mercenaries,' Mike suggested, watching the soldier get closer.

'Mercenary. Yes. Just like you, Mr Randle. We are the best. That is why we are alive and these three are dead,' he said in a Spanish accent, waving a hand in the general direction of the bodies without diverting his attention. Mike was surprised by the soldier's accent, but now knew for certain that The General was expecting him.

'You are very patient and very good, Mr Randle. But I am better,' he boasted. 'I could have killed you if I'd wanted to, but The General is anxious that you and Miss Drake should be reunited so that he can have a little chat with you – before you both die.'

'How thoughtful of him!' grunted Mike sarcastically, grimacing and holding his shoulder a little closer.

'Hurting, is it?' said the soldier mockingly. 'Too bad, such a pity that we are on opposite sides. You would be a challenge for me to prove that I am the best. I have enjoyed watching you outwit those morons who think they are soldiers just because they carry a gun.'

'So, you let them die just so you could have some fun watching.'

'Of course. They do the donkey work and I pick up the pieces.'

'Mercenary's the right name for you then.'

'Oh! So you have scruples, do you? Perhaps that is why you have a bullet in your arm and I am holding the gun. You cannot have scruples, Mr Randle, and still be the best.'

'Is that a fact?'

'Yes, and to the victor go the spoils. That is a very nice sub-machine-gun you have, and your jeep will be a useful addition to the motor pool.'

'There's something else you should have,' offered Mike.

The soldier stopped, and the expression on his face changed. He sensed trouble and tightened his finger on the trigger. Without warning, two bullet holes appeared from the P7 pistol inside

Mike's jacket when he pulled the trigger. The shots hit the man squarely in the chest and sent him reeling to the ground.

'You're not as clever as you think,' said Mike smugly. 'And you talk too much – don't pay enough attention to detail. No blood, you see.'

Mike opened his jacket and slipped it off his shoulder to take a look. The impact of the bullet had bruised him and moving his arm was painful, but the body protector had done its job. He was lucky. Another inch to the left and it would have missed the vest and shattered his arm. He got to his feet and realised that there was a niggle flashing in his brain that at first he was unable to place. He, too, could sense when something was wrong, but couldn't work out what it was – then it hit him, the same thing: no blood.

The soldier sprang to life. Both men's actions were focused, with time seeming to almost stand still at their painfully lethargic movement, like a recording shown in slow motion. The two men raced to shoot first. Mike dropped to one knee, taking an eternity to aim his pistol and pull the trigger. He won by a fraction of a second. The P7 barked once more and a hole appeared in the soldier's forehead as the force of the impact again knocked him backwards, and his gun rattled bullets harmlessly into the air.

This time, the soldier really was dead. This time he would not be getting up.

Mike stayed statue-like at the realisation that only a split second had separated him from death, and it could just as easily be him lying there. Returning the P7 to its shoulder holster, he picked up his sub-machine-gun and whispered thanks that his luck was still holding.

'Spanish also had a protective vest. Well, he won't be needing that any more,' he said, stripping the man's shirt off. It revealed a bulletproof vest the same as his own, except for a monogrammed letter 'R' on the left breast. Taking the vest and guns he threw them into the back of his jeep.

'To the victor go the spoils,' he echoed, with a sideways nod of his head.

Mike flexed his left shoulder again, remembering how Jenny had massaged all the aches and pains out of his muscles the previous day. He wished she was there now, to do the same to his bruises. He recalled the aromatic smell of the oils she used and fancied he could almost smell them again. The memory of her aroma reminded him how sweet life seems when death has come close. He daydreamed for a moment about their encounter before snapping himself back to the task in hand.

A small hollow served as a grave for the bodies. Mike covered them over and after locating their jeep, hid it deeper into the jungle, making it more difficult to find. He secured a rope round the tree trunk and dragged it aside with his vehicle, and was finally ready to continue the journey to Camp West.

He took a last, long, thoughtful look around the area. It looked no different than when he'd arrived less than an hour before, except that now four men were dead and buried there. Perhaps, before this job was finished there might be more, and with some skill and a lot of luck, he hoped to avoid being one of them.

Moving on, Mike tried putting some of the pieces together. Much had occurred in the last few days. He was now sure that Suzie was alive, and that The General knew he was on his way to rescue her. He wondered if it was *his* men who had visited Grace, and if not, then who. Perhaps Jim would find the answer soon, provided he didn't get caught and they didn't make a better job of killing him next time. Jim hadn't got Mike's experience, but maybe he would have some of his luck.

Chapter X
Which Way?

Grace began quizzing Jim immediately after their telephone conversation with Mike had ended.

'What does he want you to do? Nothing dangerous, I hope.'

'No – nothing like that,' Jim defended. 'He wants me to check on a couple of things in London, that's all.'

'Really,' enthused Grace, 'I haven't been shopping in London for ages. Is it all right if I come with you?'

Jim tried to wriggle his way out of taking her, but eventually had to confess that he might have to follow someone. It meant that he wasn't sure where he would be going, or when.

Grace insisted that she could help, and was very persuasive. Jim likened her skills to those of his father, who always managed to entice nearly everything out of him with ease. Gradually, she extracted the details and, despite wanting to go along, was eventually persuaded that it was better for her to remain at the cottage.

'After all,' Jim said, recalling a similar conversation with Mike, 'I may need to call for help, and it really would be more useful if you were next to a telephone.'

'Right. But if I can't go with you, I want you to promise to ring me every couple of hours so I don't have to worry if you're still all right.' And as an afterthought, she added, 'Apart from that, I also want to know what's going on.'

'Okay, Gracie. I'll ring if I can.'

'I expect you've got a telephone in your car,' she retorted, attempting to give weight to her appeal.

'Yes, I have… I'll ring if I can.'

'After all,' she continued, 'these are very dangerous men we are dealing with, and we know what they are capable of.'

Jim noted the 'we' in her conversation but said nothing and

instead reminded her, 'I've got my protector.' He patted his bulletproof vest.

'Yes, but you might not be so lucky next time. Suppose they shot at your head?'

'I'd prefer not to think about that, if you don't mind,' he confessed.

'What time are you going?'

'I'll have to leave about 7 a.m. to make sure I get there in plenty of time.'

'You'll need to get up by six o'clock then. What are you going to say to the policeman on duty outside?'

'Oh hell! I forgot about him. I'll have to tell him I'm going to get the morning newspapers. You don't have one delivered, do you?'

'Goodness no. We're too far out in the sticks for that. I sometimes get a *Daily Telegraph* from the local shop, but that's about all.'

'Good. That's okay then.'

Jim stared into the roaring log fire, lost in contemplation. He was excited at his first surveillance mission and wanted to prove to Mike that he was capable of handling it without any bother. He pictured himself following the bad guys and discovering vital information that would crack the case.

Grace interrupted his thoughts. 'What do you want me to tell Detective Inspector Brooke when he comes to see us later in the morning?'

'You'd better say that I was called away on urgent business and I'll see him when I get back.' He knew that Brooke would be unhappy about it, but also knew that, by then, there was nothing he could do.

Sat in front of the warm fire, Jim stroked a purring Emmy, while he gave Grace a potted history of his life. They swapped reminiscences and she talked with affection about Mike's mother and father, recalling some of the horror of their deaths, and better memories she had of bringing up her brother's two children. The evening ended, as the fire subsided to glowing embers, with a nightcap of Horlicks, a drink that Jim disliked and sipped slowly, saying nothing to avoid offending Grace.

She showed Jim to his room, promised to wake him at 6 a.m. with a cooked breakfast and said goodnight.

The spare bedroom was decorated in warm pastel shades and furnished with an oak-framed double bed, sitting on a Persian rug that almost filled the room. In the subdued glow of the bedside lamps, the room was enhanced by an oak dressing table beneath the window and a matching wardrobe in one corner.

Both settled down to a night of restless sleep, with Grace worrying about Mike, and Jim excited about his impending surveillance job.

The green Range Rover made its way towards London. Traffic was heavy, with theatregoers and nightlife seekers making their way to the capital, but Douglas Payne hardly noticed any of this. He was too busy rehearsing excuses for his boss, over and over again.

It had taken him a while to get back on to the main road, after crashing through the gate from the field behind Grace's cottage. He lost his way for a time and now muttered to himself when he discovered that one of the headlights was broken. The chance that the police might stop him for a faulty light was the last thing he needed. At the first service station he came to, Payne persuaded the mechanic, who was about to lock up, with an intimidating bribe he found impossible to reject, and had a new headlamp fitted while he waited. On the road again, he continued his rehearsals.

'At least I got what we went for,' he said to comfort himself. 'Bunny shot dead, he's not going to like that. Still, it wasn't my fault. Nothing I could do about it.'

He knew nervousness emanated from his very being, but couldn't control his worries and even thought about stopping for a drink to calm himself down, but changed his mind.

'The boss wouldn't like that either, he's sure to smell the alcohol and know. And I don't want to risk getting breathalysed by the law.'

His palms were sweaty, and he rubbed them one at a time, down his trouser leg. 'Christ, what's wrong with me! I can't be expected to know who they were,' he muttered, anticipating the question. 'Probably The General's men. Of course, they may have been the police. That would really anger the boss.'

The questions he knew would be asked kept going round and round his head, but not many convincing answers came back.

Payne drove into London, through the fluorescent-lit streets of Lewisham and Southwark, on to Waterloo Bridge, through the Kingsway underpass and turned into the dim underground car park of Orchard House. With the car parked in the residents' allocated area, he trundled across to the lift. The otherwise empty lift rose, and so did his pulse rate, with each floor he passed. Stepping out on the fifth floor, he swept along the corridor to room 505, composed himself and rang the bell.

After checking who was there through the spyhole, Al Dexter opened the door and Payne entered the warm apartment.

'Wipe your feet,' instructed Dexter, wearing a silk dressing gown despite the early hour of nine in the evening. Payne complied and followed him along the hall to the living room. The flooring was parquet, and he was aware that Dexter wore his slippers and that only *his* shoes were clicking on the floor. He found himself tiptoeing to lessen the noise and not aggravate his boss; the news he brought was enough to do that.

The living room was neat, tidy and modern, with a thick pile, wall-to-wall carpet, which sank as they walked on it. A fake Picasso dominated one wall above a desk, while the opposite wall was covered with bookshelves stacked to bursting point. Many of the books were about boats and boating, Dexter's big passion, a pastime he indulged in at every opportunity he got.

Dexter sat down in a soft, black leather armchair and motioned Payne to do likewise on the settee of a three-piece suite. Before him, a glass-topped, low coffee table stood near the centre of the room in front of the fireplace. A thirty-eight inch, widescreen television occupied the corner, staring into the room like a big eye, accompanied by five cinema sound speakers. A carved wooden mantelshelf graced the coal effect gas fire and held many small china ornaments of cats. They surrounded a carriage clock in a domed case, and in an apartment where all animals were banned, they were the only kind of cat that Dexter's wife was allowed to have.

Dexter asked, with his slightly Italian accent, 'Where's Bunny?'

Payne explained the circumstances of the evening in the best light he could, but Dexter still became angry listening to the tale of events unfold. He began shouting and paced up and down, slapping a clenched fist into the palm of his other hand.

'Can't you do even a simple job like collecting something without messing it up?' he unjustly sneered.

Al Dexter was forty-eight, clean shaven, of swarthy Mediterranean good looks with a classic Roman nose. His jet-black hair, showing a few streaks of grey lately, was neatly cut and trimmed to match his neat appearance. He preferred to wear dark suits, a white shirt with a tie, and brogue shoes with built-up heels to add height to his five feet seven inches, so that his wife was not taller than him. His fiery temperament caused him to swing quickly between a controlled calmness and rage, often lapsing into his native tongue whenever he was angry.

'You'd better pray it was The General's men at the cottage, then we can take care of it,' asserted Dexter. 'If it was the police, or worse still, Special Branch, we could be in for some real problems, especially if the man Bunny shot goes and dies. They'll start a full-scale search.'

'It's got to be The General's hoods. They wanted revenge for Bunny killing their man at Randle's flat.'

'Yes. Maybe. But what happened to the body? Who are the people Stirling said had taken the body away? I don't like the sound of that.'

'If it was the police, it's bound to be in the papers tomorrow. I'll get them and scan through.'

'But if it was them, why didn't they take him to the station afterwards for questioning?'

'That's right. So it *must* be The General's men and they took their man away.'

'I don't know. It seems a bit odd,' Dexter commented.

An attractive woman entered the room. She looked stunning in a red silk dressing gown. Her blonde, shoulder-length hair added to her good looks and full figure, which was evident from the ample cleavage showing at the neck of her dressing gown. She was tall and spoke with a slightly stronger accent than her husband.

'Ciao Douglas. Do you two men want a drink?'

'Not now, honey. We've got business to talk about,' snapped Dexter before Payne could answer. '*Vai a letto, cara.* Go back to bed, Mel. I'll be in soon.'

The blonde left the room with a slightly hurt look at the rebuttal. She loved her husband, but sometimes wished that he was a little more considerate of her feelings.

'Twelve years we've been married and she still interrupts when I'm talking business,' complained Dexter. 'Where's the watch?'

Payne held out the pocket watch taken from Mike's room. Dexter opened the desk drawer and extracted an identical watch, held it alongside and surveyed them both.

'At least we've got both watches,' he declared. 'Open it up and give me the key.'

Payne opened the back and took out a key and a piece of paper, handing them over.

Dexter did likewise and compared the keys. 'That looks okay. He's even got a note of the account number. We'll go along to the bank first thing in the morning and collect the stuff. Be here with the car at nine o'clock sharp in your chauffeur's uniform,' came the orders, a wave of his hand ending the conversation.

'Right, boss,' Payne replied, then he tiptoed his way along the hall to the front door to let himself out.

Jim had showered and dressed by the time Grace tapped on his bedroom door at 6 a.m. She fed him an enjoyable breakfast. Not like the so-called healthy food he had endured at Tramer, most of which tasted like powdered nuts and dust. After eating two fried eggs, two rashers of bacon and three slices of toast, he drank two cups of tea and then felt ready to face both the day and the journey back to London.

'I like to see a man eat a hearty breakfast. It sets him up for the day, I always say. Now remember, be careful,' insisted Grace in a motherly way. 'And don't forget to ring me.'

'I won't forget. Don't tell the inspector what they took. Say they smashed everything but nothing seems to be missing.'

'If you say so. But you know I don't like lying.'

'Yes, but it's what Mike wants,' Jim reminded.

'That's the only reason I'm agreeing to it.'

The young police constable on duty by the front door was cold, tired and grateful for a nice hot cup of tea. He simply nodded when Jim said he was off to the local shop to get a newspaper. Jim felt guilty about lying to him and wondered if he would get into trouble for not making sure that he intended to return for Brooke's visit. Not that it would have made any difference if he had.

Sinking into the driving seat of his Rolls Royce still gave him a thrill. Its luxurious comfort felt as though it was specially made to fit him. The car was so quiet, he sometimes wondered if the engine was still running, and only the dials confirmed that it was. Jim reversed in the driveway and pulled away, smiling at the policeman drinking his cup of tea, standing outside the front door.

The road to London was congested even at that early hour, but the Rolls purred along in the outside lane, and it was hard for Jim not to exceed the speed limit by too much. Other vehicles moved aside; a gratifying new experience for him after struggling through traffic for years in a Ford Fiesta.

At his destination, he frustratingly found that the streets were already full of parked cars. Circling around several times, he was still unable to secure a parking space.

'Oh damn! I must park near here in case I do have to follow someone. The only spot I can see is on a yellow line. There doesn't seem to be any traffic wardens around. Let's hope they're reluctant to put a ticket on a Rolls Royce if one of them shows up. Still, even if I got one, I can afford it! Oh, sod it! I'll park here,' he said, after he'd convinced himself of the justification for it.

All his life, he'd been careful to park legally and not feed meters – worried about having to pay a fine. Though he was now rich, he still found it difficult not to concern himself with these things. Suddenly having so much money was taking time to filter through to becoming his natural way of thinking.

Jim parked on the line, walked to the corner of the road and turned into Bishopsgate. The chill in the air made him shiver. Rubbing his hands together, he blew on them while waiting in a bus shelter opposite the building he was to keep an eye on. He stood, blending into the throng of commuters hurrying on their way to work, without attracting any attention, and he observed everyone coming and going. Minutes after nine thirty, a BMW drew up outside the building and a chauffeur bustled to open the rear door. The passenger was a stranger to Jim, but not the driver; it was Payne, alias Inspector Davidson.

'So you were right, Mike. The man who stole your watch has come here to this bank. I wonder how you knew that?' Jim asked himself.

Dexter, smartly dressed in a dark pinstriped suit and carrying a briefcase, went inside. Payne leant on the car bonnet with his back to the road, waiting for his boss to emerge.

Jim strolled back to the corner of the street where his car was parked, keeping an eye on Payne in case he turned round and recognised him. He stood and watched. The rush-hour traffic had abated but, even so, London's streets were always busy.

'It might be tricky crossing the flow of cars when they leave,' Jim murmured. His pulse rose and he could feel butterflies in his stomach as he stood waiting. He was determined not to bungle his first assignment and anxiously watched the bank entrance for movement.

Ten minutes elapsed before Dexter emerged and Jim started the dash to his car. A female traffic warden stood by the Rolls and was about to write out a ticket.

'I'm just off,' Jim announced, unlocking the car door and giving her a friendly smile.

'Okay,' she replied, eyeing him with a naughty boy look. 'You've only just escaped getting a ticket. I'll not be so lenient next time.'

'Thanks,' said Jim, giving her a quick peck on the cheek. She blushed, gave him a smile and held up the traffic to let the Rolls out.

Dexter's BMW made a hasty U-turn in the road and sped off. Jim reached the corner and saw the car accelerate down the road, thankful that he didn't have to cross the flow of traffic. Quickly nipping into a gap a few cars behind them, Jim followed the BMW across London, careful not to lose it or get too close and be spotted. He was pleased with his progress so far and began to relax a little now the first major hurdle was over. Dexter and Payne, he noticed, were too busy arguing to check if anyone was on their tail.

Dexter angrily waved his arms about and shouted at Payne, 'The bloody key you got last night didn't fit. Only mine fitted.'

'Well, that ain't my fault. I got the damn thing like you asked.'

'I felt a right prat when I couldn't get the door open. I had to tell them I picked up the wrong key. Somebody's done a switch.'

Neither said anything for the next few moments, while Dexter slowly calmed down. Payne was first to break the silence. 'There can't be many people who had a chance to do a switch,' he offered.

Dexter thought about it. 'No, that's right. Let's see... if we've got events right, only three people had the watch. First was The General's commander, and it's unlikely he'd cross his leader, especially as he ended up dead. Then there's the Drake woman, who took it when she killed him, and Randle, who brought the watch back to England.'

'That's assuming his aunt or that bloke Sterling I shot at the cottage didn't find it,' returned Payne.

'That's true. I'd forgotten about them.'

'I don't reckon the old biddy's likely to do it. But Sterling's another matter.'

'And we don't know anything about this Sterling character. Maybe he found out about the key and got friendly with Randle to get his hands on it. He might even be working for The General. We'd better check him out and search his place. If he had the real key on him when you shot him, it could be difficult getting it back.'

'I doubt if he could've got it that quickly. He hadn't been in the place long before we went in.'

'Perhaps. Searching his place may tell us. Failing that, it's got to be either Randle or Drake.'

The two men continued to discuss their problem, unaware of the Rolls following them. A few cars back, Jim was held up at traffic lights in Holborn.

'Come on lights! Why are you taking so long to change? Oh God, I'm going to lose them,' he shouted in frustration. Things had been going so well, now it looked as if it might all go wrong.

He jumped up and down in his seat until the amber light shone, then accelerated hard, catching up with the end of the queue. Five cars in front was the BMW, and he breathed a sigh of relief. They travelled along High Holborn and turned into Kingsway. Round the corner, Jim caught sight of the tail of their car disappearing down the concrete ramp of the underground car park at Orchard House, and he followed, gingerly.

Payne parked the BMW and Jim watched them enter the lift, then parked his Rolls. The doors clanged shut and the motor whirred, reeling the lift up. Jim ran across, pushed the call button and watched the indicator stop at the fifth floor for a short while, then return to the lower ground floor level. A portly lady carrying shopping bags arrived and they both entered the lift.

'Six please,' she said.

Jim pressed the illuminated buttons with numbers five and six on them, and took a deep breath to calm the nervousness starting to creep over him.

Dexter entered his apartment, closely followed by Payne. He continued to rave about the key not being the right one when they opened the door and stepped into the living room. He stopped short, and gasped at the state of the room. Furniture was overturned, papers and books littered the floor, and all the desk drawers were open with the contents spread everywhere.

'*Maledetto*! What the hell's happened here?' Dexter snarled, surveying the mess. Then the consequences suddenly came flooding to mind. 'Where's Mel? She was here when we left.'

He frantically searched all the rooms. There was no sign of her.

'They've got Mel. The General's men – it must be The General's men.'

'She may have gone out before this happened. It might just be a burglary,' said Payne, attempting to comfort his boss.

'No, I don't think so. She wasn't planning to go anywhere this morning. The office – she might be there. Let's check.'

The lift juddered to a halt at the fifth floor and the doors opened. About to step out, Jim saw Payne and Dexter hurrying along the corridor towards him. He shrunk back behind the lady carrying her shopping bags, hoping Payne had not seen him.

'Wrong floor,' he declared to her.

Payne and Dexter stepped into the lift and turned round to face the doors. Dexter punched the button to descend, but the lift went up one floor, much to his annoyance. No sooner had the woman in front of Jim got out than Dexter pressed the button repeatedly and the lift started to descend. They were both unaware that anyone else was behind them, in their anxiety to reach the third floor. Dexter fidgeted, urging the lift to go faster. Standing at the back and breathing very quietly, Jim prayed that Payne did not turn round. He could hear his pulse pounding in his ears and his mouth went dry as he stared at the backs of their necks while the lift dropped slowly. When the doors opened Dexter and Payne set off down the corridor at a pace. Jim emerged, breathing a sigh of relief, watching them turn the corner and disappear.

Orchard House was a large, seven-floor, Victorian premises, with the lower four floors converted for business use, and the top three floors turned into living accommodations. Dexter ran his business from a third-floor office and lived in his apartment two floors above.

Jim emerged from the lift and followed them down the dark, tiled corridor containing offices on both sides. All the doors had frosted glass windows in the upper halves, with only the occupying company legend on each distinguishing one from another.

Peeping around the corner, Jim saw two young ladies wandering along, but nobody else. They entered an office and closed the door, leaving the quiet corridor empty.

Moving along, Jim heard raised voices coming from an office and recognised one of them as Payne's. On the door, 'A J Dexter Import/Export' was painted in light green letters. The grumbles came from a back room and Jim listened hard at the door trying to hear what was said.

A young woman came out from an office clutching a pile of papers. She was attractive, smiling at Jim as she passed. He wanted to chat and quietly cursed his bad luck to see her at a time when he had more important things to do. He watched her enter another office, giving him a last look before she disappeared. He went back to hearing what he could and made a mental note to return at a later date.

Dexter was furious. 'Look at this mess! They've wrecked the place! Someone's searched through everything. It's got to be either the keys or the gems they're after. But there's no sign of Mel.'

Jim's ears pricked up. 'Gems, eh? So that's what all this is about. They must be worth quite a bit, considering all the trouble they're going to. I wonder who Mel is? I expect it's his wife.'

The telephone rang. Dexter snatched it up and growled into the mouthpiece, 'Dexter.'

'Ah! There you are Mr Dexter,' said a silky, deep voice slowly. 'You killed one of my men – I have your wife. Give me one good reason why I shouldn't kill her right now.'

'Wait a minute – let's talk. Who are you?'

'I'm still listening, but you haven't given me a good reason yet.'

'If you harm her, I'll hunt you to the ends of the earth and kill you. You'll always be looking over your shoulder.'

'Words, Mr Dexter, words. You don't even know who I am.'

'I can find out. I'm not without friends and influence in the underworld. You work for The General, so I've already got a start. So you'd better heed those words,' spat Dexter with all the menace he could muster.

'Perhaps. Normally I wouldn't hesitate to kill her, but I understand from my man that you've been to the bank this morning.'

Dexter remained silent, his mind racing to put all the information together and consider his options.

The voice continued, 'I might be willing to do a deal. It would save your wife's life. A swap. I'll exchange your wife for the gems.'

Dexter breathed in heavily. Silence hung in the air. He was in a corner with no alternatives.

'How do I know I can trust you?'

'What choice do you have?'

There was another pause. He was over a barrel and they both knew it.

Got to buy some time, he thought to himself, then said, 'Okay. When and where?'

'I'll ring you at your apartment this evening when I've had time to sort out the details.'

'If you lay a hand on...' Dexter started, then broke off – the line went dead. He slammed the receiver down.

'Who was that?' Payne asked.

'I don't know. But he must be one of The General's cohorts. They've got Mel and want to swap her for the gems,' he said, anger written all over his face. 'They'll never believe that Randle's key didn't fit and I couldn't get the stuff. They'll think I'm trying to string 'em along. I'll have to bluff it out or they'll kill her.'

'What's the plan, boss?'

'I want one – no, two – top, long-range marksmen. I want crossfire. The exchange is bound to be somewhere out in the open where they figure nobody can hide nearby. I want cover, in case they try something. If they're stupid enough to bring Mel with them, I want the firepower available to take them out before they realise what's happening. And I want us to get away safely.'

'I'll get on to it straight away. I know who could do it, but it's a question of finding them and seeing if they're available at such short notice.'

Dexter nodded, saying, 'Pay them whatever they ask for. Also, get all the men you can on the lookout for these scumbags. Offer a big reward to anyone who finds out who they are and where they're hiding Mel.'

'Okay, boss. I'll spread the word.'

'If they hurt her, I'll kill every last bloody one of them. I'm going to do the rounds as well and call in a few favours. Somebody must know something.'

'What about the keys?'

Dexter pondered on it then returned them to the watches. 'I'll lock them in my desk. They think I've already got the gems so they won't be looking here for them any more.'

'What're we gonna do about Sterling?'

Outside the door, Jim stiffened at the mention of his name.

'That'll have to wait. This is more important. You get on the blower, organise those two guns and get the boys on the lookout.

I'll meet you in The Boar's Head,' he glanced at his watch, 'at one thirty to see how we're doing. You lock up here.'

Jim heard him approaching and scurried along the corridor to the lift. He pressed the call button and waited. The lift was slow to arrive and he heard footsteps walking towards him. He knew that Dexter wouldn't recognise him and was grateful that the lift arrived before Payne came along. They entered together and Jim went to the back.

'Which floor?' Dexter asked.

'Sixth please,' Jim replied.

Dexter pushed the two buttons and the lift doors closed. Payne came out of the office, fumbled in his pocket for the door key and, by the time he had found it, the lift was on its way carrying one angry and one relieved man.

At the fifth floor, Dexter got out and marched up the corridor to his apartment. He hurried to his desk, leaving the front door slightly ajar.

Jim let the empty lift rise to the next floor and quietly approached the apartment. He gently pushed the front door open and heard Dexter in the living room, replacing his desk drawer and locking it. A few paces down the hall to the left was a door. With his heart thumping, Jim crept along the hall and opened it. It was a cloakroom, with a washbasin and a loo. He hid behind the door and listened to Dexter's footsteps click down the hallway.

They stopped outside.

The door opened and Dexter came in. Jim's pulse rose even higher, hearing him turn on the hand basin tap to have a wash. To his horror, the door slowly started to close on its own and Jim looked aghast at his reflection coming into view in the mirror above the basin. Dexter was bending over washing his face; Jim gingerly grabbed the door handle and slowly pulled it back open, dreading that he might look up. But he kept his head down after washing and felt for the towel. Dexter wiped his face and hands, looked at himself in the mirror, then returned the towel, combed his hair and left.

The click of the front door closing was music to Jim's ears.

'These close shaves are beginning to get to me,' he breathed. 'Thank goodness he's gone. At least I'm in the right room for what I need.'

Emerging from the washroom a few minutes later Jim tiptoed, without knowing why, into the living room. Although he was sure no one was there, it still seemed the right thing to do. He surveyed the overturned furniture.

'They made quite a mess,' he murmured.

One desk drawer was locked and he searched for something to open it with. After trying to pick the lock with a paper clip for a few minutes without success, Jim threw it away in disgust and decided that it would be quicker to force it. In the kitchen, everything was scattered all over the floor and he picked up a knife.

'It's a shame they didn't teach us how to break into desks at Tramer. Picking locks in handcuffs was easier than this.'

A combination of forcing the lock with the knife and pulling at the drawer finally paid dividends. The lock gave, revealing the two watches. Jim opened the backs of both and surveyed the keys.

'I don't know which one was Mike's anyway, so I might as well take both,' he said to himself.

He shoved them in his pocket and left the apartment straight away, glad to get out to the corridor and into the lift without being seen. Pushing the button for the basement car park, he felt pleased with the way things had gone.

'This'll show Mike I can handle things without any bother,' he chuckled to himself. 'I bet he doesn't reckon I can get both watches and keys.'

The lift bumped to a halt and the doors opened. Jim took a step forward and stopped, stunned to see Dexter and Payne standing there.

Payne looked quite shocked for a second, but quickly recovered his composure. 'Well, well, well. Look what we've got here – a Sterling ghost.'

Chapter XI

Jetuloo

Deep in the African jungle, Mike trundled along in his jeep, heading towards the army camp outside Jetuloo.

Although the rainy season was over, the ground was still boggy in places, and the jeep rocked from side to side, squelching through mud holes. The steering wheel swung violently back and forth, his vehicle following the line of least resistance. He made steady progress, and after his encounter with The General's men, kept a watchful eye out. He wasn't expecting to meet any more trouble, but knew instinctively that's when you needed to be on guard most.

Camp West was close.

It would be safer covering the remaining few miles on foot, so Mike searched out a spot to hide his jeep and covered it with camouflage netting.

He swung his backpack on, checked his guns and set off, aware that Suzie was certainly still alive, and that they were expecting him.

During a previous assignment, Mike had visited the camp when it was controlled by government troops. He was now glad to have knowledge of the layout and surrounding area. Without it, getting this far so quickly would have been almost impossible.

He stayed close to the edge of the track, keeping under cover where practical. Carefully, he picked his way through the trees and frequently stopped to check before continuing. The General's men would patrol the area this close to the camp and may well have orders to look out for him.

The General had overrun Camp West recently in a bloody battle, and government troops were certain to scout the area to assess his strengths before trying to retake it. Mike knew that he was likely to have patrols out to discourage them.

He moved to within sight of his target. Years of experience were now proving valuable in a conflict which had become very personal to him.

The immediate area around the camp perimeter fence had been cleared of all trees and foliage. This was standard practice, making it difficult for an enemy to approach unseen. From his hiding spot among the trees, the tall wire fence surrounding the compound, reinforced above with barbed wire, was visible. With the small but powerful binoculars that Paul had provided, Mike spied a wooden-framed, wire-mesh entrance gate, with more barbed wire on top and two soldiers on guard. Each lounged in a wooden hut inside the camp entrance, either side of the gate, looking bored and half-asleep.

It was late in the day and Mike waited for the sun to set before making a move. Meanwhile, he hid his backpack and reconnoitred the perimeter to learn what he could.

The camp was a hotchpotch of mainly wooden buildings and appeared to have changed little since he last saw it. He navigated the perimeter until he reached the entrance. Here, he had to return, to avoid crossing the open road in front of the main gate. Back at his hiding spot he settled down, had a bite to eat and drink, and waited. He was close to Suzie and knew it, reinforcing his feelings that the bond growing between them had strengthened a lot over the past few months.

The sun dipped below the horizon and the temperature dropped. Mike blackened his face, put on a dark jacket and took only his hand gun and knife. Floodlights burst into life, illuminating the camp and entrance, and he noted the time on his borrowed watch – 7 p.m. Only the perimeter fence, a large central square and the entrance were covered by the lights, leaving many corners in semi-darkness. This would give him much needed cover.

A handful of vehicles had left the camp during the afternoon. Mike watched and waited, hoping for a particular one to return. A jeep arrived, but it was not suitable for what he had in mind. A further wait brought another jeep back from patrol and he began to wonder if he might have to consider a different approach when a dark, canvas-backed lorry motored in. Bouncing up and down the dirt track, its headlights formed dancing shadows across the gate and fence, until it shuddered to a halt and the guards strolled out. One chatted to the driver, while his companion checked in the back with a flashlight. Mike grabbed the opportunity and scrambled beneath the vehicle, then watched the gates swing open, and held on to the underside. He searched in vain for a place to anchor his feet but found nowhere. The lorry moved forward and he was dragged along the ground, into the compound.

The vehicle chugged slowly into the almost deserted camp carrying Mike, who watched the route to keep his bearings. The lorry crossed the main, illuminated square and rounded a corner, stopping outside the armoury hut with a squeal of its brakes. The tailgate crashed down and two soldiers jumped out and began offloading ammunition supplies into the hut.

'Go easy with those boxes,' ordered the soldier with three stripes on his sleeve. 'We don't wanna get blown sky high tonight, thank you.'

'How very polite!' thought Mike.

Dropping from underneath the lorry, he glanced round and saw the motor pool compound nearby. It held several lorries, half a dozen jeeps and was in semi-darkness, ideal as a hiding place. Though surrounded by wire fencing, the gate was open, allowing Mike to slip in quietly and hide among the vehicles. When unloading finished, the lorry was driven a few yards into the compound and parked. The driver departed after padlocking the gate, and all fell into darkness and silence once more, apart from a distant noise of shouting and carousing, drifting through the still night air from one of the huts.

'So far, so good. If things had gone differently, my jeep could have ended up in here,' Mike reflected.

He found a toolbox in one of the lorries and levered the padlock off. 'No time for finesse,' he thought to himself. He replaced it to make it look undisturbed, and edged forward to observe the main square and entrance from within the shadows.

'I wonder if they bother to patrol inside the perimeter,' he mused.

They did not.

He watched for several hours, concealed by darkness, and saw only soldiers returning to their huts after an evening of card games and other noisy activities to pass the time. One patrol at midnight changed the guards on the front gate.

Although anxious to look for Suzie, Mike had learnt the value of patience. In the early hours of the morning everyone got tired, even the guards that had come on duty recently, and the odds that he would remain undetected were at their best.

Through his previous visit he recalled the location of the cells, and, as it was likely they were still in use, that was the place to start looking. Stealthily he made his way to the prison block, the only brick building on the camp, avoiding the few soldiers still around at that hour. With no sweeping floodlights, it was not difficult to move around undetected through the dark areas.

Approaching the cells, Mike waited in the shadows and kept a lookout. All was quiet and still... almost too quiet. Concerned to find no guard outside, he began to wonder if they knew he was there already and were waiting for him. They expected him to try and rescue Suzie, and it would not be difficult to guess that this was the first place he'd look.

'Nothing ventured...' he mumbled, finishing the sentence in his thoughts.

With no outside windows, the only way to see a prisoner was to peer through the small barred window in each cell door. A slight breeze wafted past Mike, his keen eyes showing white from within his blackened face, as he searched for hidden soldiers ready to spring a trap. He saw no one and crept to the door, half expecting them to surround him at any minute. A noise from within the hut came to his ears, but was too quiet for him to distinguish.

He took a deep breath, drew his knife and tried the door handle. It was not locked. Thrusting it wide he dashed inside, shut it quietly and dropped to the floor, poised to deal with any situation that faced him.

Inside were bare, wooden floorboards, and the place reeked of stale air and body odour. Mike's nostrils twitched at the foul smell enveloping him, and triggering memories of a time he once spent in such a place. In the gloom, he stared down a corridor, with cell doors on both sides, and an empty chair at the far end beneath a single, flickering, dim light. The noise was clearer now. It was a low gruff sound that came from the end cell next to the chair, where the door was ajar.

Creeping silently along the corridor, Mike peered into each cell on one side. Two or three local soldiers slept on the floor in each of the first two cells, and when he reached the last one where the noise came from, it became clear why. A naked woman was pinned to a bed by a soldier, no doubt the guard, lying on top of her with his trousers around his ankles, having his way and grunting with the satisfaction he extracted at her expense.

Even in this dim light, Mike could tell it was not Suzie, despite being unable to see her face. She was of a much smaller build, with pert breasts that the guard fondled roughly in his exuberance to satisfy himself. Despite this, she offered no resistance and uttered no sound, accepting that she had no control over her predicament. Suddenly she turned her face and looked at Mike.

She was Chinese.

Mike put his index finger to his lips in a gesture which said, please stay quiet. She stayed silent, but her eyes pleaded with him to rid her of this awful man who took what he wanted by force and left her with no pride or dignity. Mike desperately wanted to help, but his first objective was to find Suzie, and to do that he needed to stay undetected for a while longer. Killing the guard would almost certainly hasten his discovery. He gave her a 'sorry, I can't help' look and crept back along the other side of the corridor to check the rest of the cells.

At the first window he saw a soldier awake, sitting on the floor with his hands linked around his legs, staring at the ground. Mike eyed him in the murky light. He looked familiar. Then he recognised him.

'Barney?' he whispered.

The man looked up with a hint of surprise in his eyes and came to the window.

'Mike?'

'Yes. How long have you been in here?'

'Just a day or so. What're you doing in this place?'

'I'm looking for Suzie Drake.'

'Of course. They've got her in one of the officer's huts.'

'Where?' Mike asked, his expectations of finding her rising to a level he'd hardly dared hope for until now.

'Let me out, I'll show you.'

'I can't, the guard might hear me,' he whispered. 'Anyway, if they find this lot missing they'll know for sure that I'm here. I'll never get Suzie out.'

'Not this lot, just me. They're asleep. If they all got out, everybody would soon know about it.'

'Well…' Mike said pondering.

'Come on. You wouldn't let an old buddy rot in here, would you? Nobody'll miss me before daylight. Who else is gonna show you where she is and give you a hand?'

'Okay,' said Mike, 'but be quiet.'

Mike dipped his fingers into the hidden pocket in his belt and extracted the lock-picking tool. Inserting it in the keyhole, he twisted the implement, feeling for the mechanism.

'Hurry up,' complained Barney.

'I'm working on it. This isn't the sort of thing I do every day you know,' Mike protested, in an exasperated whisper.

He recalled the course he took at Tramer on picking locks and wished he'd made more of an effort to master the technique instead of embarrassing everyone, including himself.

'I never was a lot of good at doing this. Sometimes I could, and sometimes I couldn't,' Mike stated.

The grunts and groans continued from the cell opposite.

'Sounds like the guard's enjoying himself again tonight,' Barney smirked.

Mike gave him a look of disapproval, feeling uneasy at his remark. He said nothing and went back to work on the lock. The light dimmed to nothing, throwing the cells into complete darkness, then gradually flickered back on again.

'It's the generator,' advised Barney in a whisper.

'I figured that.'

'It's old and needs replacing. It frequently packs up altogether.'

There was a gentle click.

'Got it,' announced Mike, sounding pleased with himself.

The wooden door was a tight fit, squeeking when Barney

opened it, and one of the soldiers turned over in his sleep. They held their breaths and waited for a few seconds before Barney stepped out. Mike closed the door gently and they crept quietly towards the cell block entrance. The floorboards creaked under their combined weight and they both moved forward gingerly, leaving the guard still grunting as they slipped through the doorway.

Outside they inhaled the clean, fresh air, standing close to the building, blending into the shadows before moving to the rear.

'Okay, where's Suzie?' Mike asked.

'This way, follow me.'

Barney moved off into the night. Moonlight ebbed and flowed, with light wispy clouds drifting by in the almost still night air, giving an eerie look to the shadowy corners. He led Mike to one of the larger huts used for officers' quarters, where most of the windows were in darkness.

'She's in here,' he indicated, nodding towards the dilapidated hut, in bad need of repairs.

'Right. You stay here and keep watch. I'm going to take a look.'

Creeping around the hut, Mike peered gingerly through each window. He saw mainly blackness, but in a room at the back he could just make out the dimly lit outline of a woman lying on a bed.

'It could be Suzie,' he thought, 'but I can't see her clearly enough. She's facing the wrong way.'

As he watched, she turned over and he once more glimpsed her attractive suntanned features, and his heart skipped a beat.

It was Suzie.

She was covered by a blanket that slipped when she turned over awkwardly, revealing that she was manacled to the bed by both ankles and a wrist, leaving only her left arm free. Her bare shoulders became visible, suggesting that she was wearing little or nothing. After seeing the prison guard's behaviour, Mike did not care to think about what indignities she might have had to endure. His emotion was to call out to let her know he was there, but caution was still needed and he withheld the temptation. The window was locked from the inside and resisted Mike's attention. He was so close, but knew it was risky standing outside the window for too long where he might be seen.

He returned to Barney. 'I've seen her. She's chained to a bed in one of the back rooms. I'm going in to get her. Keep watch by the outside door and make sure I'm not disturbed by anyone. Okay?' Mike asked.

Barney nodded. 'Give me your gun. I may need it if any soldiers come along,' he stated.

'Okay, but try and keep it quiet if you can,' Mike replied, handing the weapon over.

They slipped quietly into the hut. Before them was a long, empty corridor, lit by two flickering lights. With Barney waiting by the door, Mike crept down the passageway, covered by a carpet that had long since seen the end of its useful life. At the room Suzie was in, he put his ear to the door and listened closely. No sounds came from within the room and he tried the handle. The door was locked, but a gap between door and frame allowed Mike to see the tongue of the lock.

This decrepit hut had seen better days and was coming apart at the seams. Nothing fitted as it should, after decades of daily temperatures in the nineties, three months of the rainy season each year, and little or no maintenance.

'The lock tongue can't be catching by much!' Mike thought as he inserted his knife in the gap, grasped the handle, and with his shoulder to the door began levering it apart. The framework was rotten, crumbling away, and the tongue pushed its way past, barely making a sound.

The door opened.

Mike closed it gently behind him and scanned the sparsely furnished room. Before him was a desk holding a few scattered items, an old armchair in one corner and two wooden chairs, apart from the bed Suzie was on. The floor was covered with a threadbare rug, and a bare forty watt bulb hung lifelessly from the ceiling, illuminating the dim room. The walls were discoloured and, like most of the camp, hadn't been touched for years, and nothing short of a total rebuild would ever improve it.

Mike approached Suzie as she slept and touched her shoulder while gently putting his hand over her mouth. She turned with a start, her eyes wide with fear.

'Sssh,' he said quietly. 'I'm going to get you out of here.'

The expression on her faced changed, her eyes turned warm, and a smile came to her lips. 'Oh, Mike. It's great to see you,' she whispered. His trusty lock pick went to work again. 'When I heard the door open I thought it was someone else. How did you know I was here?' she asked.

'I got a phone call from Martin saying that he thought you'd been snatched by two men. Your reference to a jungle holiday was the clue. I guessed the rest.'

'I was drugged. I don't remember much of what happened.'

'My room at Tramer and my flat were broken into. It's all connected with that pocket watch you gave me when I left for England.'

Suzie looked guiltily at him. 'Oh, Mike, I'm sorry. They made me say what I'd done with it. I was threatened with all sorts of terrible things if I didn't talk.'

'That's okay,' he comforted, removing the wrist manacle.

Suzie sat up and the blanket fell away, revealing, as Mike had feared, that she was wearing nothing. She grabbed it to cover herself and continued the conversation before Mike could ask any awkward questions.

'Did they do much damage?' she asked.

'Yes, I believe so. The mess can be cleaned up okay, that's no problem, but a body was left in the flat.'

'A body? Who was it? One of The General's men?'

'Maybe. Jim, a friend of mine, found him, so I'm not sure about the details.' One of the leg manacles gave up its hostage. 'Only one to go,' he encouraged.

'Why all this interest in a watch? Surely it can't be worth that much?'

'The watch contains a key to a safety deposit box. I reckon that holds something pretty valuable.'

'Ahh! So that's why.'

'Soon have you out of here.'

'Got any ideas about how we're going to get out of this place?' Suzie asked.

'No. But we'll manage. We've got a friend who's helping us.'

'A friend? Who?'

'I found him here in the prison hut. You'll remember him. It's Barney.'

Immediately the name came off his lips, Suzie drew a sharp breath. 'Barney!' she almost shouted. 'He's the slimy traitor who got me here in the first place. I thought that was him arriving when you came in.'

'What!' exclaimed Mike.

'He pretended to be a prisoner to get me to tell them about the watch. I'm not wearing anything because he's the bastard who's been raping me in the early hours of each morning.'

As the last manacle unlocked and dropped to the bed, a noise behind them turned their attention.

Standing at the door, with his own gun pointing at them, was Barney. The General stood beside him with two guards at the rear.

'It's good to meet you at last, Mr Randle,' said The General.

'The feeling's not mutual,' spat Mike. 'And you, Barney – you bastard. You... words fail me.'

Mike moved menacingly forward and Barney cocked the gun to stop him, reinforced by the two armed guards coming round to face him.

'I should have guessed when you said the generator frequently packs up. How could you know if you'd only been here a day or so. No wonder I felt uneasy. I should listen to my inner voice more closely.'

'Huh! It's a bit late to realise all that now, Sherlock,' Barney crowed.

'What a fool I've been. I was so anxious to find Suzie I didn't even stop to question how you knew where she was.'

'It wouldn't have made any difference – if that eases your conscience. I would've shouted for the guard if I'd any hint you suspected.'

'What on earth possessed you to turn traitor and work for scum like him?'

'Be careful how you choose your words, Mr Randle,' growled The General. 'If you upset me, they may be your last.'

'Anyway, the answer's easy,' said Barney. 'Money, old boy,' he smirked, emphasising the 'old'. 'Plus a few other perks – eh,

Suzie?'

'But you were locked in with the other prisoners. Why?'

Barney looked smug. 'I spend an evening in each of the cells with any new prisoners. They still think I'm one of them and talk freely. We've found it's the best way to get information. Much easier and quicker than resorting to torture – then we shoot them.'

'You nasty, money-grubbing traitor,' sneered Mike.

'Such compliments, Mr Randle,' taunted Barney. 'Then, of course, I'm let out of that smelly hell-hole in the early hours of the morning so that the others don't see me. After spending all day in that stinking place, I'm ready for some fun and relaxation. That's where Miss Drake here comes in useful.'

'You animal! I'll make you sorry for this.'

Mike moved forward again and Suzie grabbed his arm as the guns were levelled at him. 'No. Don't, Mike. He's not worth getting shot over,' she placated.

'Yes, come on, Mike,' taunted Barney, beckoning him. 'Let's see how far you get.'

The General intervened. 'You two can squabble later. I was expecting Raoul and his men to bring you in. Perhaps you changed your mind and came by another route, instead of the old jungle track?' he asked.

'No. I came that way,' Mike replied.

'I don't understand. How did they miss you?'

'They didn't. Let's just say you haven't as many mouths to feed tonight.'

The General looked shocked. 'I am... impressed, Mr Randle. Raúl is... was, good.'

'Yeah. He told me that too... just before I shot him.'

The General's expression hardened and he shifted uncomfortably. His favourite hit man, who had never let him down, had not been good enough – and it rankled.

'You have both caused me a great deal of trouble, but I will have the last laugh when you die.'

'If you kill us you'll never get into that safety deposit box,' countered Mike.

'Ah! So, you know about that, do you? That means you must

have found the key in the watch and no doubt discovered that one key is not enough. My commander was supposed to hand it over for payment after the arms were safely delivered. Not only does he let you two blow up the ammunition dump, but then he chases after you, gets himself shot and loses the watch and key!' spluttered The General, red-faced and in a voice that rose in pitch and volume.

'It's a shame he didn't have both keys, or Suzie and I wouldn't be here now. We'd be sunbathing on a holiday island.'

'Dream on, you fool,' sniggered The General. 'It doesn't matter that you found the key. Mr Dexter now has the watch and the contents of the box... and we have his wife. An exchange will be made tomorrow morning, then you and Miss Drake will be of no further use to me.'

'He may have the watch, but he doesn't have the key. Not the right one anyway. I've got that,' taunted Mike, trying to strengthen his hand.

'Rubbish,' replied The General. 'Mr Dexter has already been to the bank and collected the gems. You are lying to try and save your miserable lives. Well, it won't work.'

He did not sound totally convinced and Mike was sure a few doubts had crept into his mind. 'So. The box contains gems does it? I wondered what was in it. What're they worth?' Mike asked, only to annoy. After all, they weren't likely to tell him.

The General was angry at letting the information slip. 'That is no concern of yours. And anyway, you won't be around long enough to worry about it,' he insisted in a gruff, aggravated tone.

Barney stepped forward. 'I've enjoyed myself with the woman for the past few nights. It's a shame she must die, I was once quite fond of her. She won't agree to join us and help your cause, but she would be good sport for some of the other men before we get rid of her,' he suggested.

'Yes, Barney, you are right,' said The General, seeing an opportunity to get his own back and regain some of his self-esteem. 'The officers would enjoy having her, and I'm sure it would upset Mr Randle.'

'You bastard,' shouted Mike. The two guards rushed forward, restraining him from getting to The General.

'Language, Mr Randle!' taunted The General, looking pleased. 'How many officers do we have at the moment, Barney?'

'About half a dozen.'

'Good. Pass the word round. Those who do well in tomorrow's raid will have the pleasure of entertaining Miss Drake in the evening. I'm sure they will all do well.'

Suzie angrily interrupted, 'Don't you think I'll have something to say about that?'

'You don't have any choice, Miss Drake.'

'Maybe not, but I can still make it very difficult, ask Barney, he can tell you.'

Barney fingered several long scratches down the side of his face.

'I'm sure we can find some way of persuading you to co-operate,' The General said.

Barney agreed. 'You've got a lot of spunk, Suzie, I'll give you that. It's a pity you have to die,' he reflected. 'I've enjoyed our nightly struggles, and the pleasure I got when I inevitably won.'

'I'm sure we'll be able to find you a replacement soon,' promised The General. 'Tomorrow night, Barney, you will be the first. And if you... feel up to it,' he said with relish, 'you could be the last as well.'

Both men laughed at The General's little joke. Mike became more angry and struggled to get free. Barney smashed a fist into his stomach while the guards held him, and Mike doubled up with pain. He straightened up only to have it repeated, and buckled over again.

'Stop it!' shouted Suzie loudly. 'Stop it.'

The General moved close to her and in a quiet, smug voice, said, 'You see, Miss Drake, I've already found a way to persuade you to co-operate with my men. Mr Randle's well-being is in your hands, for the moment.'

'It's not going to stop you killing us though?'

'True. But think of it this way. While there's life, there's hope – or so they tell me.'

Mike struggled not to show any pain on his face, and straightened up.

The General pointedly turned to impress upon Mike his

words. 'You can spend all day thinking about what will happen to Miss Drake when the evening arrives.' He turned to the two guards. 'Take him away. Strip and search him thoroughly, then put him in the pit.'

Chapter XII

The Chase

In the underground car park of Orchard House in London, Jim stood in the lift, staring in disbelief at Payne and his boss.

'Who is he?' asked Dexter.

'Mr James Sterling, friend of Mr Mike Randle,' was the reply. 'I thought you were dead.'

'No. I went on a combat training course and they taught me how to be Superman,' Jim said dryly.

The two men looked at each other and smiled.

'So where's your red knickers?' spluttered Payne.

They both burst out laughing.

Jim's finger was poised over the lift button and he gently pressed it. Before Payne and Dexter realised what was happening, the doors started to close.

'Get him,' shouted Dexter, trying in vain to stop them shutting and almost getting his fingers caught. His smile turned to anger. 'Up the stairs – I'll wait here. He's gotta come back for his motor,' Dexter instructed.

Payne dived through the door and took the concrete stairs two at a time. The lift stopped at the ground floor, and Jim pressed the button for the top floor and hurried out. He walked smartly past the desk in the plush, carpeted reception area, through the glass-fronted doors held open by the uniformed doorman, and into Kingsway. Payne dashed through the stairway door, too late to see Jim walk along to the car entrance and down the vehicle ramp. Dexter was standing by the lift, watching the floor indicator, unaware of Jim tiptoeing briskly to his Rolls. The door closed with a gentle click, the engine turned over with barely a murmur, and the car moved quietly away.

The lift doors opened and Payne stepped out. 'There he goes,' he yelled, pointing towards the vehicle accelerating up the ramp and disappearing into Kingsway.

They ran to the BMW, their echoing footsteps clattering round the car park. The rev counter span to 5000, tyres squealed, and a shower of sparks cascaded behind them from the underside scraping on the exit ramp, in their haste to catch up with the fast disappearing Rolls.

'What vehicle's he driving?' questioned Dexter, motoring down the road in undue haste. 'Is he the one with the Roller?'

'Yeah. That's right. It's a silver Rolls Royce. You can't miss it.'

'Who the hell is this bloke anyway? What's his connection with Randle?'

'Don't know. First I saw of him was when he took Randle to the airport. We lost him and were lucky to pick him up again going home. Next day we followed him to Rye and Bunny was killed. I got out and shot him at point blank range. I don't understand why he's not dead.'

Jim's Rolls sped down Kingsway and into Aldwych, with the BMW close behind. He turned into the Strand, and was heading towards Trafalgar Square when his car phone buzzed. His father came on the line and Jim hurriedly explained his predicament.

'Make for my club in the West End,' his father suggested. 'I'll ring and let them know you're on the way, and I'll join you there in about half an hour. I want a little chat with you anyway.'

'Okay, Pop,' he replied, trying to sound casual about the whole thing.

Moving into Trafalgar Square, Jim encountered heavy traffic, delaying him, but he pushed his way through. The BMW had trouble getting past the jam, allowing Jim to put space between the cars in his effort to lose them before getting to the club. In desperation he shot through an amber traffic light, passing close to a crowd of pedestrians eagerly thronging onto the road. It allowed him to get out of sight of the BMW before turning into the street where the club and car park were.

Albert, the aged parking attendant, raised the barrier and saluted when the Rolls entered. Jim gave him a nod and a smile, and parked his car among the many other expensive vehicles.

The main entrance to the club was fifty yards back down the street. The BMW came cruising along and Jim ducked back into the car park and hid behind a vehicle, pretending to inspect it. Albert gave him a quizzical look and raised his eyes to the sky as if to say, 'Crazy rich people.'

The BMW stopped at the entrance and they surveyed the cars.

'Christ, look at all them Rollers in there!' declared Payne.

'And there's his car in the corner. Our boy moves in exclusive circles. Even I'd have a job to become a member of this place. I don't get it. Something don't seem right.'

'What're we gonna do?'

'Nothing for the moment. We've got more important things to take care of. He'll keep.'

Jim watched them drive away, then hurried along to the club and made straight for the bar. He ordered a Scotch, then remembered it was about time that he kept his promise to ring Grace.

'Hallo, Gracie, it's Jim. I'm just giving you a quick call to let you know I'm still all right. I'm at my dad's club in the West End.'

'I'm pleased to hear that. Any developments?'

'A few. I saw that bogus inspector and followed him. I'll tell you all about it tonight.'

'Oh good! That sounds as if it could be interesting. Detective Inspector Brooke was not very pleased when I told him that you'd left on business. He still wants to see you soon for a chat about last night.'

'Okay. Thanks, Gracie. I've got to go. I'll speak to you later.'

Jim replaced the receiver as his father climbed the steps and was ushered through the doorway. He looked his usual unperturbed quiet self, immaculately dressed in his pinstriped suit, bowler hat and umbrella, and Jim reflected how well he fitted into the Victorian club's surroundings.

The club covered five floors. The ground floor contained the members' room, restaurant, lobby and washroom. On the first floor was the reading room, where the occasional cough was the only sound to be heard, and the smoking room. Here those who indulged, and that was most of them, could lounge in the shiny red leather upholstered armchairs and puff away at their cigars. The remaining floors were for members who wished to stay overnight, and the staff quarters and kitchens were in the basement. All the rooms had fine Victorian furniture, typical Victorian high ceilings with an ornate cornice, and beautiful intricate chandeliers. Large paintings, mainly portraits of past PM's and royalty, hung on every wall. There was a hushed atmosphere, with members speaking in low tones. The chiming of clocks and the clinking of cutlery in the restaurant were the noisiest sounds to be heard, and the whole place had an air of calm and easy pace to life.

Sir Joseph greeted his son with a warm handshake, then ordered himself a whisky with ice, after Jim politely refused a top-up to his drink. They moved to a corner of the members' room to sit and talk.

'It's good to see you looking so well after last night's encounter,' his father began.

'Yes. That was a bit scary,' Jim replied.

'I thought we ought to have a little chat about it. Tell me how it all started.'

Jim told his tale of the past few days, ending at the previous night's events, though his father knew most of this already. He neglected to mention the pocket watches in his explanation.

Sir Joseph nodded. 'And what about this morning?' he asked.

Jim hesitated, then replied, 'How about you telling me something first? How is it that you seem to know so much about this, and how did you get involved?'

'I got "involved", as you put it, because you rang me to ask if I could find the whereabouts of Suzie Drake. During my inquiries, I discovered that Special Branch already had an open file on The General and Alfonso Dexter, and that there were references to Suzie Drake and Michael Randle added recently. It made fascinating reading.'

'I see. And why were Special Branch interested in this General and Dexter?'

'Dexter runs an import/export business but is also an arms dealer, which is why the Branch keep an eye on him. He recently supplied a consignment to The General for his rebellion in Africa. But it appears that something went wrong with the deal and there's disagreement between them. The General, for some reason, is interested in Drake and Randle, though I've not yet been able to ascertain why. He is, as I told you a couple of days ago, holding Miss Drake in his recently acquired headquarters at Camp West. Randle, of course, is on his way there. He must surely realise the possibility that it's a trap to capture him as well.'

'Yes, I'm sure he does, but he reckons he's smart enough to outwit them.'

Sir Joseph nodded in acknowledgement. 'I hope he's right. I'm trying to find out why The General wants them so badly. Do you have any clues about that?'

'I expect you know that Mike and Suzie are mercenaries?' Jim asked.

'Yes, it had come to my attention.'

'Well, they blew up The General's arms dump recently. Mike reckons he wants to get even. It was probably that consignment you spoke of.'

'Ah! So that's why Miss Drake was snatched. If so, then it's definitely a trap for Mr Randle.'

Jim looked at his father, hoping to discover if he really believed that was the only reason, but he couldn't. His father could read him well, but the reverse was not true. Jim had divided loyalties and kept things back, but was worried in case his father found out.

'Mike and I were followed on the way to the airport by a green Range Rover, but I thought we lost them,' Jim said. 'It must have been the same pair that showed up at Gracie's cottage.'

'Yes. They may have been watching Randle's flat and saw you leave. Events took a nasty turn when you rang to tell me you'd found a body there. One killing often leads to retaliation and can escalate out of hand. I checked on the two policemen who interviewed you and found they were bogus. That's why I asked Special Branch to send Brooke and a colleague to Silverdale Cottage. I wanted them to keep an eye on you and Miss Randle. You were clearly in something deeper than you were aware of. No sooner had they arrived than they were involved in the shooting.'

'Yes, how is your policeman?'

'Bill Harding will live, but he'll take time to recover. It'll be a while before he comes back to work.'

Jim now had most of the puzzle and wondered how much to tell his father.

He began hesitantly. 'I… overheard a telephone conversation to Dexter's office earlier. His wife has been kidnapped and held to ransom.'

Sir Joseph peered over the top of his glasses, wide-eyed and with his brow creased. He removed his spectacles and with one arm of them tapped his teeth.

Jim continued, 'He told his henchman, the bogus detective, to hire two hit men to take care of it. He thinks it's… The General's men who did it.'

A worried expression fixed on Sir Joseph's face at this latest development. He sipped his drink, then put the glass down.

'That could cause a lot of trouble. Now why would they kidnap his wife? It sounds as if either Dexter's reneged on his arms deal and they want revenge, or he has something The General's men want, so they've snatched her to barter for it.'

'It's got something to do with some gems.'

'Ah! Now that might have been payment for the arms and what their disagreement is all about. That type of deal is usually paid for in an untraceable currency. Perhaps Dexter's got hold of them and The General wants them back.'

'But I heard Dexter say that he hadn't got the stuff and was going to bluff it out. That's why he's hiring the gunmen.'

'Really? But they must *think* he's got his hands on the gems,' Sir Joseph said, slipping his glasses back on.

'So they snatched his wife to do a trade,' Jim suggested, swallowing the last drop of his whisky.

'Exactly. It explains why there's been so much activity recently, both here and in Africa.'

'You seem to be very well informed about all this,' remarked Jim, with a sneaky regard for this new-found image of his father's international dealings.

'We have an active operator in that part of the world who sends us information regularly. Now, who was chasing you this morning when I telephoned? I presume from what you've told me that it was Dexter?'

'Yes, I think so. The bogus detective bloke spotted me going back to my car after I'd eavesdropped on them and heard about the kidnapping.'

'And what were you doing there?'

'Eavesdropping!'

Again, Sir Joseph peered over the top of his glasses, but this time he gave his son a 'don't get smart with your father' look.

Jim recognised the look and continued, 'When Mike phoned from Africa, he asked me to keep an eye on Dexter.'

'I see. I wonder why he did that.'

'I'd rather you didn't get Mike too involved with this. He's got enough on his plate to worry about at the moment.'

'I'll see what I can do. But no promises.'

'Thanks, Dad.'

'Well, I'd better get those two closely watched and try to stop this bloodbath. What's your next move?'

'Back to Gracie in Rye, I guess. I didn't do a very good job of looking after her last night. Perhaps I'll do a bit better, this time.'

'I'll tell Colin Brooke that you're returning there this afternoon and get him to call on you. I think he's still got some questions to ask you. I shan't tell him what your "business trip" was about. You'll have to find your own excuses to explain this morning's events and how you came to be where you were.'

'Okay, Dad,' Jim replied, slightly embarrassed.

Sir Joseph Sterling finished his whisky and left. Jim stayed for lunch at the club. The food there was good, and he wanted to allow the men chasing him plenty of time to give up and leave the area.

Dexter revised their plans and told Payne to meet him at his apartment at 5 p.m., and dropped him off in the East End of London to tackle the task of finding two marksmen.

Payne trudged from pub to dingy club, renewing acquaintances and asking after the men he sought. He was careful whom he spoke to. In the East End of London, there were those who would sell information to the right people – for the right price. If the men holding Melissa Dexter found out that her husband was looking for a couple of hit men, any edge he might gain by hiring them would be lost.

At the same time, Al Dexter was also renewing old friendships and exerting all the pressure he could to get eyes and ears on to the streets, in the hope that somebody would see or hear something. He told them to spread the word about the reward he was offering to anyone who found Mel. It would be difficult for any new gang in town to stay undetected for any length of time. He was banking on hearing some sort of whisper of their whereabouts.

Later, he met Payne at his apartment. They cleared away the mess and straightened the room. Dexter was pleased that contact had been made, and a deal done by Payne with two contract killers. The Peten brothers were known in the underworld for this type of work and had the reputation of being ruthless and efficient.

Finding them had not been easy, and Payne had used bribes and threats to set up a meeting with the pair. The fact that he was successful so quickly was a tribute to his tenacity and a measure of both the fear he engendered and the respect he commanded in the underworld.

The Peten brothers were credited with several grizzly murders and were renowned for being cold-blooded and brutal to their victims. Arriving in England with their parents as refugees from the Hungarian uprising, they had bullied their way through school. Later, they drifted into petty crime and became involved in gangland killings. They enjoyed it, but relished more the feeling of power it gave them. It encouraged them to take up the art of intimidation and contract killing. A healthy bank balance grew fast, along with a nasty and well-deserved reputation.

'I've also been busy,' said Dexter, 'spreading the word about Mel, and getting as many people out looking for her as I could. So far, there's no word on her whereabouts. In case we don't find her in time, I've also made other arrangements,' he announced, spreading out a large map of London on his desk.

'What's the plan, boss?' Payne asked.

Dexter produced a list and began marking the map. 'I've got ten men with mobile phones spread around London in cars, waiting at these locations,' he said, ringing each vicinity and writing a telephone number alongside. 'Jerry's at the exchange waiting to trace the call. I'm banking on them being in the London area. When they ring, we'll trace it and get a man there fast to follow them. They're unlikely to use a phone at their hideout, they're too clever for that, so I'm hoping they'll use a public call box and think they're safe.'

'Sounds good to me.'

'I've got to keep them talking long enough to get the call traced and someone there before they hang up. That's your job. When we find out where their hideout is, the boys are ready to go in. Everything's prepared. Now we just wait...'

Jim enjoyed lunch at the club, eating steak and kidney pie with chips, and finishing with a half-pint of weak shandy to wash it down, conscious not to drink too much before his drive. The club was proud of its reputation for good food and boasted having one of the top city chefs. This excellence was reflected in the menu prices, which were only slightly below those of major London restaurants.

At half past two, Jim began his journey to Rye and searched cautiously up and down the street for the BMW. It was nowhere in sight, so he collected his car, putting out a hand and glancing skywards as it began to spit with rain. A wave to Albert produced another salute when he left and, keeping a watchful eye on his mirror, he motored through the city and across Vauxhall Bridge, leaving London behind. Every mile that passed with nobody tailing him helped Jim to relax a little more.

During his journey, it rained on and off. The intermittent, dark grey Nimbostratus clouds trailing across the sky brought wet weather, then eased for a short while, only to return again. Jim took his time on the trip, enjoying the lovely Sussex countryside drifting past, thinking about the day's events and delighting in the silky-smooth ride. He wondered if Mike was okay, and what progress he was making. By the time he reached Rye, darker clouds had filled the sky and rain lashed down so hard that it was difficult to keep the windscreen clear.

Parking outside, Jim dashed to the front door, but was quite wet by the time he entered the cottage. Grace greeted him warmly, took his jacket to dry over the Aga in the kitchen and handed him a towel.

After combing his damp hair and wiping his glasses, Jim sat in front of the fire, warming himself, and was immediately pounced on by Emmy, as ever looking for a comfortable lap to sleep on.

A wet Detective Inspector Colin Brooke arrived a few minutes later, and Grace made a fresh pot of tea for them before they settled down. Jim answered Brooke's questions about the previous night's events, but was unable to add much to what Grace had already told him and what he'd seen for himself.

'And what about today? I gather you have more news. Sir Joseph didn't say much about your business trip. He was anxious for me to get back here quickly when he knew you were returning. What happened?'

Jim was not sure how best to fudge his business trip, along with the events of the morning, and before he could begin Grace interrupted, 'Yes. Tell us about your good fortune in spotting one of the men who was here last night.'

Taking his cue from her, he told them the same story he had related earlier to his father, but began with his 'good fortune' to see Payne in Bishopsgate. Again he made no mention of the bank or the watches.

'Sounds like a spot of blackmail,' proffered Brooke. 'Dexter must have something valuable that the other men want. And they want it badly enough to snatch his wife to get it. That's my guess.'

Jim nodded in agreement. 'That's right. Dad said the same. Trouble is, Dexter doesn't have the stuff they want, so they're hiring two gunmen to take care of it.' He sipped his second cup of tea and helped himself to an 'After Tea' biscuit.

'That's nasty. If these two start a war, Special Branch could get caught in the middle. Just like last night. Miss Randle – Gracie – did you check to see what they took yesterday?'

'Yes,' declared Grace. 'They smashed a lot of things, but nothing seems to be missing.'

'Really? I wonder what they were searching for then?'

Grace shot a glance at Jim, wondering whether she sounded convincing or not. Telling fibs was not easy for her, but she wanted to avoid getting either Mike or Jim into trouble.

Brooke finished writing in his notebook and returned it to his pocket. He spoke deliberately.

'Due to the seriousness of the case, and no doubt because Jim is involved, Sir Joseph has asked me to keep watch here for a day or two. Would it be okay if I stayed and slept on the couch?'

'Of course. You can sleep in Mike's room if you'd prefer. I've tidied up the mess.'

'Thanks, but I'd rather sleep here in the living room if that's all right with you. If anyone does try to enter the premises I want to be down here ready for them,' explained Brooke, drifting into his official jargon.

'As you wish,' Grace agreed. 'Is that it?'

'Yes, thanks. For the moment.'

'Good. Enough of this serious talk, then. It must be dinner for three.'

'Thank you,' said Brooke. 'I'll speak to Sir Joseph about this information first,' he informed, punching the buttons on his mobile telephone.

'Of course.'

After dinner they settled down to an evening of chat, and the two men were persuaded to play a game of cards. They sat in front of a cosy log fire, while the rain patted against the windowpanes. Grace's passion was reading books and listening to the radio; she refused to stagnate in front of a television each evening, so had never bothered to get one.

By eleven thirty, after a nightcap of Horlicks, they settled down for the night. With Brooke now staying, for the moment at least, Jim was unable to talk to Grace about his exploits to find the watch.

'Perhaps it's better she doesn't know – less for her to worry about,' he thought.

Outside, the rain became a storm lashing against the windows, with lightning flashing and thunderclouds clapping. Inside the cottage, Brooke checked all the downstairs doors and windows, and his gun, which he laid on the coffee table beside him. He made himself comfortable on the couch, in front of the dying embers of a flickering log fire, producing dancing shadows on the wall mixed with sudden bursts of light from outside. Emmy settled herself down next to him to sleep, warm by his side.

Dexter waited anxiously in his apartment for the telephone to ring. A couple of calls came in from friends enquiring about progress in finding Mel, but no good news. The carriage clock chimed the hours and half-hours away.

He paced up and down and looked at his watch every few minutes. 'Why don't they ring?' he asked nervously.

'They just want you to suffer a little. Relax. They'll ring soon,' said Payne, trying to calm him.

The hands on the clock approached 10 p.m. when the call finally came. On the other end of the line was the man with the same deep, confident voice.

'Good evening, Mr Dexter. We speak again. My name is not important, but you can call me… Nick,' he said with a laugh.

Dexter didn't smile at the pun. He motioned to Payne that this was the call they were waiting for. Payne immediately contacted Jerry, monitoring their telephone, then listened in on the extension.

'Is my wife okay?' Dexter asked.

'So far. She'll be returned when we get the gems that you collected this morning. Oh, and don't think you can trace this call. I'm phoning from a rented car on a mobile phone, driving around London. How's that for caution?'

Dexter quietly cursed. 'I want to talk to my wife before we do any deals.'

'Tomorrow. You can talk to her tomorrow,' the voice said, slowly and deliberately.

'How do I know she's still alive? You might have killed her already.'

'Would you like me to send her back to you in little pieces?'

'No, no, don't hurt her. What arrangements have you got in mind?'

'That's better. We'll meet at the old railway sidings in Shoreditch at noon tomorrow. You bring the gems. We'll bring your wife and we'll do a straight swap.'

'All right. But only if she's not harmed.'

'And no tricks, Mr Dexter. If I see the slightest sign of a double-cross, your wife will be the first to die, and you will be the second. Do you understand?' he said, in a cold, threatening tone.

'Yeah yeah! I understand. Tomorrow at twelve then, but you

hear this. If you lay a finger on her – you're dead, Nick, or whatever your real name is,' Dexter spat. The phone went dead without a reply.

He slammed down the receiver and stood there, infuriated. Going over the arrangements with Payne, he said, 'He's a cautious bastard, thinks of everything. Anything on that phone trace?'

'Nothing of any use,' he replied despondently. 'Jerry confirmed it was a car phone in a vehicle registered to Arnie's Autos in Shoreditch Road.'

'Shoreditch again,' mused Dexter, with a slight cock of his head. 'Get someone to check it out right away and tell the boys to concentrate on the Shoreditch area. It's not much, but it's all we've got at the moment.'

'Consider it done.'

'And let everyone know about the arrangements for the exchange tomorrow, especially the Peten brothers. Tell them to get there at first light and find a good, high spot to survey the area. That Nick's clever. I wouldn't put it past him to try and hide someone there himself before the meeting.'

'Right.'

Payne punched the buttons on the telephone as Dexter, folding the maps on his desk, noticed damage to the middle drawer. He opened it, rummaged through and discovered that the watches were gone.

Cursing and swearing, he smashed his fist down on the desk in frustration. 'Am I working with a bunch of idiots or what? First somebody walks in here and snatches my wife, and now someone's nicked the bloody watches.'

'That's not possible,' protested Payne. 'Nobody knew they were there! It can't be that Nick, he's already searched the place, and anyway he wouldn't phone to make the swap.'

'I know that, stupid. Question is – who was it?'

'Don't forget we saw that bloke Sterling coming out of the lift this morning. I bet it's him.'

'That's right. We've got unfinished business with Mr Sterling. Get on the blower and organise a search for him at first light. I want him found, and quickly.'

'What, now?'

'Yes, now!' shouted Dexter.

Payne nodded his compliance, rattled the phone lugs and punched the buttons again. It took him half an hour to make all the calls and give out the instructions.

Afterwards, they talked into the early hours, mulling over the various situations they could face at the exchange. They discussed tactics and options, and tried to anticipate any crafty move Nick might make at the meeting, and counter it. By the early hours, they'd exhausted all the possible scenarios they could think of. Both were tired, feeling the stresses of the day, and couldn't think clearly. There was no more they could do. Dexter told Payne to sleep in the spare bedroom, and they went wearily to bed as the clock chimed twice.

Neither slept very well. Dexter had a bad dream about a man with a featureless face about to push a naked Mel over a cliff. He ran at top speed to try and save her, but couldn't get any closer. The man laughed, pushing her over the edge, and her screams woke Dexter up. His heart thumped away in his chest and he was perspiring. He switched the bedside lamp on. It was almost four in the morning. For a while he lay there, thinking about his wife, then got a drink and went back to his restless sleep.

At 6 a.m., Dexter woke and looked at the empty place beside him in the bed. He could smell Mel's perfume on her pillow and felt frustration and anger at his inability to find her. She was not very strong and would be scared, but it would all be over soon, and they would pay dearly for snatching her. He used his hate for these faceless men to push himself forward and block out thoughts about the ordeal that his frail wife was forced to endure.

He rose at half past six and had a shower. Payne got up at seven and did likewise. The storm had passed and left a clear morning, overcast with grey skies to match the mood they felt.

Both men had toast and coffee for breakfast but talked very little, and tension hung heavily in the silence. With breakfast over, they dumped the dirty crockery in the sink and left it.

The doorbell rang, making them jump. They were edgy and Payne grabbed his gun before answering it. He peered through the spy hole and shouted to Dexter.

'It's okay. It's only the postman with a registered parcel. I'll get it.'

'A registered parcel,' echoed Dexter shakily. 'They wouldn't.' The horror of Nick's words made him feel sick to his stomach. He sat with his head in his hands, picturing all manner of grotesque thoughts that flashed through his mind.

Payne tucked the gun in his belt at the back and opened the door. He signed the book and stared in horror at a gun, stuck into his ribs by the postman. His heart began to thump when he realised his mistake, and fear engulfed him as he waited to find if he would live or die in the next few seconds. His apprehension subsided when the man jabbed him in the midriff with the gun and ordered him to be quiet, and to step back slowly into the hall.

Two more men appeared from the side and one held on to a very frightened Melissa Dexter. She looked pale and tired. Gone was the beauty seen the previous evening, replaced by a woman with red eyes and a drawn haggard look. Payne was relieved of his gun and ushered quickly into the living room, where Dexter was startled by the intrusion.

'Hallo, Mr Dexter. I'm Nick,' announced a short, stockily built man with a pockmarked face, in the superior tone of one who knew that he had the upper hand. He wore a light suit and his blonde crew-cut hairstyle and cold blue eyes gave him a hard and ruthless look. He carried an air of authority that the others acknowledged.

'I see you've cleaned the place up.'

Dexter moved towards his wife and brushed aside the gun pointed at him. He didn't like hired help who tried to intimidate him, and it showed in his expression of contempt.

He gave his wife a hug. '*Come stai, Mel*?' he asked gently.

'*Bene, Dex,*' she replied shakily.

'Speak English!' barked Nick.

'Anyone touched you?' Dexter asked.

'No. Nobody touched me, Dex. I'm just tired, and scared.'

'Mr Dexter, *please!*' Nick said, with an exaggerated tone of offence, spreading his arms in a gesture of innocence. 'How could you think I would allow any of my men to touch your beautiful wife? At least, not after we knew you'd been to the bank for the gems.'

'If it wasn't for that, you'd have killed her without batting an eyelid.'

'That's different. That would be to teach you a lesson. This is business. You would not be as co-operative if you knew you were getting soiled goods back.'

'My wife's not goods.'

'Merely a figure of speech, Mr Dexter.'

Dexter stared hard at Nick with an acrimonious look. 'I thought we were meeting in Shoreditch at noon?'

'I decided a change of plans would be much safer, just in case you were foolish enough to try and be clever. Now, where are the gems?'

Dexter was in a tough spot and knew it. He had no option but to explain that when he tried the second key to the box it wouldn't fit. When he then said that the watches and keys had been stolen, he could see Nick thought he was lying, even after he was shown the damaged desk.

Nick gritted his teeth. 'I'll kill all of you if this is just a con to try and pull the wool over my eyes.'

'It's not,' assured Payne, attempting to add weight to his boss's argument. 'We saw a bloke called Sterling leaving the building yesterday, and we're sure he's mixed up in it somehow. He may be working for Randle. He's probably the one who's taken the watches.'

'May be! Probably!' screamed Nick in a rage, pacing around the room. 'You don't seem to be very sure of anything.' He turned to his men. 'Search the place,' he ordered.

Nick's men rummaged through the apartment. Dexter and his wife watched, with suppressed exasperation, at every room in their home turned upside down and wrecked again. Nick found the map of London and smiled with satisfaction that his precautions had outwitted Dexter's attempts to trace him. One of his men went down to Dexter's office to search there.

Nick thrust his face into Dexter's and their noses touched, and with quiet anger he demanded, 'And what are you doing about this Sterling character?'

'I've got men trying to trace him now. They're checking the three addresses where he's been seen recently.'

'Which are?'

Dexter picked up a map of southern England from the floor, where it fell after the desk drawers were emptied. He spread it on the desk and ringed three areas.

'A detached house in Weybridge, his home. My men followed him there after he dropped Randle at London Airport. The second address is Randle's flat in Surbiton.'

'Oh yes,' said Nick tersely. 'Where you killed one of my men. That's why we called on you yesterday. Unfortunately, you were out and we only found your missus. You were lucky we decided to take her with us to teach you an agonising lesson, instead of killing her there and then.'

'I was at the bank trying to collect the gems.'

'Yes, I know. After I learned you'd been there, I assumed you'd picked up the stuff and I decided to do a swap instead. Killing my man wasn't very clever. The boys expect me to do something about that, and I have a reputation to consider.'

'Yes, well that was Bunny. He took revenge for your man stabbing his mate Jack when they searched Randle's room at Tramer, where he works. He reckoned your mob were also looking for the key and had the same idea about turning the place over.'

'My men didn't go to Tramer. I didn't know he worked there. Ray searched Randle's flat and, when he didn't return, my man checked the place and found him dead, just before some bloke arrived.'

'That must've been Sterling.'

'He gets around, doesn't he? I figured you got there first, found the key and killed my man when he interrupted you. The only way of getting my hands on the gems after that was to watch the bank and pay you a visit.'

'So did one of your men kill Bunny at this last address, the cottage near Rye?' Dexter asked, ringing the spot.

'No. Not one of my men, Mr Dexter. You seem to be crediting me with a lot of things I'm not guilty of. I know nothing about a cottage near Rye.'

'It belongs to Randle's aunt. Bunny and Payne found the watch and key there before Bunny was shot. If it wasn't your men who did it, then who? The police? Special Branch?'

Nick's frustration worsened. 'Special Branch,' he raged. 'That's all we need. How the bloody hell did they get involved?'

'I don't know,' snapped Dexter. 'Maybe this Sterling bloke called them when he found your man's body in the flat. Or maybe he even works for them.'

'So what was he doing there in the first place?' demanded Nick, who was horrified that news of the keys and gems looked like becoming common knowledge.

'I don't know, do I?' shouted Dexter, in a voice that had gone up an octave. 'We think he may have got friendly with Randle to steal the key. He's certainly not short of a bob or two. He runs around in a Roller.'

Nick's brow creased. Now he was really puzzled.

'What sort of crook runs around in a conspicuous Rolls?' he asked himself. 'What're your men gonna do when they locate Sterling?' he questioned.

'They'll ring me.'

Nick's man returned from Dexter's office shaking his head.

'Okay. We'll wait for your man to ring then. Everybody make themselves comfortable.'

Tension in the air was high. Nick told Mel to make coffee for them all, and they waited in an atmosphere that was ready to explode.

With each call that came, Nick listened in on the extension. Dexter tried to cut short anyone who enquired about arrangements for the exchange, but it became obvious a lot of activity was going on. Men who checked the addresses in Surbiton and Weybridge rang in with nothing to report. Listening to these calls gave Nick some assurance that Dexter might be telling the truth.

Time wore on; Nick's men filled the air with cigarette smoke. Dexter hated that and normally wouldn't allow anyone to smoke in his apartment. But times were not normal and he had no choice. They all waited, the silences charging the air with electricity. Dexter tried to calm his wife, saying that things would be okay, but she looked very nervous and tense. She needed sleep and looked close to breaking point.

It was shortly before midday when a call came from Dave Collins at Rye. He reported that Jim's Rolls was outside the cottage, but said that he could see no sign of anyone there at the moment.

Dexter relayed Nick's instructions. 'You stay and keep watch, follow Sterling if he leaves, and ring me on my mobile phone. I'm on the way there.'

Nick put down the extension and nodded to his two men. 'Right then, it's all down to Rye, after I've rung The General with the latest news.'

He telephoned The General to keep him abreast of their progress. Dexter could see that even Nick chose words carefully to try and impress upon him the ease and certainty with which he expected to obtain the gems soon. Dexter was well aware from his own dealings with The General that he was shrewd, and fooling him was not easy. He knew that this would put Nick under a lot of pressure, as failure was not an option. Aware of this ruthlessness, Dexter had already set up an escape route for himself, Mel and Payne to use if things became too hot after he got his hands on the gems.

Turning to Dexter and Payne, Nick stated, 'We'll use my car and my man will drive. That leaves two of us to watch three of you, and you have another man already there. I don't like the odds. Could be a bit tricky,' he said, pointing his gun at Payne and pulling the trigger.

The silenced weapon gave a muffled spit, and Payne grunted as a hole appeared in his chest and blood coloured his shirt. He staggered back against the glass-topped table, smashing it as he fell to the floor, staining the carpet red with his blood.

Mel Dexter screamed and had a hand clasped over her mouth.

'Shut up,' shouted Nick.

'That wasn't necessary,' choked Dexter, watching Payne shaking on the floor. He coughed up blood and it trickled from the corner of his mouth. The shaking stopped and he exhaled for the last time.

'Like I said, my men expect me to take care of things. And anyway, it leaves more room in the car for the rest of us and serves as a warning in case you were thinking about trying any more smart moves,' he cautioned. 'Let's go.'

Chapter XIII

The Pit

Camp West had held a surprise for Mike that he wasn't prepared for. A traitor, his one time comrade – Barney.

Mike was searched and relieved of his weapons. Even the lock pick hidden inside his belt was found. They were very thorough. He got back his T-shirt with the pocket half torn, his trousers without the belt, and nothing else. His wrists were bound in front of him with wire, cutting into him, and he was marched along, barefooted, and unsympathetically thrown into a six feet by ten feet hole in the ground. A barred metal framework was dropped over the top, crashing down with a resounding thud of finality and padlocked shut. Things looked bleak.

'Look what they've done to my shirt,' he jested to himself, 'another one ruined! Still, at least it's in one piece – just.'

The night was warm and the humidity high. Mike settled in the corner and tried to get some sleep on the hard ground. With the discomfort, and his mind racing to calculate all possible scenarios still open to him, sleep never came.

Slowly the hours drifted by, taking an age to drag the morning into daylight. The first shafts of light hurried across the compound, heralding the rising sun, bringing with it fresh hopes. Mike found it useless to struggle with his bonds, and the more he did, the worse it cut into his wrists. Apart from a guard checking on him from time to time, staring through the bars, he saw no one, and as the day progressed, the heat increased, becoming almost unbearable. There was no shade and no escape from the now blinding sun that seared down on him.

The tramp of many feet plodding past heralded soldiers wandering, rather than marching, on the way to their vehicles taking them on a raid. Sitting in the corner with the sweat dripping from him, the hours drifted past without a visit from anyone or a drop of water to quench his thirst. By mid-afternoon, his face was beginning to blister and his lips were dry and cracking.

The General, still looking dishevelled, came to gloat at his captive's unease. 'I hope you're not suffering too much,' he crowed, sucking an orange to antagonise his prisoner.

'No, no. It's just like being on Brighton beach, soaking up the sun,' Mike said facetiously. 'I don't suppose you have any suntan oil on you?'

Throwing the orange away in anger, The General remarked, 'Make your jokes, Mr Randle, you may not have time to tell many more. My man in England tells me he will have the gems by tonight.'

'Oh, really. As I recall, you said last night that some bloke called Dexter had the gems and you were going exchange his wife for them in the morning. Now you're talking about getting them tonight, so what's gone wrong? Could it be that they're still in the vault and he hasn't got the right keys? Just like I said!'

The General seethed at the smug look Mike gave, but knew that until his men got hold of the gems he would have to be patient – just in case.

He conceded, 'There may be some truth in what you said, but don't bank on it saving your hide.' Then, to torment Mike some more, he added, 'It seems that the keys are at your aunt's cottage in Rye, held by Mr James Sterling. My men are on the way there right now.'

It provoked alarm in Mike who yelled, 'You leave my aunt and Jim out of this. Somebody's already paid them a visit and searched the place. There's nothing there, and they know nothing about the keys or the gems.'

'We shall see, very soon. Meanwhile, you can be thinking about the fate your lady friend will endure shortly. However, if you were to tell me where you've hidden the key, I will try to make this evening... less arduous for her,' he offered in a condescending tone.

'Go boil your head in oil,' was the defiant reply.

'I seem to have heard that remark before. I can't think who could have said it,' added The General mockingly, and then departed.

Barney was informed about the call from Nick and agreed it was wise to keep Randle alive until the gems were secured. After all, he was in no position to cause any problems and was probably half-dead with exhaustion already.

Mike lay in the pit and suffered the sweltering heat of the glaring afternoon sun. He heard vehicles returning and soldiers wearily trudging back.

'Perhaps all the officers got shot. That would mess up The General's plans for Suzie tonight,' pondered Mike, 'but that's wishful thinking.'

Early evening approached and the temperature, encouraged by a slight breeze, dropped, to give him some relief from his blisters. With no opportunity to escape he became more concerned about Suzie, the fatal hour getting nearer. She had already endured a lot and, just as freedom looked possible, it was snatched away. But she was resilient, he reminded himself, and their luck had to change some time.

The guard approached and unlocked the cage to allow a Chinese man to hand Mike a bowl of what looked like dirty hot water and a crust of bread. He gave a look and tried to convey something, which made Mike wonder whether the food was poisoned, but he seemed to be encouraging him to try it.

With a questioning expression, Mike took the bowl and saw the guard kick the Chinese man to encourage him to hurry along with his task. The hot liquid spilt onto Mike's hand and burnt him, almost making him drop the bowl, to the Chinaman's alarm.

The cage top was slammed shut again and locked.

Mike supped the hot broth carefully through his cracked lips, precariously holding the bowl between his knees. It tasted better than it looked, and when he scooped the next mouthful, he saw his lock pick on the wooden spoon. He dropped it back into the broth immediately and checked that he wasn't being watched before fishing in the liquid for it.

A wry smile crossed his lips. His luck was beginning to change.

'I don't know how you got hold of this, Chinese, but thank you very much,' he said to himself as he tucked it in his pocket and enjoyed the rest of the broth, reorganising his thoughts and making plans for his and Suzie's escape.

Later the Chinese man returned for the bowl and saw that it was empty, and their eyes met in mutual recognition of the significance. Mike gave him a small 'thank you' nod, before the smile was wiped from his cheeky face by the guard's kick to speed him up.

The sun became a large orange ball balancing on the horizon, sinking into a few straggling clouds that drifted by at the end of the day. Mike set to work on the padlock, but it resisted his attention. He struggled to open it between stops for passing soldiers, knowing the floodlights would burst into life soon, illuminating the area and making it harder to continue unseen. Frustration started to get to him in his failure to make any progress.

'And I said I was getting good at this,' he moaned, taking a swipe at the lock.

Frequent stops added to his difficulties, but he ignored the pain inflicted by the wire cutting into his wrists, leaving blood trailing down his arms.

'Come on, you bitch – undo,' he swore under his breath.

The lock clicked. The cage was finally open. Mike lowered his aching arms and blew out a lungful of air in gratitude that the task was finally accomplished. To give the impression that he was still locked in, he left the padlock in place, sank to the ground and took a much needed rest, allowing the ache in his shoulders to subside.

When the guard returned to make another check, Mike stood and pointed at the lock with a quizzical expression on his face. Intrigued by this, the guard bent down to look and froze with amazement when Mike whipped the lock off. He thrust the cage top up, smashing it into his face, breaking his nose with the iron frame and knocking him out cold. His knees buckled and he keeled over, allowing Mike to grab him by the belt and drag him into the pit.

He relieved the guard of his knife and, with the blade held towards him, started cutting his bonds, ignoring the pain. The wire gouged deeper into his wrists at each stroke of the blade and blood dripped to the ground and disappeared immediately, soaking into the dry earth. He'd cut most of the way through when the soldier began to rouse. Frantically, he tried to break the last few strands, but the man recovered quickly and made a lunge towards him. Mike span the knife round and the guard ran onto the blade, stopping suddenly and staring at the knife buried deep inside him. With a look of disbelief on his face, his grip on Mike's arm released and he sank slowly to the ground with barely a murmur from his lips.

Shoving him aside, Mike quipped, 'Sorry about that, but there's no time for heroics. Anyway, you shouldn't have kicked the Chinaman.'

The floodlights burst to life.

Mike resumed hacking away at his bonds and, after cutting through the last strands and freeing his hands, changed clothes with the guard, placing him in the darkest corner of the pit. With his face turned away, anyone casually looking in would think it was the prisoner sleeping. The guard's shoes were a little tight and Mike complained – but he slipped them on anyway, knowing that they would have to do, and he unbuckled his gunbelt and knife.

Checking the pistol and donning the guard's cap, Mike lifted up the top a short way to peer out. Soldiers approached. He lowered it quietly and flattened himself against the side. After they'd passed he checked again. This time the coast was clear and he climbed out, locking the cage. He turned to see one of the guards on the main gate in the distance watching him. Tugging the peak down, he gave him a wave and grinned at the acknowledgement he received with a wave in return. His desire was to run to safety, but he knew that would be fatal. Instead, he turned and walked slowly away. Each step took him further from the guard, and he kept moving.

At the edge of the first hut, the Chinese man stepped out from the shadows and beckoned him.

'Me Charlie. I cook.'

'Me Mike. I fight.'

Charlie smiled and they shook hands. He had a firm grip for such a small man. A sign of a strong character, thought Mike. Charlie asked Mike to follow him. They took a quiet route to the kitchens where he worked. There he noticed Mike's wrists were bleeding badly and offered to bandage them. Mike tore off a piece of his shirt for Charlie to use.

'Another shirt ruined. Even if it wasn't mine to begin with. One of these days I'll get to wear one without having to rip it up,' Mike quipped.

Charlie looked slightly bemused, but continued to bandage the cuts.

The kitchen was at the rear of one of the larger huts that served as a dining hall for the eighty soldiers on the camp. The smell of cooked food and grease lingered in the air. These conditions were far superior to those that Charlie had encountered when cooking for the men in jungle hideouts, moving from makeshift camp to makeshift camp. The log-burning stove he now used was a luxury compared to the open campfire he previously had to cope with.

When he finished bandaging Mike's wrists, Charlie said, 'There is a Chinese lady in the prison cells. They do what they want with her.' He spoke in a quiet voice with lowered eyes, masking a lot of hidden anger.

'Yes, I know. I've seen.'

'She is my wife.'

Mike felt sorry for him. He could see the pain and anguish he was suffering, picturing the humiliation his wife was forced to endure.

'I helped you escape. You help us get away?'

This had not been a part of Mike's plan and, although it complicated things, he was indebted to the little man for helping him. He recalled the woman's eyes, pleading with him to help her, attempting to ignore the guard mauling her. Mike knew he had little choice. The Chinese man's help had resulted in the guard's death, and someone was sure to find out how he'd escaped when they discovered that the lock pick was missing. There was no going back for either of them.

Charlie looked longingly at Mike, waiting for an answer. His face broke into a wide beam when Mike said, 'Okay.'

No one could pronounce the Chinese pair's real names, so he was called Charlie, and his wife, Mrs Charlie. They were both slim and only five feet two inches tall.

Charlie was devoted to his wife. It was almost ten years since they had left China and taken to the high seas to work as cook, cleaner and an all-round odd job pair. Treated like slaves, they jumped ship in South Africa to gain their freedom and worked their way across the continent before being captured by The General. For almost a year now he'd forced Charlie to cook and used his wife for the pleasure of his men, keeping her chained or locked up to prevent them from leaving. Despite being in their early thirties, the hard life they'd endured had aged both of them, and the African sun had turned their pale complexions darker.

'Okay. First I want to help Suzie. Can you get in to see her?' asked Mike.

'I take her food in. She is to be fed soon… before the men visit her,' he said in a sheepish tone, avoiding the angry look in Mike's eyes which he knew would be there.

Mike controlled his temper. 'Can you get a weapon to her or give her a message?'

'Maybe. But it is very difficult. Since you arrive, many men now guard her. One on main door, one on door to her room, and one inside room, and they search me before I go in.'

'They're not taking any chances, are they? What food are you taking to her?'

'A bowl of hot broth and a crust of bread. Same as I gave you. I am preparing it now.'

Mike thought out loud, 'It worked once, why not try it again? Charlie, have you got a short length of thin wire and a small wooden peg?'

He nodded, rummaged through the drawers and found a length of wire and a pencil.

'Okay?' he asked, holding them up.

'Perfect.'

Mike cut the pencil to a short length for the peg, made a slip knot in one end of the wire and fixed the peg to the other end. He coiled the wire up and dropped the whole thing into the bowl. Charlie poured the broth in and covered it over.

'Show it to Suzie, then hook it underneath the bed by her free hand where she can reach it. Okay?'

'Okay.'

'She'll know what to do... I hope.'

Charlie left with the bowl on a tray.

Mike waited anxiously for him to return. The minutes ticked by and he began to wonder if the gadget had been discovered and Charlie caught. He sat in a corner of the kitchen in the dark clutching a gun, prepared to repel any soldiers who burst in on him.

'Come on, Charlie, don't let me down. This could be our only chance to get out,' he quietly muttered.

After almost twenty minutes, Mike tensed, hearing footsteps approaching the door. It opened and Charlie came trotting in with the tray and empty bowl.

'I took a long time because the lady is now manacled by both hands and feet. I had to feed her.'

'Damn,' Mike cursed, looking to the ceiling in mock anger at the heavens upsetting his plans. 'Did you manage to show her the gadget?'

'Just. I fixed it under the bed by her left hand. She looked very pleased when I whispered to her that you were free. Just before the guard's boot told me to leave.'

'Well done, Charlie!' Mike enthused, clapping him on the shoulder. 'I'm going to get a jeep ready for us to get away in. You make another bowl of that broth. I'm going to need it shortly.'

Charlie nodded enthusiastically, thinking that at last someone appreciated his cooking.

Pulling down the peak on his cap and grabbing a torch, Mike walked to the motor pool area, casually nodding to a passing soldier.

He thought how fortunate he was to find Charlie, and wondered why all the guards seemed to want to kick the little man.

Let's hope he has the last laugh.

At the motor pool area, the canvas-backed lorry that was last to enter blocked all the jeeps.

'Sod! Nothing's going right. Can't push the damn thing out of the way, and I daren't start it. Might arouse someone's suspicions,' he cursed.

Mike climbed into the lorry, tore the wires from the starter switch to disable it and left them hidden, needing only to join them together to start the vehicle. He returned to the kitchen to find that Charlie had prepared the broth.

'Charlie, I want you to take this bowl of broth to your wife. The guard is used to seeing you and won't be alarmed so quickly. If you can distract him for a moment, it'll give me a chance to deal with him without making any noise or attracting attention. Okay?'

He nodded.

'Let's go.'

Charlie scooted off to the prison hut with Mike in close attention. They passed a couple of soldiers who took no notice of them, confirming that Mike's luck still held and his escape was, as yet, undetected.

At the hut, Charlie entered with Mike behind him, his nostrils twitching at the foul smell that enveloped him once again. The same guard that he'd seen the previous evening was sitting on his chair beneath the dim light at the far end, with his sub-machine-gun propped against the wall. His black face and beard blended with the dark surroundings, leaving only the whites of his eyes and teeth showing, making him hard to see.

They walked towards him.

'What are you doing here, Charlie?' he barked.

Charlie replied meekly, 'Please sir, I have some broth for my wife.' They continued to get nearer.

'Broth? Why?' he laughed. 'So she can keep her strength up for a night of passion?'

Mike could sense the anger rising in Charlie, and he touched his elbow to calm him. They were only a few feet away when the guard recognised him.

'You,' he shouted, reaching for his gun.

Mike drew his commando knife and threw it underarm in one movement. The knife plunged into the guard's midriff almost to the hilt, and an expression of hate and defiance came to his twisted face. He was propelled back into the chair, overturning it, and slumped to the floor.

Charlie dropped the tray and gave a jubilant shout, jumping up and down and clapping. Mike calmed him down and tried to keep him quiet.

'Sssh, Charlie! We don't want to wake the whole camp up.'

'Sorry, Mr Mike. You don't know how many times I've wished for him to be dead.'

'Sure, okay, I understand. Let's just keep things quiet.'

Mike took the ring of keys from the guard's belt and unlocked the cell. Charlie released his wife and they embraced and jabbered to each other in Chinese.

'C'mon Charlie,' Mike said, tugging at his elbow. 'We're not out of the woods yet. There's still a bit to do before we're all free.'

They crept out of the cell, but the noise had woken other prisoners and faces appeared at the grill in each door. They all wanted to be let out when they realised what was happening.

'You gotta let us out or we're gonna scream blue murder,' one of the soldiers threatened. 'This ain't an opportunity we can afford to miss.'

'Okay,' Mike reluctantly agreed, 'but only if you're all very quiet and do *exactly* as I say.'

There was a general murmuring of acceptance, with heads nodding, and Mike opened all the cells. They were free – a dozen men.

The guard was perched back on the chair and Mike retrieved his knife and grabbed the pistol and sub-machine-gun. He took the men, a few at a time, back to the motor pool area. Along with Mr and Mrs Charlie they all climbed into the back of the lorry. Mike was now pleased it was at the front of the line.

'Perhaps my luck's okay after all,' he whispered.

One of the soldiers spoke up, 'We'd all like to help you for getting us out of that hole.'

'Thanks, but we don't have enough weapons, and the more of us there are creeping around, the more likely it is that somebody will spot us. It's best that you all stay here and wait quietly for me. I've got to free one more person. Take these guns, but don't use them unless absolutely necessary,' he instructed, handing over the pistol to Charlie and the sub-machine-gun to the soldiers. 'If you do have to use them you'll wake the whole camp up, so get out any way you can, I'll do the same.'

Taking a deep breath, Mike closed the tarpaulin on the lorry and started out on the most dangerous part of his quest. The part that he'd come over four thousand miles to achieve.

Suzie lay on the bed shackled by both ankles and wrists. Staring at the ceiling, she wondered what Mike was planning and how long his escape would remain undetected. She'd heard no alarms or commotion, so she guessed he was still free for the moment. It was encouraging that he'd managed to escape, but she worried that he might get caught again, attempting to free her. Barney would arrive soon. Mentally she began preparing herself to cope with the ordeal that would follow if her scheme didn't work out. She knew that it needed a lot of luck for it to succeed and wanted to keep Barney occupied to give Mike time to put his plan into action – he would have a plan and might need all the time he could get.

Dismissing the guard, Barney entered the room and stood gloating over his conquest. He gave a sickly smile. 'Well, Miss Drake, and how are we looking forward to this evening's marathon love-in? Lots of soldiers did very well. I bet you wish now that you hadn't spurned me so often when we were back at Camp Grey?'

Suzie smiled back sweetly, trying to give the impression that she'd accepted the situation. 'You're right. I should have taken more notice of you,' she said, whilst thinking, 'I might then have realised that you were such a nasty shit, capable of something like this,' then added, 'I've resigned myself to the inevitable and decided I might as well make the best of it.'

'Good,' he gleamed, with an expression of some surprise. 'I'm pleased to see that you're being sensible at last. It's a pity you couldn't have come to that conclusion before all this became necessary,' he argued, with a tinge of regret in his voice that he put quickly behind him. 'But, if you just lie back and relax I'm sure you'll find it's not so bad after all,' he mocked, in a condescending tone that made Suzie's stomach churn.

'I expect you're right,' she lied. 'How about freeing my hands then?'

'Oh no. I'm not that stupid. You might be tempted to try something, and that would be foolish. Wouldn't it?'

'Just one hand then. Surely that can't do any harm. It would enable me to caress you, and you did say I should try and enjoy myself.'

Barney looked suspicious – Suzie smiled at him, trying to look willing and inviting, without overdoing it and wrecking her chances. She half sat up allowing the blanket to fall aside and reveal a shapely bosom that sent Barney's pulse rising.

'Okay,' he said, 'but no tricks.'

'What could I possibly do with both ankles and one arm shackled against a tough soldier like you?' Suzie expostulated, lifting her right arm to be freed.

Barney took a bunch of keys, clipped to his belt, and started to unlock the manacle, then changed his mind. 'No, not this one, your left wrist I think,' he said, undoing the lock.

He removed the blanket from her, and the sight of her shapely naked body and firm breasts quickly aroused him. He grasped them in both hands and began to kiss and nuzzle them with his face. Suzie played along, stroking the back of his head and making noises of enjoyment, despite his roughness, and the sick feeling she had inside.

He was eager and disrobed, dumping his clothes and gunbelt on the desk. He climbed on top of her, kissing and petting her frantically in his enthusiasm to enjoy himself.

'God, I'm going to miss you when you're gone. It's a shame you couldn't be more co-operative and join us, then we could have done this more civilly – every night.'

The thought of having Barney make his demands on her every night appalled her, but she needed to keep him interested and divert his attention away from the movement she was about to make.

'Perhaps you're right. Maybe I should look out for myself more and savour the things you could provide for me.'

'Good,' he said, kissing her hard. 'We'll discuss it later.'

Suzie's hand dropped down the side and she fumbled for the gadget, but couldn't find it. She resumed caressing his hair while he slobbered all over her, to avoid him becoming suspicious.

She tried again.

Her fingers ran along the edge of the bed. She felt the gadget and with great dexterity and skill released it, putting her thumb through the loop. Barney was about to enter her when she clasped her fingers around his erection and put her thumb on top, as if to guide him. Quickly she slipped the loop off her thumb and down his member, slid her fingers down the wire to the peg and pulled the slipknot tight.

'What the hell...' he began.

'Steady, lover boy. One wrong move and it's goodbye to any more loving days for you,' Suzie taunted, gripping the peg tightly. 'And I know how you want to make love every night,' she said, in a tone that had changed from subservient to masterful anger.

He looked in horror at the wire around him. 'Where in blazes did that come from?'

'Prince Charming! Now, unlock the shackles and don't even think about shouting for help. They'd never get here in time,' and to emphasise the point she tugged on the peg. 'See what I mean?'

'Yeah. Yeah, okay. Just take it easy with that thing. Stop pulling it, will you?'

'Just taking up the slack. We wouldn't want you to slip out just because your ego's getting deflated. Would we?'

Barney reached for his clothes on the desk and pulled his trousers towards him. Loose change, cigarettes and a lighter fell out of his pockets. He grabbed the bunch of keys clipped to his belt – his every move closely watched by Suzie. The shackle on her wrist clicked open.

'Put it on your wrist and lock it.'

'But...'

'Do it – now.' A further tug emphasised her order.

He grudgingly did as he was told. Suzie shoved her feet towards him. A look was all it took to convey her words and Barney undid the ankle shackles.

She slipped off the bed and pulled the peg. 'On to the bed, Rover.'

He complied, an angry glare on his face, the wire tugging at him.

'Put them on,' she ordered.

He reached down to his ankles, then made a grab at her hand holding the peg. He clasped Suzie's wrist with his free hand to prevent her pulling the gadget tighter and tried to prise the peg away from her with his other hand. With the wrist chain extended to its maximum, her fingers were just out of reach, but he was strong and pulled their hands together. Suzie smashed a fist into his face but he held on, trying desperately to peel her fingers away. Again she hit him, and again, and he had to let go. A final time she punched him, he slumped onto the bed, stunned.

Dropping the peg, she quickly grabbed the wrist and ankle shackles, snapping them on him.

Their positions were now reversed.

Suzie took a couple of deep breaths and licked her sore knuckles, glaring at him with a look of contempt. 'So far, so good,' she muttered, donning his shirt and trousers. He came round and sat up.

'I've a good mind to use that gadget on you after what you've put me through. And you had the gall to ask me to stay with you!'

Barney pleaded, 'No, don't do that. Please, take it off.'

'Oh, no. That stays right where it is. If you don't do exactly as I say, I can still use it before anyone else gets in here. That's my insurance.'

'I know where the gems are hidden. They're worth a lot of money. If you let me out of this, we could get them and share the proceeds. What do you say, Suzie?'

'You must be kidding. Do you think I'd trust a weasel like you after what you've done to Mike and me?'

'Okay. Maybe not. But at least take this thing off now you're free. Anything might happen if I'm caught with it like this. Please.'

Suzie buckled on his gunbelt and knife and saw him trying to wriggle the gadget off.

'Naughty, naughty,' she chastised, pulling it a little tighter and making him wince. 'We must stop this slipping off.'

Among the things scattered on the desk was a roll of sticky tape. Suzie wrapped several layers around him to stop the wire from slipping.

'There. That's better. Isn't it?' she tormented, patting it. 'Now, how many guards are there?'

Eager to help, he was hoping to appease her. 'One in the corridor and one on the outside door,' he said.

'The one in the corridor must think you're having a whale of a time with all the slapping and grunting going on in here.'

Barney made no reply.

Suzie stood behind the door and told him to call the guard. He came in and froze at the sight before him, just before the gun cracked down on his head knocking him unconscious.

To ensure that Barney remained quiet, she jammed his underwear into his mouth and secured it with sticky tape. 'That should give you something to chew on,' she spat.

He issued a lot of muffled groans. Suzie surveyed him and smiled at the comical sight. She turned the door handle, then hesitated before opening it wide, hearing footsteps coming down the corridor.

'You stay quiet,' was her order, pointing the gun at Barney to emphasise her point. 'No muffled noises.' She closed the door and hid behind it, poised to deal with any intruder.

Chapter XIV

Escape

Mike left Mr and Mrs Charlie and the soldiers in the back of the lorry, with instructions to keep quiet and wait for his return. He retraced his steps to the officers' hut, crept to the corner and glanced around it towards the entrance. This time there was a soldier on guard outside the door, leaning back in a chair perched only on the rear legs, with a rifle lying across his lap. Mike cursed and drew back.

Ideas on how best to tackle the problem were sifting through his mind when a cold, steel gun barrel touched the back of his neck.

'What are you doing sneaking around here?' a voice from behind demanded.

Mike turned to face the individual, but before he could answer, the soldier said, 'You're a friend of that female? You're supposed to be in the pit, ain't you?'

Without waiting for a reply, the soldier dug his rifle into Mike's ribs. 'I'll take those,' he said, relieving him of his weapons. 'Let's go. We'll see Barney. He should just about be finished, and I'm next in line to savour the lady's pleasures.'

The expression on Mike's face changed to anger, and it showed. But all he got for his hesitation was another dig in the ribs.

'I said let's go.'

He was marched into the hut, past the sleepy guard who barely bothered to flick his eyes open to see who was passing, and pushed along the corridor to the room that Suzie was in.

'Hey, I thought there was supposed to be a guard on this door!' the soldier exclaimed.

'Perhaps he's inside enjoying himself,' taunted Mike. 'He could be a queue jumper.'

The soldier looked puzzled, creasing his brow. 'He'd better not, if he knows what's good for him,' he replied angrily, opening the door and pushing Mike through.

'Hey! Watch my back, will you,' Mike shouted, tripping into the room and falling over the unconscious body on the floor.

'What the...' was all the soldier said before Suzie's gun came crashing down, spread-eagling his unconscious body alongside the prostrate guard.

'Quite a party you've got going in here,' said Mike, getting to his feet and brushing himself down with a flick of his fingers.

'Yes, and if you hadn't spoken as you came in, you might have been lying on the floor with them.'

Mike nodded. 'I figured that possibility when I saw that the guard was missing.'

'Look at your poor face.'

'What's wrong with my poor face?' Mike light-heartedly replied.

'It's a bit blistered.'

'Oh that. Just an overdone suntan – care of The General. He had no suntan oil, you see.'

'And look at your wrists,' Suzie said in dismay, seeing the blood-stained bandages.

'Never mind that. They'll heal. We've got to concentrate on getting out of here. It's good to see you're okay.'

Mike gave Suzie a hug, looked at her and nodded. She smiled. They were pleased to see each other, glad that they were both alive and relatively unscathed.

Mike wandered over to Barney. 'I see my home-made version of the chastity belt for men worked okay.'

'It's a good idea. What made you think of it?'

'Oh, I don't know. It's just my vivid imagination, I guess. What made you realise how to use it?'

'Oh, I don't know. It's just my vivid imagination, I guess,' was Suzie's cheeky reply.

'I like the sticky tape keeping it in place.'

'Yes, I didn't want it to fall off,' Suzie chuckled.

'What's that in his mouth?'

'His underpants.'

Mike smiled. 'Good thinking. By the look of the bruises on his face, I'd say you had a bit of trouble,' he said, his expression changing to contempt for his one-time colleague.

'Just a little. Nothing I couldn't handle,' she exclaimed, blowing on her bruised knuckles.

Mike gave them a kiss, saying, 'There, there, it's all better.'

Suzie pouted. 'I didn't make a fuss... unlike you,' she quipped, recalling the time she bandaged his injured leg.

'I was wounded, that's just a bruise,' Mike defended.

Suzie pressed tongue into cheek and said nothing.

'Okay. What are we going to do with this toad?' Mike asked.

'Leave him. If The General's the sort of person I think he is, I'm sure he'll find a suitable punishment for him when he finds out we're...'

A loud, wailing siren suddenly shattered the peace.

'...missing,' Suzie said, finishing the sentence.

'Shit. Somebody must've found one of the guards,' Mike explained, jamming the door shut with a chair and grabbing his weapons back. Suzie unlocked the window and climbed out. Mike was halfway out when he asked, 'Any matches in here?'

'Barney's lighter,' offered Suzie, pointing to it amongst his things scattered on the desk.

'That's great,' Mike said, slipping back to collect it.

Barney frantically mumbled something in desperation, with all the volume he could muster.

'Got no time to listen to your moans now. Gotta go,' said Mike, grabbing the lighter and sub-machine-gun, and hurrying through the open window.

Outside, he lead the way to the motor pool, dodging soldiers running in all directions, most of them wondering what was happening.

The General, alerted by the siren, went to the room and found the two unconscious guards and Barney shackled to the bed. He approached, saw the gadget and ripped the sticky tape and gag away.

'Shit!' yelled Barney. 'That hurt.'

'Not as much as the other one would,' he chided, fingering the peg. 'So, you let the little lady get the better of you?'

'She had help. Mike Randle was here. He's managed to get out of the pit somehow,' offered Barney nervously.

'They won't get far now the alarm's been raised,' The General asserted.

'Good. I want to deal with Mr Randle and friend myself. They've caused us enough trouble already. We should do away with them both right now, to stop any more problems. I reckon he's bluffing anyway. He hasn't got any information we need,' Barney expounded, desperately attempting to bluster his way out of the precarious position he was in.

'Is that so? You've changed your tune. You were all for trying to persuade the woman to join us.'

'No, not really. It just seemed a bit of a waste of a good-looking female, that's all.'

'Well, I've recently heard that Mr Al Dexter has been getting a lot of information about our activities from someone.'

'Not from me, General,' Barney said shakily, with a quivering voice.

The General took hold of the peg. 'Nasty little device this. You are the only one who could have provided the information, Barney. I'm very disappointed in you...'

Outside, the quiet early morning was disturbed by considerable activity. Soldiers, still half-asleep, ran around in confusion at the conflicting instructions yelled at them.

In the semi-darkness, Mike and Suzie crouched at the back of a hut, where men searching for them blocked the route to the motor pool.

'The vehicles are on the other side of this hut. We're nearly there,' said Mike.

'Nearly – but not quite. Those soldiers look like they plan on staying there.'

'That's okay – I've an idea how to move them. I saw soldiers unloading ammunition and storing it in this hut when I arrived. If I can start a fire it'll give them something else to concentrate on. I'd planned on using it as a diversion anyway.'

A soldier wandered across on his own to the far end of the hut and spotted the pair. He shouted for them to identify themselves.

Mike swore.

'I'll handle this,' offered Suzie.

'Make it quiet, will you? Gunfire will only tell the rest of them where we are.'

'Okay,' she said, standing up and taking off her shirt, dropping it to the ground.

She stepped into the light and walked towards the soldier. He stopped in his tracks and gawked at her. He was mesmerised seeing this gorgeous female, naked from the waist up with firm breasts gently bobbing up and down, as she strode towards him. It was too late by the time he snapped out of his dreams. Suzie transferred her weight to the left leg, turned sideways and her right leg shot out like the crack of a whip. Her foot caught him underneath the chin and the force jerked his head back, breaking his neck. He crashed to the ground but his pistol went off, firing into the air.

Suzie picked up the gun and ran back to Mike who had a fire going. 'Sorry about the shot. I couldn't help it.' She looked at the flames. 'You bastard! That's my shirt you're burning.'

'Correction, it's Barney's shirt. Anyway, I'll buy you a dozen shirts when we get home.'

'You mean *if* we get home. That shot's likely to bring more soldiers hurrying this way.'

'No, I mean when we get home. I can't wait to see you wearing a clean, white silk shirt.'

'Silk? Okay, it's a deal.'

'Nothing else – just a silk shirt,' he said, with a devilish grin on his face.

'Men!' said Suzie.

'Gorgeous, aren't we?'

Only silence greeted him.

Mike shrugged his shoulders and lifted the burning shirt on the end of his gun barrel, smashed a window and threw it onto the wooden boxes. The tinder dry wood was quick to light and the flames spread.

Moving to the front of the hut, Mike and Suzie peered round the corner. They were met by a fusillade of bullets that splintered the woodwork around them.

'Damn! It looks like half the garrison know where we are.'

Mike returned a few short bursts in their general direction, then threw the empty weapon away in disgust. 'You'd better go easy with that gun. Those are our last shells.'

Suzie fired at anyone brave enough to stick their head out on the opposite side, but their route to the motor pool was covered by crossfire and she had only a few bullets left.

Meanwhile, the fire had taken hold and the wooden hut was well ablaze.

A high-pitched scream rang out over the whole camp.

Suzie cringed. 'What the hell was that?' she asked.

'Don't know, but it came from the direction of the officers' hut. If it's what I think it is, I wouldn't like to be in Barney's shoes right now.'

Soldiers began closing in on them when an explosion sent them scattering back for cover. Mike and Suzie ducked when a second explosion blew part of the roof off.

'If we don't get out of here soon, we're gonna get blown to bits when the rest of this little lot goes up,' Mike yelled above the noise, anxiously searching for a way out. He peered round the corner, and shots peppered the woodwork around him.

'What I wouldn't give for a couple of grenades right now,' he wished. A soldier appeared at the corner of the hut opposite.

'Look out,' shouted Suzie, squeezing a shot off that sent him scurrying back. But with few bullets coming their way the soldiers were getting braver, realising that their quarry was short on ammunition.

Just when all looked lost, a lorry came crashing round the corner, knocking a soldier down. Sub-machine-gun fire from the back sent others scampering for cover.

The lorry screeched to a stop in front of them.

The door burst open and Charlie shouted, 'Get in quick, Mr Mike.'

Suzie and Mike jumped into the cab. Charlie stared at Suzie's naked body in bewilderment.

Mike barked, 'Eyes front, Charlie, and step on it!'

'Yes, Mr Mike.' Charlie crashed the vehicle into gear and stamped his foot on the accelerator, swinging the lorry round towards the exit.

He could barely see above the steering wheel and didn't need to duck the bullets that smashed the glass. Mike grabbed the gun from Suzie and thrust it through the window, firing bullets in all directions and emptying the chamber. Another big explosion lit up the base, throwing debris up into the sky, and dropping all around them as they motored towards the exit.

'Foot down hard as it'll go, Charlie,' encouraged Mike. They gathered speed, scattering the sentries on gate duty and demolishing their huts and the gates. All went flying before them as the lorry crashed its way through and sped into the darkness.

Sub-machine-gun bursts faded into the distance, and with each yard they covered down the dark bumpy road came shouts and cheers from the back of the lorry.

Mike took off his shirt and gave it to Suzie.

'Oh, gee thanks. I've always wanted a one armed shirt.'

Mike looked at Charlie, who was grinning all over his face. 'Well done, Charlie! You saved our bacon back there. I've emptied this gun. Have you still got the pistol I gave you?'

'Me give it to Mrs Charlie. She shoot at nasty soldiers.'

Mike threw the empty gun through the window. 'Shan't be needing that any more – I hope.'

Shouting erupted from the soldiers in the back of the lorry, with Mrs Charlie's voice amongst them. Charlie yelled out in Chinese and a reply came.

'Mrs Charlie's hit by bullet, Mr Mike. She says it is not serious and to keep going.'

'We'll take a look when we stop, Charlie. If the fire keeps them busy it might take a while before they start chasing us,' Mike said, more in hope than expectation. Another explosion roared in the distance.

'And there's still another arm on this shirt that we could use as a bandage,' said Suzie, with tongue in cheek.

'Right,' agreed Mike, giving her a knowing look, a smile crossing his lips. 'How did you get this lorry started, Charlie? I disabled it.'

'I found broken wires and joined them up. I soon get lorry going.'

'Clever clogs,' said Mike with a grin.

Charlie looked at him and laughed, and they crashed over another big rut in the road, making them jump out of their seats.

'And talking of clever clogs, how did you get your hands on my lock pick?'

'It was on the desk after they searched you. When I took food in to the lady, I stole it.'

'You took a big risk. Thank you.'

'And thank you from me, too,' said Suzie, kissing him on the cheek. The darkness covered his embarrassment.

An almighty explosion erupted, lighting up the sky, and they all instinctively ducked. Looking at each other, they giggled at their nervousness.

'They must have had a hell of a lot of explosives in that hut,' suggested Mike. 'There may not be much of Camp West left now. It needed rebuilding anyway.'

'Do you think we're in the clear?' Suzie asked hopefully.

'Don't know. I wouldn't count on it just yet. The soldiers may have already left the camp to chase us. I'm sure The General won't give up easily.'

The lorry started to misfire and Mike tapped the petrol gauge. The tank was empty.

'Turn off the road here, Charlie,' pointed Mike, at a narrow path leading into the jungle. 'We must hide the lorry.'

They drifted to a halt.

'What do you guys want to do?' Mike asked the soldiers, emerging from the back.

They elected to make their own way back to their headquarters. Mike wished them good luck, and they disappeared into the night. Suzie took a look at Mrs Charlie's wound, which was a flesh wound and not serious. Mike made a makeshift bandage for it with the other arm of the shirt Suzie was wearing.

'I'm sure you don't want me to wear this shirt,' Suzie complained, in mock anger. Mike opened his mouth to speak and Suzie added, 'And before you say it, I know, you'll buy me a dozen when we get home.'

Mike grinned and said, 'My jeep's not far from here. It'll be quicker if I go alone to get it. Mrs Charlie's leg will make it difficult for her to walk,' he explained. 'I reckon it's about a mile away, maybe even less, so I shouldn't be long.'

'If they're following us, will they look along this track?' enquired Suzie.

'Probably. The General knows I came by the old jungle route. He's likely to think I'll use it on the way back.'

They heard the sound of vehicles approaching and watched, concealed by darkness and the jungle. An armoured jeep and two trucks clattered past, bumping along the unmade road.

'When they don't catch up with our lorry they'll realise we turned off somewhere,' stated Mike. 'It's just a question of how long it takes them to find out where. It'll be safer for us to assume they're not very far behind.'

Suzie nodded. 'Do you want your half a shirt back?' she asked.

Mike declined the offer. 'Later, maybe.'

She smiled, and he gave her a wink and moved off to collect his jeep.

Stumbling along in the half-light, Mike wished that he had a torch. The sky was clear and a full moon helped, but the going was difficult, squelching through rutted vehicle tracks filled with water in shoes that didn't fit very well.

After twenty minutes, he reached his jeep and was alarmed to find it uncovered. Anxious to get back quickly, Mike glanced round, but in this light it was impossible to see much of anything. He approached cautiously and peered inside. All looked okay, but it was hard to tell. Nothing obvious was out of place.

He climbed into the jeep.

Suddenly, torchlight shone on him and a familiar voice from behind said, 'Hallo, Mike. Good to see you again.'

Mike's hand automatically went to his holster. It was empty. Then he remembered that he'd thrown the gun away after using all the shells.

'Is that you, Paul, ol' buddy?' he said, turning to face the light. 'What're you doing here?' he asked, shading his eyes from the glare of the torch.

'Looking for you, ol' buddy,' he replied, holding a pistol at the ready.

'Why the gun?'

'By the sounds of all the explosions I've heard recently, you've caused The General quite a bit of trouble, even if it did cost you your shirt.'

Mike looked disappointed. 'Not you as well!' he exclaimed.

'I think it might be better if you stepped out and raised your hands. I know from old what a tricky customer you can be.'

'I thought one traitor in the camp was enough,' Mike grumbled, obeying the instruction.

'Ah! That'll be Barney. How is he?' Paul's Irish accent becoming broader with his nervousness.

'If my guess is right, he was cut off in his prime, just before he was blown to hell.'

Paul looked bemused. 'That's too bad. Between us, we had a good thing going, supplying The General and Dexter with information we got from each other, and getting a nice price for it.'

'You've got your sticky fingers in a number of pies it seems.'

'Well, I hear lots of things in the bar, and the girls are always anxious to sell me titbits they hear between the sheets, from their customers. We had a nice little business trading information, and heroin.'

'Drugs? You deal in drugs as well?' Mike spat in disgust.

'Don't knock it. It's a good money-earner. Brings more people into the pub, and a crowded pub's the perfect place to handle the business. Everything was fine until we got a bad batch. One or two dealers got a bit upset when some of their clients died. It didn't look very good,' he said with contempt.

'Ah!' observed Mike, past things dawning on him. 'So the hit men in the Austin were after you, not me.'

'That's right. There was I, scratching me brains to try and find a plausible explanation for you, when you go and take the blame and apologise to me. I couldn't believe my luck. The only problem with that, of course, was that they weren't hit men – just local drug dealers. And you went and killed them all.'

'What a shame! If I'd known, I'd have invited them in for tea,' Mike said mockingly.

'It's going to take me a while to re-establish contacts and get the trade going again.'

'I'm all broke up. But how did you find me here?' asked Mike, his hands dropping slowly towards the handle of his commando knife.

'You asked about this track, remember? So I knew you'd come this way. It wasn't too difficult to spot where you turned off, and I soon found the jeep.'

'But why come looking for me at all?' Mike asked, to keep Paul talking.

'Barney came over and said you'd foiled the ambush they laid for you, but then you walked right in and practically handed yourself over to him.'

'I didn't know what a rat he was then.'

'He confirmed that you'd taken this route. He also said you mentioned to The General that you have the key to the safety deposit box.'

'Ah! And you thought I might have hidden it in the jeep before I went in… just in case I got caught.'

'It was a possibility. I've searched it thoroughly and can't find it, and you didn't leave it in your room. Where is the key?' asked Paul hopefully.

'I haven't got it. That was just a story I made up to confuse them and buy time.'

'Well, I didn't expect you to tell me, and if you drop your hands any lower, I'll be forced to end this conversation rather abruptly.'

Mike took the hint and raised his hands.

'I suppose it's pointless to offer doing a deal with you?' Paul asked tentatively.

'We would never trust each other.'

'That's true. So now it looks like it's all come to an end, thanks to you. At least, The General will reward me for catching you, though you'll have to be dead, or you're likely to tell him nasty things about me.'

'That's if he's still alive after most of the camp was blown to kingdom come.'

'Well, you won't need to worry about that. I know The General's a wily old bird and isn't so easy to kill as that. We went through a lot together and had our moments in the past… so I really am sorry about this, Mike.'

Paul levelled the gun.

With nothing to lose Mike went for his knife, but before he could grasp the handle, a shot rang out.

Paul, stood for a second; a patch of blood soaked through his shirt. He dropped his gun and torch, and fell to the ground.

The area plunged back into darkness. Mike stood for a moment wondering what had happened, when from behind a tree someone stepped forward holding a gun, picked up the torch and approached him.

Mike stared almost in disbelief. 'Jenny?' he asked incredulously.

'Surprise, surprise.'

'You're right. I am surprised, and grateful.'

'All part of the service,' she said.

'Service! What service?'

'The British Secret Service. I work for Sir Joseph Sterling.'

'Sterling?' Mike almost shouted. 'Everywhere I turn he crops up. I can't seem to get away from him.'

'Lucky for you he does. Especially this time.'

'You're right enough there,' Mike conceded.

'It's a good job you haven't got a shirt on or I might not have recognised you in this light, especially with all those cuts and blisters. What on earth's happened to you?'

'I'll tell you some other time. Right now, I've got things to do.'

'I didn't think I'd see you again this soon when I watched you leaving the pub two days ago. Things seem to be happening fast.'

'They are.' Mike briefly explained about Suzie and Mr and Mrs Charlie waiting for him to return with transport. He donned Raúl's monogrammed vest to use as a shirt, and lifted the bonnet of his jeep to hot wire it.

Jenny checked Paul's jeep and found an Ingram model 10 sub-machine-gun, two handguns, a box of dynamite and a box of hand grenades.

'So. He was able to get an Ingram after all,' murmured Mike.

'I heard all the explosions. Did I hear you say Camp West was blown sky high?'

'That's right,' agreed Mike, slamming the bonnet shut.

'And The General? You're not sure if he's alive?'

'No. Maybe he's dead. Maybe he's not. But I'm not waiting around to find out,' said Mike, looking at the items which Jenny had found. 'Paul brought quite an arsenal with him. We could maybe use some of this. Soldiers are chasing us.'

'Soldiers chasing you?'

'Yes. We may have lost them. Don't know for sure.'

'I'll put these weapons in your jeep,' Jenny suggested.

'No, I haven't got time now. I'll go back and get the others and pick you up on the way past. You can drive Paul's jeep. We'll take both. It'll save time transferring the stuff. Meanwhile, you could bury him. Despite what he did, he was a friend once, and I'd rather not leave him here like this.'

'Okay. I'll see to it,' Jenny replied.

Mike set off and charged back. The lorry stood out starkly in the blackness picked out by his headlights. The beams rose and fell as if on a ship in a stormy sea. He shouted to identify himself and three figures emerged. The sound of approaching vehicles disturbed the night as Mike helped Mrs Charlie into the back of the jeep and they set off with Suzie driving.

'That's got to be The General's men. They'll stop and check the lorry, but that'll only give us a few minutes' start,' declared Mike, the jeep gathering speed.

Jenny was waiting for them on the way back. Mike stood for a few brief moments by Paul's grave.

'Goodbye, ol' buddy. It's a real shame things didn't work out, but thanks for all the good times.'

Suzie eyed this good-looking ex-beauty queen, Jenny, suspiciously, particularly when they moved off and Mike got into Paul's vehicle to talk to her.

'How come you were on the spot to help me?' he asked. 'This isn't exactly Piccadilly Circus.'

Jenny explained, 'Paul got a telephone call this afternoon and hurriedly loaded up a jeep with supplies. I hid a small tracking device on it so I could follow at a distance. I tracked him into the jungle and, when he stopped, I hid my jeep and proceeded on foot. It was dark by the time I saw him searching your vehicle.'

'Do you know what he was looking for?'

'I didn't, but I heard him ask you about a key.'

'They're all after a key, so I told them I had it to keep them guessing,' Mike lied.

'Well, anyway, I lay low and watched. I think he was about to leave when the first explosion erupted. He hid his jeep and waited. I stayed put and only came in closer when you arrived.'

'I'm glad you did.'

'So am I,' Jenny smiled.

'Err… there's something I'd like to ask you,' Mike began hesitantly.

'Something to do with the friend you had on your mind – the one that I asked about after your massage?'

'Yes, something like that. That afternoon… I was tired from the long journey and…'

'It's okay, Mike. I wasn't expecting you to give up everyone else for me. It was a very enjoyable interlude, and didn't gain me much information. But I won't tell her what happened between us. That can remain our little secret.'

'Okay, thanks.' Mike breathed easier now.

The two jeeps bumped along the rough track at a pace so tortuously slow, that they felt certain the soldiers would catch them soon. On the way, Jenny explained that Paul was suspected of being a go-between for drugs and arms deals. Her job was to find out what she could about him and his friends, and send back all the information she could gather.

Mike wondered what she'd told them about him, and whether they knew the methods she used to obtain it…

Mr and Mrs Charlie looked worried. They were scared what would happen if the soldiers caught up and recaptured them. Mr Charlie was holding his wife tightly, and Mrs Charlie still clutched the pistol he gave her, too scared to let go.

While Jenny drove, Mike prepared some sticks of dynamite and hand grenades. 'Can't you keep this vehicle a bit steadier?' he chided, the vehicle rocking from side to side.

'You like to try?' she retorted.

No reply came – Mike struggled on.

'Look out for a tree trunk we can drag across the path. I want to delay them.'

'Okay,' Jenny murmured.

Headlights occasionally shone through the trees in the distance behind them.

'They can't be more than five minutes back, I reckon,' said Mike, leaning out of the window to scan behind.

'That tree trunk okay?' pointed Jenny.

'That's perfect. Stop the jeep. I'll hook it with the rope.'

Mike waved Suzie's jeep through then tied the rope to the tree. 'Go, go, go!' he shouted, and the jeep's wheels span round, throwing mud into the air. The tree trunk slithered across the path, and Mike rigged dynamite under each end with a hand grenade primed to set it off. He covered it over with wet mud and leaves, and heard vehicles getting close by the time they hurried off.

'Is that going to work, Mike?' Jenny asked.

'Don't know for sure. It depends how careful they are. It's dark and not easy to see anything clearly. If they're careful they'll find the dynamite, but it'll take time to remove the hand grenade without setting it off, and look for others. If they're not careful… that should slow them down as well.'

'I hope you're right, or we've just wasted valuable time.'

Jenny's face screwed up at the problems she was having controlling the jeep. The vehicle wanted to go its own way and she struggled to keep it on the track.

'What's the matter?' asked Mike.

'Not sure. Something's wrong.'

They stopped to check and discovered one of the tyres was flat.

'Sod! No time to change the wheel. Transfer the guns and explosives to the other jeep quickly while I fix it up with a present,' Mike said, grabbing another stick of dynamite and a grenade. 'I haven't heard anything yet, so I guess they found the other dyn—'

A loud explosion ripped through the jungle, cutting his words short.

'Well, they might have found one and missed the second. That's good. If they're still following us, they'll be a lot more cautious when they come across this jeep. That'll cost them more time.'

Before moving off, Mike spoke to Charlie and his wife in the back, and gave them a reassuring smile. 'It's going to be okay,' he said. They both nodded without replying.

Mr and Mrs Charlie stayed in the rear of the jeep, with the guns and explosives at their feet. It was a situation that disturbed them, but it was one more horror they would have to put up with if they were to accomplish their dream of escape.

Jenny and Mike squashed into the front with Suzie. Mike sat in the middle, between the two women, who looked each other over, unsure how to react. The problem of getting out alive was more important at that moment, and they smiled at each other and set off again on their arduous journey.

Jenny remarked, 'Shame we couldn't use the main route. It'd be a lot quicker.'

'Yes,' agreed Mike. His expression changed, a nasty thought coming to mind. 'How many vehicles are behind us?'

'I've only seen one set of headlights,' remarked Suzie, turning to Mike with an expression that showed she'd had similar thoughts. 'Are you thinking what I'm thinking?'

'Yes. And I bet The General thought of it too. He's only sent one or two vehicles back. The remainder are using the road to get to the other end first, and he won't let border guards stop him. That way we're trapped between them, and he can lay an ambush for us. And I bet I know just where that'll be.'

Chapter XV

The Fight

Mel and Al Dexter were still shaking from the horror of seeing their old friend Douglas Payne brutally murdered in their apartment. Ushered into the underground car park, they were unceremoniously shoved into the back seat of Nick's plush Jaguar car, with one of his henchmen to guard them.

They were all too busy to notice two men sitting in a Ford Escort parked in a dark corner, eyeing them and checking photographs. They drove off, watched by the men as one of them punched the buttons on his mobile telephone and spoke to his control officer.

'Mr and Mrs Dexter are leaving in a Jaguar with three men, Sarg, and look as if they're going under protest.'

'Okay,' said the voice from control. 'One of you search the flat and office, and the other follow the Jag. But observe only. No approaching anyone. Okay?'

'Understood,' said Detective Constable John Green.

He and Detective Constable Ray Teal had been transferred to 'The Branch' recently, and so far had found things rather dull. Both had completed a long spell as constables on the beat in East London, and struck up a friendship when Green had found himself in difficulties with a crowd of youths and Teal had arrived to help.

In their mid-twenties and single, they were eager for promotion. The East End beat had provided them with good experience, and both did well and showed promise. Looking after themselves became second nature, and good policework earned them the opportunity to join Special Branch. New boys were always given mundane jobs like surveillance that no one else cared for. This morning they'd waited in the car park for several hours and both were bored with sitting and checking faces against photographs. At last there was something to do, a welcome opportunity!

Teal jumped from the car as Green gunned the engine and charged up the exit ramp into Kingsway. Traffic was light and, spotting the Jaguar, Green settled in two cars behind to shadow it and strapped on his safety belt.

Riding the lift to the third floor, Teal gained entry to Dexter's office with a skeleton passkey. The front office contained only two desks and four filing cabinets. All the drawers were open and papers were scattered everywhere. The rear office was much the same, and even the small cloakroom had not escaped the frantic search. The cistern top lay smashed on the floor. Whoever searched had not worried about any damage they caused.

Teal couldn't be bothered to wait for the lift. He climbed the stairs, two at a time, up two flights to Room 505. After ringing the bell several times to be sure the place was empty, he entered the apartment.

Green reported that the Jaguar was heading southwest out of London when Teal rang in with news. Dexter's office and plush apartment had been ransacked and he'd found a body.

'From the photos we were given, I can identify the victim as one Douglas Payne, an associate of Alfonso Dexter. The body's still warm, so he was shot very recently. Oh, and on the desk is a map with circles drawn around Weybridge, Surbiton and Rye.'

'Good work, Ray. You stay there until the lab boys arrive.'

'Okay, Sarg.'

The sergeant turned his attention to the shadowing car. 'Don't lose that vehicle, John, but be careful,' he communicated to Green. 'Teal's found a body in the apartment. The suspects are thought to be armed and dangerous.'

'Right, Sarg,' replied Green enthusiastically. 'Something decent to do at long last,' he told himself. Searching in his top pocket he pulled out his sunglasses and donned them. He was ready for action.

The operations room buzzed with activity. Sir Joseph Sterling entered and was informed about the discovery of Payne's body. He also learned that the suspects were being followed and asked about the Jaguar's direction. Green called in to say the car had turned on to the A21 and was heading south towards the coast.

Sir Joseph became concerned when he was told about the circles on the map. He knew where the suspects were going, and the map confirmed his fears. He conveyed his orders in a firm and precise manner, changing from an interested spectator to a man of authority and purpose.

'Get on to the ARVs. I want six armed officers and a marksman straight away. They're to get to Silverdale Cottage in Rye, in double-quick time.'

'Yes, sir,' replied the sergeant, picking up the telephone and repeating the orders to the commander in charge of Armed Response Vehicles.

'Do we have a helicopter available?' Sir Joseph enquired.

'No, sir, not at the moment. They're still using it on the drug-smuggling bust. It probably won't be back for an hour or two, depending on how smoothly things go.'

'Hmm. Yes, okay. When it does, I want it available to fly me to Rye straight away.'

'Yes, sir.'

'Get those men on the way now. Tell them to keep in contact with Green and get directions from him. Let me know immediately if there's any further developments.'

'Yes, Sir Joseph.'

'I'm going to ring the cottage and talk to Detective Inspector Brooke.'

In Sussex-by-the-Sea, the stormy night drifted into the memory of yesterday, and the sun rose in a clear sky, on a clean fresh morning in Rye. A slight breeze fluttered in the air; perfect conditions for the invigorating walk that Grace, Jim and Colin Brooke were to take around the countryside, ending in the local pub at lunchtime.

A small cupboard under the kitchen sink provided the home for Grace's working boots and shoes. She rummaged through and found a pair for each of them. The walk took them through woods, still glistening with raindrops slipping from trees onto soggy ground scattered with fallen leaves and puddles. Grace pointed out local landmarks to Brooke during their walk, wandering along a well-established footpath, climbing stiles and navigating fields in a large circle that brought them back to the far end of the village, shortly after noon.

They strolled along the path chatting and laughing, enjoying peaceful surroundings. Colin Brooke kept alert, his ever-watchful eyes scanning continually. Jim was blissfully unaware of this, but Grace, though not letting on, soon noticed his vigilance.

She regularly took this path for exercise, especially when she was able to persuade visitors to accompany her. She loved the countryside and got great pleasure from a leisurely stroll.

It served to enhance all their appetites. A bar meal with a pint in the local sixteenth-century inn, The Swan, completed an enjoyable morning, despite Colin Brooke banging his head on the low wooden beam when they passed through the old, solid oak door. They drank real ale with a ploughman's lunch, sitting at a plain oak table, in a smoky atmosphere.

The cosy pub boasted tapestry-cushioned pews and a large brick inglenook fireplace. The walls were decorated with paintings and early photographs of the pub, and an assortment of wooden truncheons hung from one of the beams. Colin Brooke eyed these, wondering how many were used in the name of the law! He was grateful that the Force now had better weapons to tackle lawbreakers with.

Their lunch over, and now fully refreshed, they ambled their way back to the cottage. Dark clouds were beginning to gather again, changing the sparkling morning into a gloomy afternoon.

After ambling up the cottage pathway and barely getting through the front door, Brooke's mobile rang. He entered the living room, listened attentively, nodding in agreement, confirming what he heard.

'Yes, sir. Don't worry. Yes I am,' he said, automatically patting the bulge by his left arm, making it obvious what he'd been asked. 'I noticed a car parked down the street when we came back, with the driver just sitting there. It may mean something, it may not, but I'll keep an eye out just in case.'

Grace looked at Jim with a worried expression on her face. Memories of the previous evening came worryingly to mind.

When Brooke had finished his call Grace tackled him. 'What's the problem now?' she asked anxiously.

'Oh, nothing,' he replied. 'It's just Sir Joseph fussing.'

'That's crap,' spurted Jim, looking slightly embarrassed at his own language, and giving a quick glance at Grace. 'My father doesn't fuss. He rang for a purpose.'

Brooke looked at them both thoughtfully, then said, 'Okay. Your dad thinks there might be a few gang members, possibly armed, paying us a visit soon.' He was trying, unsuccessfully, to emphasise the unlikelihood of it all.

'Great. So now what do we all do? Go back to the pub?' said Jim.

'Not quite. You two should return. I'm waiting here for them. I'm armed, and there's an armed squad on the way.'

Grace confronted Brooke. 'This is a quiet village. We don't want a gun battle here.'

'It's because it's a quiet village that makes it the perfect place to nab these villains. There aren't a lot of innocent bystanders around who might get hurt.'

'True,' conceded Gracie. 'So what can we do to help?'

'This is police business. There could be some shooting, and I'll have enough to do without worrying about you two. It would be better if you both left. And as I'm not sure about the man in the car along the road, I think it might be better if you went out the back way.'

Grace looked indignant. 'Leave my own home because of a few ruffians? Not on your life! And there *is* no back way out. Not unless you want to count the route carved out by that loutish driver last night when he smashed his way through to the field. Anyway, I don't come from a family of quitters who sneak out by the back door.'

Brooke opened his mouth to say something but, after seeing her determination, he changed his mind.

Jim chipped in, 'If she stays, so do I. I promised Mike I'd look out for her.'

Brooke exhaled hard through his nostrils and in a resigned tone said, 'All right. But you must both please go upstairs and keep out of the way.'

They reluctantly agreed, and tramped up the stairs in a manner that left Brooke in no doubt that they were not very happy about being relegated to the side lines, when eager to help.

The Jaguar sped along the road towards Rye. Green followed at a safe distance, hoping that they were not watching for a tail. Feeling macho in his sunglasses, worn to avoid the glare of sunlight which was streaming between the clouds and through the trees, Green saw this as his opportunity to make an impression. He was anxious not to lose the car and got annoyed when his path was temporarily blocked by another vehicle.

'Come on, get out of the way. Bloody Sunday drivers,' he hissed under his breath.

The Jaguar overtook the majority of other vehicles on the road, and Green was forced to stay in the outside lane most of the time to keep them in sight.

After passing through Flimwell, they turned onto the A286 heading towards Rye. Control told him this was the probable destination, which helped on the few occasions that he lost momentary sight of them. Green confirmed that Rye still looked the likely destination. Way behind him, two more speeding cars and a van with sirens wailing, carried the armed policemen ever closer.

Meanwhile, Dave Collins had sat in his car and watched Silverdale Cottage for several hours, drinking a can of beer which he always kept with him. He saw Jim Sterling and two others return from their walk, and now awaited the arrival of his boss.

His bladder was starting to complain, and he decided to ease his discomfort behind some nearby bushes. As he did, the Jaguar turned the corner at the end of the road and pulled up behind his car.

Moments later, Green came into the lane and parked his vehicle where he could see the Jaguar, Collins's car and the cottage at the far end. He spoke to control, giving them the latest information and asking for further instructions.

'Just keep watching and let us know of any further developments, John. The hit squad are well on the way.'

'Okay, control. Hit squad! What a name.'

Collins pulled up his zip and was about to step out when he saw Mel Dexter in the back of the Jaguar and noticed she'd been crying and was very distressed.

'The boss never brings his missus with him on this kind of business,' Collins thought, 'and whose car is it, anyway? I don't recognise it, or any of the men. Something looks fishy.'

In the Jaguar, Nick turned to Dexter. 'So where's your man?' he asked.

'How the hell should I know? That's his car. Perhaps he's checking the back of the cottage,' he replied tersely.

Nick looked at his driver. 'You take the front. I'll take the back. Kill anyone who gets in the way. I'm through with messing about,' he said, then turned and thrust a gun barrel into Al Dexter's face. 'Any trouble out of either of you, and you're dead. Got it?' he said in an aggressive tone, glancing at his man sat next to them, whose head nodded imperceptibly. Everyone understood what he meant.

Collins watched this from behind the bushes and could see his boss and wife were in trouble. Nick and the driver closed their car doors quietly and, after a glance around, made their way towards the cottage. Collins watched them until they were out of sight then drew his gun and sneaked up to the Jaguar. Glancing through the window, he saw that the Dexters were covered by Nick's accomplice with a gun.

His movement caught the gunman's eye, who turned to see Collins and swung his gun round at him. Dexter seized the opportunity to grab him and they tussled in the back seat. Collins reacted instantly, flinging the door open and firing once, hitting the guard in the back. The force of the shot knocked him onto Al Dexter's lap.

Dexter shoved the blood-spattered body away from him contemptuously and grabbed his gun. 'Good man, Dave. Well done,' he said, turning to his distraught wife whose mouth was open to scream – but nothing came out. Grabbing her by the shoulders he turned her towards him and said firmly, 'It's okay. Everything will be okay. You stay here. Dave, you come with me.'

Grace and Jim stood at the upstairs windows peering through the curtains. Jim was watching the back and Grace the front. She saw the driver approaching.

'There's a man walking up the garden path, and he looks a bit unsavoury,' Grace stated.

'And there's another man coming round the side to get in the back way,' added Jim, 'and he's got a gun. Colin is caught between them. We must do something.'

Then the shot rang out.

Everyone froze for a moment, uncertain about what was happening.

Green saw Dave Collins shoot, and he frantically rang in speaking at twice his normal speed. 'Some bloke's just opened the back door of the Jag and shot someone inside the car. He and Dexter are now making their way towards the cottage. Where's the armed squad, for Christ's sake? If they don't get here soon, there's gonna be a massacre. That's four blokes I've now seen, all probably armed, going to the cottage. I can't just sit here doing nothing.'

'Calm down, Dave. The squad's nearly there. Don't get involved. You're not armed and we don't want you getting shot. Brooke knows the situation and he's got a gun.'

'Well, tell them to hurry up.'

The driver took out his gun and tried the front door. It was unlocked, so he pushed it open and entered.

Inside, Colin Brooke, hidden behind a chair in the living room, shouted, 'Armed police. Drop your weapon.'

The driver backed out through the doorway, firing two quick shots in the general direction of the voice. In the rear bedroom, Jim opened the window and was climbing onto the ledge when the two shots resounded. Nick was directly below him trying the handle of the back door and didn't know what hit him. Jim fell on him like a ton of bricks, sending both men crashing to the ground, with Jim rolling over clasping his stomach, the part of his anatomy that had taken most of the force of his first attempt to be Superman.

At the front of the cottage, the driver turned to run back down the path and was surprised to come face to face with Dave Collins. Before he could react, Collins fired once, killing him instantly.

Brooke appeared at the edge of the doorway. 'Armed police.

Throw down your weapon,' he demanded, pointing his gun steadily at him in the classic 'Cooper-Weaver' stance, looking determined and willing to shoot.

Collins thought for a split second about taking a chance, but decided that the odds were not good and dropped his gun. Brooke handcuffed him to the wrought-iron gate.

By the back door, Nick was first to recover and get to his feet. Retrieving his gun, he pointed it menacingly at Jim. His finger tightened on the trigger.

'I don't know who you are,' he said, 'but if you know any prayers, you'd better say them right now.' He started to squeeze the trigger when a shot rang out, knocking him back against the door.

'That's for Mel,' spat Dexter with undisguised anger. 'And this is for Doug.' He fired deliberately, twice more.

Nick, wide-eyed and disbelieving that this was happening, crashed back into the kitchen door. The bullets drove into him, each one jerking him back, like a rag doll being tossed in the air. His blood-soaked body, shaking uncontrollably, slid to the ground and slumped over at Brooke's feet as he opened the kitchen door.

Wailing police sirens filled the air and cars screeched to a halt outside the cottage.

Dexter saw that Brooke was armed and fired at him. Brooke ducked back into the cottage, the bullet shattering the window in the door, spraying him with glass.

Jim grabbed at Dexter and yelled, 'No, you bastard.'

Dexter turned the gun on him.

'No, Dex, please don't. No more killing,' pleaded Mel, who'd run across from the car. Sitting in the back seat with a blood-soaked body at her feet was too much for her. It was making her sick. She'd had to get out.

Al Dexter hesitated, hearing her voice. Armed policemen, wearing body protectors with the word POLICE emblazoned across them in large dayglow letters, ran towards him from both sides of the cottage. He thrust the gun into Jim's face.

'Do exactly as I say if you want to live.'

Jim nodded nervously and was hauled to his feet by the shoulder.

'If anyone gets any closer, Sterling here gets a bullet,' he threatened.

The armed police stopped and waited.

'You can't get away, Dexter. Give it up,' demanded the police commander.

He was not about to give it up.

'I've gone too far to lose everything now. Back off, or Sterling's a dead man.'

'Okay. Take it easy. Back away men. Let's talk, Dexter.'

'No talk! Just get out of my way.'

The policemen all backed away slowly, watching Dexter move down the side of the cottage towards the Jaguar, using Jim as a shield.

'Come on, Mel,' he instructed. 'You,' he gestured to a policeman, 'give her your handcuffs.'

The policeman looked at his chief, who nodded compliance. The handcuffs were handed over.

'Don't try to follow us, or else,' Dexter said defiantly, marching Jim to the car. He pushed him into the driver's seat and got in behind.

'Do you want me to take him out?' the police marksman asked his chief. 'I can do it now with one shot.'

'No. Not yet. I want this to end peacefully if possible. This place already looks like the OK Corral. Get ready to track them,' the chief instructed.

Mel got into the back seat next to her husband. He bundled the dead body out of the door and told Jim to reverse back down the road.

The Jaguar screeched around the corner and away, watched by Green, with two police cars following at a safe distance. A helicopter buzzed overhead and landed in Grace's back garden. Sir Joseph emerged and was disappointed to hear about the shootings and alarmed when told his son was taken hostage. They took off immediately, with Brooke also on board. Both donned headsets, to communicate to each other and the pilot, over the deafening noise of the helicopter's engine. They were patched through to the cars on the ground shadowing the Jaguar, after they spotted it, and began to follow unobserved from their high vantage point.

The two trailing squad cars were kept briefed on every move that Dexter made.

Jim drove on to the A259 coast road and headed west, at Dexter's instructions. From the back seat, he was more interested in checking to see if they were being followed than watching Jim. He carefully took the watches out of his pocket and slipped them under the driver's seat.

Mel was shaking with fright and the mood in the car was sombre. The weather echoed this, the sky filling with dark clouds and spots of rain spattering the windscreen. Inside the helicopter, they viewed this with concern.

'If the weather gets any worse, we'll have to put down, sir,' the pilot informed Sir Joseph over the intercom.

'Yes, I was afraid of that. We mustn't lose sight of them. My son's life may depend on it.'

They watched the Jaguar enter Brighton and join the throng of other vehicles. Progress in the heavy traffic was slow. They merged with cars, buses and lorries in the stop-start procession of vehicles caught up in jams and negotiating traffic lights and zebra crossings. Dexter knew Brighton and directed them through side streets, away from the throng of vehicles clogging the main roads.

The light was fading fast, engulfed by thunder storm clouds rumbling across the heavens.

'That's strange,' remarked Brooke, following them with his binoculars. 'They've doubled back and look to be heading towards Rye again. I'd better inform the lads they've changed direction. The problem is, they're stuck in the heavy traffic and daren't use their sirens or Dexter will know they're trailing him.'

'He's being very clever. He's going to a lot of trouble to make sure no one knows which direction he intends to take,' remarked Sir Joseph.

'Damn!' exclaimed Brooke. 'I've lost them. The light's poor, and with all this blasted traffic, I can't see them any more. Do you think they've realised we're tracking them and deliberately tried to give us the slip?'

'No, I don't think so. I'm more inclined to believe they went into Brighton to play safe, just in case anyone's following. The heavy traffic provides them with an ideal opportunity to give anyone the slip. We've got to pick them up again. He's twisting and turning. He could take any direction.'

'So where are they going now?' Brooke murmured. 'And why go back? It doesn't make sense if he thinks he's lost any tail in Brighton. Why not go on?'

Sir Joseph scanned the whole vista and noticed a small sailing boat scurrying towards the shore to avoid the waves, now becoming higher and rougher. It was racing to beat the full fury of the impending storm that was approaching fast.

'A boat!' Sir Joseph exclaimed. 'I'll bet he's got a boat in Brighton Marina. We passed the marina just a couple of miles back. Inform the others, Colin, and tell them to get on to the marina officials and find out if Dexter keeps a boat moored there.'

'Right,' he agreed, switching frequencies to contact control.

'Can we put down anywhere near here?' Sir Joseph asked the pilot.

'There's a helipad at the marina, sir. I'll radio them and say we need to land there.'

The pilot contacted the marina, then spoke to Sir Joseph. 'They've told me the pad's being resurfaced and is out of commission for a couple of days.'

'Blast!' said Sir Joseph. 'Is there anywhere else?'

'Shoreham, sir. They've got a small airport there. It's only a few miles away.'

'Okay. Get us there quickly. Colin, get one of the squad cars to meet us and tell the other one to get to the marina straight away.'

In the meantime, Jim drove into Brighton Marina and along the jetty, past the harbour shopping precinct clock striking the hour, three times. Seagulls squawked, and dark clouds moved overhead, like a curtain being drawn across the sky. He stopped alongside a boat named *Lucky Lady*. She was a forty-eight foot, six-berth, blue water cruiser, capable of ten knots or more, and was bobbing gently up and down in the water.

Mel climbed the steps and Dexter pushed Jim aboard.

'Come on, hurry up,' Dexter instructed. They were greeted by a damp musty smell, tinged with varnish and diesel, filling the air. Jim was taken below and his wrist was handcuffed to the berth in the after cabin.

Dexter cast off and slipped out, to the clap of thunderclouds overhead turning the afternoon into night. Lightning flashed, illuminating the marina for a few seconds before it fell back into darkness once more, creating an eerie and foreboding atmosphere. Once into the Channel, Dexter passed the wheel to Mel for a few minutes while he went below to check on Jim.

'You might as well get some rest,' Dexter told him. 'You could be here for quite a while. And while we're at it, I want to know what you've done with those two watches.'

'What two watches? I don't know what you're talking about,' pleaded Jim innocently.

Dexter searched him, emptying his pockets onto the berth, and was disappointed not to find anything.

'If you didn't take them, then who did?' he muttered to himself, going topside.

In a gusty wind, the police helicopter landed at Shoreham Airport. The storm had broken, and rain dropped from the sky in bucketfuls, soaking everything almost immediately. A squad car raced across the tarmac to meet Sir Joseph and Brooke, its wheels sending a spray of water arcing behind them from the large puddles already forming. They bundled in and set off for the marina. On the way, a radio message from control confirmed that Dexter had a berth there for a boat called *Lucky Lady*, but it was missing from its moorings.

'Damn!' groaned Sir Joseph. 'I'm sure they've escaped. That boat's certainly got an appropriate name.'

By the time they reached the marina, the storm, in full flow, had thunder and lightning crashing, and rain pelting down hard enough to sting the face of anyone unfortunate enough to be caught out in it. The waves rose and fell twenty feet, whipped up by the high wind. Even in the shelter of the marina, boats moored there tossed up and down, and lines clinked against their masts, fighting to be heard above the roar of the wind and thunder.

In the marina manager's office, Sir Joseph asked if it was possible to pursue *Lucky Lady*.

The silver-haired manager, Bruce Mowatt, told them, 'It's possible. Your police boats are just as capable of navigating the storm as anyone else. The problem is knowing which direction to take. It's almost impossible to catch visual sight of them in this ferocious weather, and without confirmation of which way he's heading, you could waste a lot of time and effort in a fruitless search. I suggest it's better to wait until the storm has passed.'

Sir Joseph nodded in agreement. Nothing could be done to continue the chase until the storm abated. 'I'll get a general alert issued with a description of the boat and occupants,' he said.

They all sat in the manager's office for the next few hours, collecting information about Dexter's cruiser, and waiting for the storm to die down. The manager described *Lucky Lady* as a versatile boat with an 85 hp diesel engine, its own generator, GPS radar, autopilot and air-conditioning. In it, Dexter could go anywhere in the world, and in almost any weather.

The information was depressing, but much as expected, and although the storm was dwindling, darkness now approached and they were forced to postpone the search.

'There's nothing more we can do tonight,' stated Brooke. 'We'll continue the search at first light.'

On the drive back to London, the day's events occupied Sir Joseph's mind and he prayed that his son had come to no harm, or at least that he was still alive.

Chapter XVI
Retribution

The fire at Camp West lit up the charcoal sky. For Mike and his group, attempting to escape from the clutches of The General, the quietness of the early morning jungle served to amplify the roar of their jeep's engine. The five occupants spoke little during their bumpy ride over the rough track on their nightmare journey. The spot where Mike had been ambushed less that two days before was close, and they halted.

'Jenny, you stay with Mr and Mrs Charlie while Suzie and I reconnoitre ahead,' Mike instructed, examining the weapons in Paul's armoury. 'Keep your eyes peeled. They could still be tracking us, unless that blast destroyed their truck. If they get close, you'd better move forward. We should have checked ahead by then.'

'Okay. Do be careful,' she said, glancing at Suzie and wondering if she'd guessed that they'd slept together.

'Sure,' Mike replied, continuing his search without looking up. He could almost feel Suzie's eyes boring into the back of his head, as the question of how close he had got to Jenny went through her mind. She knew him well enough to guess right, he knew that. What he was less sure of was why it bothered him so much that she would guess. Words like 'love' didn't come easily to him. 'In this profession you can't afford to go soft,' he always maintained. But he knew that he was only trying to kid himself.

Mike picked up a pistol, several hand grenades and a few sticks of dynamite. He handed the Ingram and several spare clips to Suzie and avoided looking her in the eyes. The clips were taped together in pairs, each pair with one upside down to assist in quick replacement. They started out on foot, with only the diffused illumination of the moon to light their way.

'She seems very concerned about you. You two got a thing

going?' Suzie questioned.

'Don't be silly,' insisted Mike. 'She's just worried about everyone getting back safely, that's all.'

They stopped for a moment.

'Look, Mike… I don't expect you to be a saint, and I just want to say… you know, just in case…'

'I know,' he said, caressing her cheek with his fingers. 'Me too.'

They looked into each other's eyes in the gloom. Words were not needed. They knew what each felt about the other, and despite the suspicions about Jenny, the problems of the last few days had reinforced the bond between them.

Mike gave her a quick kiss on the lips. 'C'mon. Let's go. Let's get it done. You watch my back and I'll watch yours. Just like we've always done.'

Suzie nodded.

They moved on, plodding through slushy puddles. Each step sounded noisy and magnified in their minds. Mike thought about the time that he taught Jim tracking at Tramer. Jim was unable to move quietly and unobtrusively through the undergrowth, no matter how hard he tried. Now Mike felt like he was doing the self-same thing, except that the circumstances were very different and much more depended on him.

Stealing towards the clearing, Mike motioned Suzie to follow him to the top of a ridge. They picked their way carefully through the undergrowth, neither speaking, conscious of each step they took and every rustle they made. Their close partnership on previous missions gave them an understanding of each other that was vital in such difficult situations, where a careless noisy movement could mean the difference between life and death. This understanding had grown quickly and was why they worked well together, and it gave rise to much envy by others.

They crawled the last few yards slowly to the ridge top on their stomachs, making no sound at all. The smell of the damp jungle filled their nostrils and the wet seeped through to their fronts, knees and elbows. In such critical circumstances they hardly noticed the discomfort, ignoring it and peering over the ridge top.

Below, the terrain was barely visible in the moonlight. The

tree trunk was back across the track again and Mike pointed to it. Suzie saw it and nodded, understanding the significance.

'See?' whispered Mike, indicating several glows in the dark. 'Cigarettes.'

Suzie nodded again. 'Yes. Now what?' she asked.

'It looks as if most of them are on the far side. There's just a few below us.'

'Any ideas?'

'We need a diversion to get them in the open.'

'Don't look at me,' was Suzie's indignant reply. 'I'm not taking my shirt off *again*! Even if it is soaking wet.'

Mike raised his eyebrows at the thought. A cheeky grin came to his face. 'Wouldn't be any use. They couldn't see you well enough in this light to know what a glorious sight they were missing, and anyway, I can't afford to keep buying you shirts!'

'I haven't had the first one yet,' complained Suzie in an exaggerated whisper, giving him a playful punch on the arm, a smile lighting up her face for a moment.

Mike watched and calculated. 'We don't have much time. I reckon there's about ten or a dozen.'

'We could just start shooting. The Ingram's a powerful weapon and we've got the element of surprise.'

'Too risky. We need to flush them all out in one go. We can't afford to get into a long-running battle in case there are more soldiers chasing along behind us. They'll hear the shooting and know what's happening. It may even spur them on.'

'Okay. What then?'

'I've got an idea. Follow me,' said Mike.

They quietly retreated a short distance and took a wide berth across the track to the place where Mike had hidden Raúl's jeep. To his relief, it was still there. He briefly explained about the encounter and said that before he moved on he'd concealed the bodies and equipment.

The jeep was undisturbed, and uncovering it revealed a full can of petrol strapped to the back. Mike lashed several sticks of dynamite to it while Suzie kept watch.

'That ought to be enough. Do you think you can see it well enough to hit it from the ridge?'

'With this gun, I can hit anything,' she replied, patting the Ingram. 'And besides, they don't call me Annie Oakley for nothing.'

Mike raised his eyebrows and inhaled deeply. 'I should have known better than to ask,' he quipped.

Suzie's teeth showed white with the exaggerated grin she pulled.

They crawled back to the high ground and Mike took out several hand grenades.

Suzie took aim at the explosives on the jeep, and Mike stood and yelled, 'There they are.'

The Ingram spat out a volley. The dynamite exploded with a thunderous roar, and the jungle lit up like a fireworks display.

The jeep burst into flames, triggering a mass exodus by soldiers emerging from their hiding places, rushing towards it, firing at dancing shadows.

When the first men reached the vehicle, Mike hurled a grenade, and the explosion ripped lumps from everything nearby, tossing bits of jungle and men alike into the air. The rebels were taken completely by surprise and scrambled in all directions for cover. Light from the burning jeep uncovered their cloak of darkness and exposed them to the Ingram's rapid firepower. The gun's deadly speed enabled it to spew out bullets at the rate of nine hundred rounds a minute, equal to the combined rate of several weapons, and gave the impression that there was more than one enemy soldier firing. The weapon scythed its way through anything and anyone unfortunate enough to be in its path, giving little opportunity to retaliate.

The thirty-two round magazine was quickly empty, and Suzie pulled the clip out, turned it upside down and jammed in a new clip while Mike lobbed more grenades. Bodies were flung aside, with confused soldiers dashing for cover in the mêlée and wildly firing back at anything. The Ingram rattled again, and more soldiers were hammered into the ground, not knowing what had hit them.

The scrambling soldiers were by now still, their blood-soaked bodies at rest. The sickening sound of battle was brief and the noise melted away, dissipating into the night and followed by an unfamiliar quietness.

It looked as if it was all over.

Mike and Suzie gingerly emerged and were surprised when a fusillade splattered the trees near them. Suzie replied with another volley aimed at two soldiers, firing a heavy calibre machine-gun mounted on the back of a camouflaged armoured jeep which had them in their sights. They dropped quickly to the ground as more bullets ricocheted around them.

'Blast! I didn't see that thing hidden in the bushes,' Mike cursed. 'I should have guessed. We saw it go past on the road.'

Suzie, raising her head to fire, had to duck again fast, at another burst taking more chunks out of the tree. 'They've got a bead on us. I can't get a clean shot at them from here.'

'No. I've got to get close enough to lob in a grenade.'

'Okay, Mike. I'll move away and draw their fire.'

Suzie slid down the ridge and moved along to the track by the fallen log. Mike went in the opposite direction to get behind the vehicle.

The soldiers caught sight of Suzie and a volley of shots sent her diving behind the tree trunk for cover, the firing pinning her down.

'What the hell am I doing here?' she muttered, spitting soggy leaves from her mouth, with bullets continuing to slice lumps out of the tree above her head. 'C'mon, Mike, get me out of this mess!'

Mike could see the impossible situation Suzie was in, but was unable to find a quick route that would get him close enough to the jeep without being seen and picked off. He fought his way through thick undergrowth, scratching at his face and arms, in a desperate attempt to carve a way down.

Suddenly, the crack of a rifle filled the air and one of the soldiers was hit and fell. The other responded by grabbing the gun and turning it towards Jenny, standing in front of her jeep with the gun poised. Another crack sounded, and the force of the shot catapulted him from the back of the vehicle, to hit the ground with a dull squelch.

The noise of battle stopped. Everything went quiet once more. Only the sound of flames licking the burning jeep could be heard, its flickering light illuminating death and destruction.

Suzie got up. Now it was all over.

They approached Jenny.

'That was good shooting,' complimented Mike.

'I had ambitions to be in the Olympic shooting team once,' she confided.

'Seems I owe you... and Sir Joseph, yet another vote of thanks,' he said. Jenny opened her mouth to speak and Mike interrupted her. 'Yes, I know. It's all part of the service.'

'Right,' she replied, her smile showing gleaming white teeth. A look flashed between them.

Suzie noticed the look – and wondered what else was all part of the service. 'I'm glad you didn't wait for us. I guess the sound of gunfire changed your mind,' she said.

'We heard the shooting and explosions, and I thought you might need a hand. This rifle was among the weapons Paul brought, so I decided to see if I could make good use of it.'

'I'm glad you did.'

Mike and Suzie surveyed the scene for any signs of movement. The slaughter before them was ugly, but events were out of their control.

Mike put a reassuring hand on Suzie's shoulder and gave a squeeze. 'It was them or us. We had no choice.'

'Yes, I know, Mike. But it was another dozen lives snuffed out because of one ruthless despot. I've got to get away from this senseless butchery, and soon.'

'You and me both. But what else do we know how to do? Come on, I'll clear things up.'

Mike went among the bodies cautiously, checking to see if anyone was still alive. None were; the Ingram had done its job frighteningly well.

He moved the bodies out of sight and covered them with bracken. 'The General wasn't among them, so he must be with the group following us,' Mike suggested. 'The way's clear now.'

'We mustn't delay any longer,' urged Jenny, 'the soldiers aren't very far behind us.'

'I'm very pleased to hear that,' said The General, quietly emerging from a camouflaged dugout. He put an arm around

Suzie's throat and a gun to her temple.

Mike was taken by surprise. 'Where the hell did you spring from?'

The General was smug. 'There's a few tricks left in the old dog yet. Drop your weapons or Miss Drake will die,' he threatened, kicking the Ingram away from Suzie.

Her back was arched by this dumpy man, his grip tight around her throat, choking her. He looked menacing; flames from the jeep created dancing shadows across his chubby face, showing a look of evil, grim determination.

Mike and Jenny threw down their guns.

'Move away from them,' barked The General, throwing Suzie forward onto her knees.

Mike helped Suzie to her feet, then moved away, circling around, with Jenny following his lead. The General faced them as they moved and now had his back to their jeep.

'Okay, Charlie,' shouted Mike. 'Cover The General with the gun I gave you.'

'Charlie!' exclaimed The General. 'The little Chinese cook? Surely you don't expect me to fall for an old trick like that, do you, Mr Randle?' he laughed.

'No, General, of course not, only… it's no trick.'

Mrs Charlie popped up from the back of the jeep, holding the gun she'd been given with both hands. She pointed it at The General and with a look of hate in her face spat, 'Shit General.'

A hint of surprise came over his face. His expression changed and hardened, then he span round and two gunshots sounded as one.

A bullet whistled past the side of Mrs Charlie's head, and The General's eyes opened wide in shock as her bullet tore through his neck. He dropped his gun, clasped his throat and staggered, not hearing Mrs Charlie's words, repeated with venom.

'Shit General!' she cursed, the gun barking again and again, putting two more bullets into his ample body. He crumpled to his knees and slowly toppled forward on his face.

They all stood in shocked silence for a moment.

Charlie emerged from the back of the jeep and stared at the body. 'She get pretty mad, Mr Mike.'

'Yeah. So it seems, Charlie. So it seems,' he repeated, not knowing what to say.

The sound of shots died away, and their attention turned to the roar of an approaching vehicle.

'Come on quick. We'd better go,' urged Mike. 'We can't go into town in a jeep with a gun mounted on it, so we'll use it to move the log and block the way.'

Everyone galvanised into action and a gap was quickly opened wide enough to let their vehicle through. Mike left the gun jeep as a barrier and shot two tyres out.

Mrs Charlie was shaking, and Mr Charlie tried to calm her down. They all bundled into their jeep and motored away, bouncing up and down violently in their haste to retreat.

The dense jungle gradually thinned out, the closer they came to civilisation once again. The audible throbbing of the vehicle following them melted into the night, with each mile that they put between themselves and the dead General.

'I guess they've found him. Let's hope they give up the chase now,' Mike said optimistically.

Jenny turned to him. 'Better get rid of the guns and explosives, Mike,' she advised.

'Yes. Good idea. I'll bury them. Wouldn't like to leave any of this stuff lying around.'

'And I need to call in at the pub for a few moments to collect some things before we go to the airport, then I'll try and get us on a flight to London.'

Mike dug a hole away from the track and buried the guns and explosives. 'I seem to have done a lot of this lately,' he commented to Suzie, who was watching him fill in the hole.

'Let's hope this is the last time,' she reflected.

With the dense jungle behind them the bog-filled ruts evened out. They all relaxed a little now they were over the border and close to Roseburgh. The ease in tension showed, especially in Mr Charlie and Mrs Charlie, who even managed a nervous smile. She patted her husband's hand, grateful that their ordeal was almost over.

Roseburgh was quiet. Mike drove in at 5 a.m. through deserted streets. Most inhabitants still slept, while the almost clear sky, full of stars and a glowing moon, gave the town a spectral atmosphere.

Mike pulled into the back yard of Paul's Bar and yanked on the handbrake. 'Suzie, okay if you stay with Mr and Mrs Charlie while Jenny and I go in? We'll only be a few minutes.'

Suzie nodded, aware that this time Mike had asked rather than told her what he was doing. 'Does he actually feel guilty?' she pondered. 'Maybe, but doesn't want to spoil things between us. Poor Mike. I bet he'd be different if he knew about Martin. Still he needn't worry, but I won't let him off the hook that easily. Perhaps it'll teach him a lesson.'

Jenny opened the back door and climbed the stairs to her room, while Mike wandered into the dimly lit bar where the smell of beer and cigarettes still hung heavy in the air. Most punters had left only a short while ago, and the last was still with a girl upstairs.

Suddenly aware of someone else in the room, Mike turned to see Manny standing behind the bar.

'You gave me a start. I didn't realise anyone was still up,' Mike said.

'Sorry. I didn't mean to make you jump. I was just finishing some of the glasses while I wait for the last girl to leave. Have you seen Mr Paul? He took off after you.'

'Yes. I saw him a couple of hours ago,' Mike hesitated, not sure how much Manny knew about Paul's business. 'We... er... ran into some trouble. There was some shooting and... well, Paul won't be coming back.'

Manny looked shocked. He stopped wiping the glass he held, and spoke quietly and slowly.

'Oh! I'm very sorry. He was good to me. Gave me this job. Let's me sleep here – when the girls have finished with the bedrooms. What am I going to do now?'

'I don't know, Manny. I just don't know.'

Jenny emerged, carrying a small suitcase. 'Hallo, Manny. How are you?'

'I'm fine, Miss Jenny. Much better than Mr Paul, it seems.'

'Oh! Mike's told you...'

'Yes,' interrupted Mike quickly. 'I told Manny we ran into problems and Paul didn't make it.'

'He was a good man,' insisted Manny. 'I think he knew there may be trouble. He left a package with a note asking me to give it to one of you if he didn't return,' he said, lifting it from beneath the bar and handing it to Jenny. She took it and started to pull the sticky tape away.

'Stop,' shouted Mike. 'Put the package down on the table gently and move away.'

Realising what Mike was thinking, Jenny gingerly put it on the table and took a few steps back. 'He wouldn't. Would he?' she asked.

'He might. He was a cunning devil.'

'What are you saying? You think he left a bomb?' Manny sounded incredulous.

'No, of course not,' said Mike, not wanting to hurt his feelings. 'But Paul was a great trickster. He may have left a surprise for us. Could you turn the main lights on, please, Manny? And do you have a pair of scissors?'

Manny handed him the scissors. Mike approached the table. The lights came on and brightened as the dimmer switch was rotated to full. He sank to his knees, putting the package at eye level and began to slice through the sticky tape very gently. Cutting the top flaps free, he lifted them slowly, peering underneath to look for anything attached. The room was deadly quiet, with both of them hardly daring to breathe, watching Mike lift the four top flaps up.

Suzie entered the bar. 'You're taking a long ti… is that a bomb Mike?' she asked, stopping in her tracks.

'Hi, Suzie. We don't know what's in the package,' Mike said, without removing his eyes from it. 'We're just making sure. Perhaps you should all take cover behind the bar – just in case.'

Mike peered into the package. A bead of sweat ran down the side of his face. 'It looks like a cash box,' he declared, 'and there's a key taped to the top of it.'

Gently grasping the handle, he gingerly lifted the box out and put it on the table. He wiped the sweat from his brow and dried his palms on the thighs of his trousers while he took a short breather. Glancing at the girls and Manny peering over the top of the bar, he started to splutter with laughter.

'If Paul's watching us now, I bet he's having a good laugh.'

'You be careful,' said Jenny.

'Yes. Concentrate on what you're doing,' said Suzie. They looked at each other with a feeling of rivalry passing between them.

After peeling the sticky tape off, Mike inserted the key in the lock. He wiped his lips on the back of his hand and tasted the salty sweat. The key turned easily and the lock snapped back, echoing around the silent room, making them all jump.

A clank of footsteps came down the stairs, and the last girl came into the room with her client. They took in the scene, quickly realised what was happening, and rushed for the back door with the woman screaming. The screeching faded into the distance, past Mr Charlie, who came in to see what was going on.

'Go back to the jeep, Charlie, and stay with your wife,' Mike ordered.

Charlie stared, wide-eyed, at the group cowering behind the bar and backed out through the door. 'Yes, Mr Mike.'

Using the scissors, Mike cautiously lifted the box lid and peered inside. He stood up and flipped the lid wide open.

'There's just some papers in here,' he breathed with relief, taking out an envelope with 'To Jenny or Mike' written on it.

He opened it and read to himself:

Dear Jenny or Mike,

If you are reading this letter then I must be dead, ol' buddy. I didn't want to go without making sure the pub was in good hands, so the deeds are enclosed. If either or both of you have a mind to stay on, then the place is yours. I'm not totally sure Jenny is quite what she seems, but she's great for business.

Good luck.
Paul

Jenny read the letter. 'Makes me feel quite sick now,' she said.

'Don't. You know the score... and what the result would have been otherwise,' stated Mike.

'Yes. I guess so, and this is really sweet of him, but this is not for me. England's my home. I don't want a pub in Africa.'

'Me neither. How about you Manny? Do you fancy owning this pub?'

'Me, Mr Mike? It would be an honour. It will stay as Paul's Bar and continue in the way he would have wanted.'

'That's settled then,' he said, slapping the deeds down on the bar. 'How about one for the road, and for Paul?'

'I'll drink to that,' Manny said, pouring them all a drink of Paul's favourite strong Irish whiskey.

Back on the road, they sped their way towards the airport. Mr and Mrs Charlie couldn't understand why they were all so happy and smiling when they came out, until they smelled the whiskey on their breaths.

Traffic lights appeared, and a few vehicles were around when they motored through the city centre. Here, some of the girls were finishing their work for the night or standing near street corners hoping for one more customer, while keeping an eye out for the police or military. Soliciting was against the law, but was still a thriving business in some quarters.

Passing through the centre they journeyed on to the airport, along the unlit but only good road in the area. Airport lights shone out like a beacon standing alone in the wilderness of the night.

Mike recalled the interrogation he had gone through on arrival and suspected that it was arranged by The General's men. There could be trouble if news of his death had reached them. However, he figured that they were unlikely to be aware that a seemingly frail Chinese woman had pumped three bullets into him, in retaliation for the torment he'd caused her for such a long time.

They parked the jeep in a corner of the terminal car park and entered the building. Jenny contacted security and was escorted to the same room that Mike had occupied on arrival. She needed great powers of persuasion and argument before she was allowed to telephone London. After explaining the situation, without telling them that The General was dead, and threatening to call the British Consulate with a complaint about the treatment that they were receiving from airport officials, they agreed to consider her request.

At this early hour the airport had few visitors, with only a trickle of people arriving to catch the first flight out. Mike's group sat outside the office, waiting, watching a cleaner sweep away the never-ending stream of dust that blew in through the open doors. Footsteps echoed around the building, and the few people there spoke in whispers as if afraid of disturbing anyone.

It was a long while since any of them had eaten, and they were all feeling a bit peckish, but the only cafeteria in the airport was shut.

'Let's hope we get something to eat on the plane,' Mike remarked, holding his gurgling stomach. 'In fact, I wouldn't mind a bowl of your broth right now, Charlie!'

Charlie looked pleased. It wasn't often that his cooking got any sort of praise.

Nearly an hour passed before Jenny was called back into the office. She emerged after a few minutes to say that she'd spoken to Sir Joseph Sterling.

'Everything is finally arranged. We're on our way home. We can board the aircraft going to London via Nairobi. It's due to leave in less than an hour.'

'Sterling again,' said Mike. 'He's getting to be a real boy scout.'

'Like I said before, lucky for you.'

Mike nodded in agreement, conceding the fact.

'Sir Joseph also said he's very worried about his son Jim. An arms dealer called Dexter, and his wife, are holding him hostage. It seems he was taken by boat, possibly out of the country. They'll resume the search when it gets light. It's about four in the morning over there at the moment.'

'Oh no!' exclaimed Mike. 'That could be my fault. I asked him to do something for me. I shouldn't have got him involved in this, it's too dangerous for an amateur. God, I hope he's okay. Any chance I can make a quick call to England? Surely Sir Joseph's operative can arrange a simple thing like that?' he asked, in a mocking tone that only drew a hurtful look from Jenny. 'Sorry. I'm a bit concerned about him, that's all,' he added.

'That's okay. I understand.'

Mike made his call to Grace who was relieved to hear from him, even at that hour of the morning. She had a lot to tell him.

Chapter XVII

Flight

The quiet calm of late evening came as a welcome relief to Mel and Jim. It was in stark contrast to the rough lashing that *Lucky Lady* had taken from the storm when they left Brighton Marina that afternoon. Al Dexter was an experienced sailor and the storm hadn't worried him. On the contrary, he was pleased. He knew that even if the police traced him to the marina, they were unlikely to chance following him in such awful conditions, when they were unsure which direction he had taken. He was confident that he'd eluded them, and after one short stop for fuel and provisions, he would disappear with his wife to live a life of modest luxury on a small, sunny Mediterranean island. He regretted not having the gems to take with him, but had salted away enough profits in the nearby Palermo bank not to have to worry too much about that. He'd always planned to retire there and, when problems arose over payment for the arms, he had simply brought forward that plan and turned it into an escape route. Now he'd activated it, and they would vanish into thin air without a trace.

The only fly in the ointment was Jim Sterling.

'What am I going to do with him? I should kill him, but that would only upset Mel, and she's been through a lot in the last two days. Best to kill him, but let her think that I've put him ashore where he can make his way home,' he decided.

The morning arrived. Jim hadn't slept much. He'd dozed on and off, but every time he turned over the handcuffs yanked his wrist and disturbed him. Mel slept in the single cabin after the storm abated, while Al Dexter stayed at the wheel, forging on towards his destination. He could sleep later. Right now, all he wanted to do was put enough distance between them and the English authorities to make him and his wife safe.

Jim felt the boat bump alongside a quay and heard the sound of distant voices and traffic. Mel came below and brought him a cup of coffee.

'Where are we?' he asked. 'I know we've tied up somewhere.'

'I can't tell you. Anyway, it doesn't really matter, we won't be here for very long.'

'If it doesn't really matter, why can't you tell me?'

'My husband is going to put you ashore, safe and sound in a remote spot, where we can get away before you can call for the police. So don't worry.'

Jim stared at this lovely-looking woman and saw the beauty she possessed for the first time. Seemingly out of danger and with a few hours' rest, she was much more attractive than when he had first seen her at the cottage. He noticed her shapely figure and smelled her strong perfume. She stared into the mirror, brushed her long hair back over her ears and clipped it in place.

Al Dexter came in. 'Come on, Mel. I want to get the food and booze aboard. The sooner we get away from here, the better I'll like it.'

'Okay, Dex. I'm being as quick as I can.'

He sighed loudly.

'*Dio mio!*' she cursed, dropping a hairgrip and searching the cabin floor for it.

'Leave the bloody thing. Let's get going to the supermarket.'

Mel patted and fussed her hair, then followed her husband on deck. Jim heard the door lock and footsteps recede as they went ashore.

He looked for the hairgrip and saw it underneath the opposite berth at the far end. Laying on the floor, he stretched to the limit the handcuffs would allow, but still couldn't reach it with his outstretched foot.

'Bugger,' he muttered to himself. 'I've got to get it.'

He tried again, stretching until it felt as if his arm and leg would come out of their sockets. He was tantalisingly close and could almost brush it with his shoe. With another effort he touched the grip but only managed to push it a little further away.

'Oh sod!' he exclaimed, relaxing and letting his muscles return to normal. He squirmed – gripped by cramp in the top of his

Flight

shoulder – and massaged it with his free hand, flexing the shoulder to ease the discomfort.

Looking around for something to help, he noticed his things on the berth, where Dexter had thrown them. He had an idea.

Taking off his shoe and sock, he grabbed his ballpoint pen and lodged it between his big and first toes. Trying again, he found that he could reach the hairgrip, but when he put pressure on the pen to pull it towards him, it began to slip away.

'Damn!' Jim uttered, breathing out heavily in sheer frustration. After several attempts, and coming close to losing the pen, he looked for something else that might manage better, but there was nothing within reach.

Then he had a brainwave.

He tore the plaster off his forehead, swearing as it ripped away. 'Bloody Dexter. That hurt!' he yelled, rubbing furiously at the spot in an attempt to ease the pain.

Jim used the plaster to stick the pen between his toes and tried again. Slowly, gradually, the hairgrip moved a little, then a little more, until finally he could reach it with his big toe. He pulled it towards him, returned the pen, and put his sock and shoe back on, anxious to hide what he'd been doing in case they returned.

The boat swayed a little, and he thought they were coming aboard. He waited, a little apprehensive, but it was only movement with the tide. Hearing nothing, he began working on the handcuffs.

'Come on. I was the first to get these off in class. It seems a lot harder when it's for real,' he muttered.

Jim tried over and over again to undo the lock, but without success.

'Bugger! Bugger!' he cursed, yanking at the handcuffs. But they only pulled against the rail and hurt his wrist.

'Slow down. Do it right,' he told himself, recalling some of the instructions he'd received during his training.

He tried once again, taking his time and concentrating – the way they had taught him at Tramer. The minutes ticked by, then came a click. He was so elated when the cuffs came off that he stood and shouted, 'Geronimo! I've got to get out of here quickly, they could be back any minute.'

He pocketed his things and ran up the steps to the outer doors. They were locked, which he expected. Gripping a ledge on either side, he gave the doors an almighty kick. They started to give, and a second kick was all he needed to burst them open.

He was free.

The boat was tied to the quay in a small harbour. From the signs Jim could tell he was in St Helier, in the Channel Island of Jersey. Storm clouds had vanished, and it was a bright sunny morning with just a few white wispy clouds in the sky. The Dexters were nowhere in sight – luck was still with him.

Jumping onto the quayside, he made for the town and hailed a taxi to take him to the nearest police station.

In a converted house on the outskirts of St Helier, and only a few minutes away, Jim rushed into the Jersey States Police station. He explained his tale to the desk sergeant first, then to a DC in the interview room, and finally to DI Parker. By this time, telephone calls to London had confirmed his identity and story. Contact was made with Sir Joseph, and the good news of his son's escape was conveyed to him. He spoke with DI Parker and explained the situation, feeling a lump in his throat when Jim came on the line. He'd been mentally preparing himself for the worse and was more pleased than he cared to admit that his only son was safe again.

'This is the second piece of good news I've had today. The first one got me out of bed at 4 a.m.'

'Oh! What was that?' enquired Jim.

'Your friend, Mike Randle, and his lady friend, Suzie Drake, are safely on their way home.'

'That's great!' said Jim, punching the air. 'I'm so pleased. I never doubted he'd do it.'

'Oh! Really?'

'Well… just a little doubt. Now if we can only nab the Dexters before it's too late, that'll make a perfect climax to the day.'

'Good luck. Tell Parker to keep me informed of any progress he makes.'

DI Parker was a skinny man with a thin face and pointed chin. His dark, wispy hair, combed straight back, had receded, leaving him with a wide forehead wrinkled in a permanent frown. A pencil moustache above his thin lips gave him a weasel-faced look. He was a thorough man and took his time, much to Jim's frustration. Nearly an hour had passed since his arrival at the police station.

'The Dexters will escape. We must go to the harbour straight away,' pleaded Jim.

'Yes, sir. So you keep saying. Everything's been taken care of. We'll pop along there now, and the police launch will meet us in a few minutes.'

The police car sped to the harbour with lights flashing and siren wailing carrying Jim and DI Parker.

'This is all a bit late,' Jim mumbled under his breath, the car screeching to a halt on the jetty.

Lucky Lady was gone.

Parker went to investigate while Jim sat in the car listening to a throaty roar signalling the arrival of the police launch.

'Harbour master says she left about twenty minutes ago,' Parker said, holding the squad car door open and poking his head into the vehicle to inform Jim. 'We'll go out in the launch and see if we can spot them. I've called for a helicopter to help us with the search.'

'I heard them talking this morning before they went ashore. I couldn't hear very well, but I'm sure they mentioned the Mediterranean,' Jim commented.

'Hmm yes. It makes good sense for them to head that way. They're unlikely to go back to England at the moment. Too hot for them, I fancy. So if we assume that's their plan, they'll have to proceed in a westerly direction,' said Parker in typical police jargon, 'then round Ushant island off Brittany before turning south towards Portugal. I'll pass that information to the helicopter pilot. He can search in that direction and we'll follow along in the launch.'

Jim and Parker jumped aboard the launch and it sped to sea with two other policemen aboard. Gathering speed, after clearing the harbour, they headed west, spray lashing against the windows. Jim held on to the rail tightly, the craft rising and falling, crashing into the waves and reaching nearly twenty knots, cutting its way through the water.

Staring out to sea, he looked for the Dexters' boat. Wind rushed through his hair and salt spray covered his face, smearing his glasses. The helicopter buzzed over them and flew ahead to begin its search. Parker contacted the pilot by radio and told him they'd picked up a fast moving boat on their surface radar, and gave the location.

To Jim, the excitement of the chase mixed with the smell of the salt sea air was invigorating. The sun beat down and the wind took away his breath. A crackly message came over the launch loudspeaker from the helicopter pilot. He'd spotted *Lucky Lady* less than three nautical miles ahead, crashing through the white-tipped waves and making around ten knots.

Parker handed Jim a pair of binoculars and pointed to the horizon. 'There. Three miles ahead,' he said.

'Yes. I see them. We're catching up fast,' Jim enthused excitedly. 'But he's a desperate man, and he's armed.'

'Yes, I know. Your father told me.'

Spurred on by the sighting, the police launch seemed to find a little extra speed, and their quarry came into clear view and was quickly reeled in.

Parker called through a loud hailer, 'Ahoy, *Lucky Lady*. This is the Jersey States Police. Slow down and come alongside. We wish to board you.'

All he got for his efforts was a bullet whistling past him which splintered the woodwork. Parker took a pistol from his briefcase and called another warning, adding that he was armed. He got the same reply: another bullet dug its way into the launch. He thought about returning fire, but the rise and fall of the two boats, travelling at nearly ten knots, made accurate aiming difficult, and he wanted this to end without bloodshed.

On his instructions, the launch was moved in closer and Parker fired a shot in the air.

'I will fire, if necessary, Mr Dexter,' he yelled, above the roar of the engines and the crashing of the waves. 'Slow down and come alongside.'

But Dexter, who was at the wheel, turned and fired a volley of shots, emptying his gun at the policemen. A bullet hit Parker, and he slumped to the deck, dropping his gun and clutching his side, blood oozing from the wound. One of the policemen picked up the gun and prepared to shoot.

The launch pilot veered the boat away and slowed down. 'We must return at once,' he said. 'The inspector looks badly hurt. We've got to get him to hospital quickly.'

He span the wheel round and headed back, radioing for an ambulance to meet them. Jim knew there was no other choice. He watched *Lucky Lady* speeding off into the distance. The frustration he felt at being so close, and still losing the Dexters, swamped him with disappointment. They made Parker comfortable and sped back to the St Helier.

The helicopter returned to base because *Lucky Lady* was out of their jurisdiction and into international waters.

Blue lights were flashing on waiting police and ambulance vehicles at the harbour. The inspector was conscious but looked to be in some distress.

'He'll be back. We'll get him,' he told Jim.

'Yes, I expect you're right,' he replied, thinking it was unlikely.

The ambulance rushed the inspector straight to hospital. Jim returned to the police station to ring his father with the news, then made arrangements for a flight home.

With a few hours to spare before his plane was due to leave, and suddenly realising that he hadn't eaten for a while, Jim wandered into St Helier, looking for somewhere to have lunch. He found a small restaurant overlooking the harbour, where the salty smell of fresh fish hung in the air. He plumped for fish and chips, and after a delicious lunch caught a taxi to Jersey Airport. While there, he rang the hospital to ask about Parker and was told that he was in the operating theatre having the bullet removed. He thought about Al Dexter who had put him there, and the anger and frustration in him worsened.

'Still, best to be grateful it's not me, and just forget him,' he thought. 'I wonder if he really would have let me go, or would I have ended like Parker, with a bullet in me?'

Jim's journey to England took less than an hour, and he was soon staring at a grey, London skyline through the cabin window. The weather might not be so great, but it was home, and good to see England again, after thinking just the previous night that he might not.

Mike and his group were last to board the Airbus A320 at Roseburgh airport. The temperature had not dropped below 22°C and was now starting to climb back to nearer the 35°C it reached each day. They would all notice the difference on arrival in London, especially Mr and Mrs Charlie who were unfamiliar with the English climate.

Suzie sat next to Mike, with Jenny and Mr and Mrs Charlie several rows behind them. Mike was glad the girls were not together, because it stopped them from comparing notes and asking each other questions that might be a little awkward for him, if Jenny let anything slip by mistake.

'Not that I'm married or tied to anyone,' he told himself. 'What I do is my own business.' But he didn't want to do anything that might lose him Suzie, so he was still pleased they sat apart.

The aircraft climbed into the ether, at the rising of the sun, silhouetting the buildings against the skyline with a golden halo. Sleeping in the aeroplane was not easy, but they were all exhausted and got some rest before they reached Nairobi. After waiting for more than an hour in a holding area, the 747 was finally ready to take them on the remainder of their journey. Mike became apprehensive each time the girls spoke to each other while they waited and did his best to keep them apart. Still tired and anxious to be on their way, the announcement to board the plane came as a welcome relief to them all.

When the flight resumed, they were all seated together, with Mike and Suzie in the outside row, and the others in the centre row. Mike's luck was holding, the two girls were still unable to chat together easily, but Suzie had noted Mike's reluctance to leave them alone, and this only confirmed her suspicions.

Over the constant drone of the engines and between meals in plastic trays, Mike and Suzie went over the events of the past few days.

'I gave you the watch as a get well gift and reminder of me when you left for England… and because you were continually asking me what the time was,' Suzie confessed.

'Yes, I thought that was probably the real reason.'

'I never dreamt that it would cause so much trouble. When did you find the key?' she asked.

'Shortly after I telephoned you about my new job at Tramer International. I knew the watch wasn't new, because you told me that it was a little something you'd picked up. What you failed to mention was that you picked it up from the soldier you shot. I was curious about it and opened the back for a look. I found a key and an account number on a piece of paper. I checked the type and key number at the library and came across only three places where that type was used, and they were all London banks. I opened a safety deposit account in each, so I could check them out. I found the right bank okay, but then discovered that you needed two keys to open each box, and the manager didn't hold the other key, as I'd expected.'

'I bet that was a disappointment.'

'Of course. It meant I couldn't find out what was in the box. I guessed somebody would want the key and might come looking for it. I had a duplicate made and hid it at Gracie's among a bunch of old keys she keeps over the fireplace. I carefully filed a couple of teeth off the original, so it wouldn't fit but still looked okay unless very carefully inspected, and put it back in the watch,' Mike explained.

'Sneaky. Did you not think that I might have given you the watch for safekeeping, and knew the key was there?'

'No. Not you, Suzie. If you'd wanted me to look after it I'm sure you'd have said so,' answered Mike with his impish grin.

'Okay, but wasn't it dangerous for Grace to have it hidden at her place?'

'Not as far as I knew. But I didn't know you'd taken the watch off the dead soldier then. I intended ringing you to ask where it came from, but events overtook me...'

'And how do you think The General found out that I had taken the watch from the soldier?' Suzie asked.

'Barney. He must have sneaked a look at your report before he went AWOL. When he read that you'd shot the soldiers following us, he guessed that you'd also taken the watch but not reported it. They thought you'd still got it and snatched you when that woman couldn't find it in your room.'

'Hmm. I wonder how long Barney'd been in The General's pay.'

'Not too long, I reckon. If he had, we might have found a reception committee waiting for us when we got to the arms dump.'

'That's true,' Suzie agreed.

'It was probably the loss of the watch and key that persuaded The General to recruit someone in the government's army to get him some answers. That's where my friend Paul came in. Lots of the soldiers used his bar, and he's sure to have known Barney and his persuasions.'

Mike and Suzie made way for a passenger sitting by the window, who wanted to squeeze past.

They settled back into their seats and Suzie asked, 'So who has the other key?'

'I don't know for sure, but I reckon it could be a guy named Dexter that The General spoke of. Jenny said he was the one that snatched Jim.'

'I hope he's okay.'

'Yes, me too. I feel a bit guilty about involving him. Apparently, Dexter is an arms dealer, so I reckon it was his shipment to The General that we destroyed.'

'Aha!' exclaimed Suzie, as pieces of the jigsaw fell into place. 'So the gems in the deposit box are probably payment for those arms.'

'Looks that way. Arms that he now hadn't got, thanks to us, and gems that he probably needed to pay for replacements, or at least didn't want to part with for something that was now blown to smithereens.'

'Right,' said Suzie. 'No wonder he was desperate to get the key back, and presumably he tried to steal the other one as well.'

'That's right. Both Dexter and The General wanted both keys.'

'The 64,000-dollar question is, who has the keys now? Is your duplicate still at Grace's?'

'Yes, I think so. I haven't told anyone where I hid it. I don't know about the other key. It was four in the morning when I rang Gracie, and she was still half-asleep, but she told me she'd had a visit by several nasty men with guns. Three were shot and Jim was taken hostage by Dexter and his wife. All of them must have been looking for the keys. Some were The General's men, I know, because when I was in the pit he delighted in trying to aggravate me by telling me they were going there.'

After moving once again to let the passenger back into his seat, Mike and Suzie talked about their narrow escape from The General, between bouts of dozing, eating and half-watching the film. They were showing *The Bodyguard*.

Jim's flight landed at Heathrow Airport at 3 p.m. He was met by his father and Grace, who had driven to the airport in his Rolls and enjoyed the 'fabulous ride', as she put it. After a subdued but nevertheless emotional meeting, they went into one of the many airport bars for a drink.

Jim graphically filled in details about his abduction by the Dexters, and how his incredible skills learned at Tramer had helped him to escape. His father smiled inwardly, listening to him. In his diplomatic career he'd heard many tales of daring deeds. Jim's exploits would hardly rate even a mention, but then it was the first time he'd encountered anything like this, and all things considered, he'd done quite well. Jim related his account of the exhilarating chase after the Dexters and how close they had come to apprehending them.

'It was really frustrating watching the Dexters cruise into the distance, after being close enough to almost touch them,' he grumbled.

'That's the way it goes sometimes,' said Sir Joseph. 'Interpol has been alerted. Even if they don't find them this time, they'll be back, and we'll get them.'

'Yes. Inspector Parker said that.'

'I must ring and find out how he's doing,' said Sir Joseph.

'When you do, give him my best wishes and thank him for all the help that he gave to me. Tell him that I hope he'll be on his feet again soon.'

'Of course.'

'Where's Colin Brooke?' Jim asked.

'He's busy doing a job for me at the moment, as a matter of fact. We caught Dexter's henchman, Dave Collins. Brooke handcuffed him to Miss Randle's wrought-iron gate during the fracas. Collins confessed that they were all looking for two watches that contained keys to a bank safety deposit box holding a lot of gems. And what's more, they seemed to think you'd got them.'

'Not me, Dad. It's funny, but Dexter asked me the same question. I don't know anything about any stolen watches or keys.'

'Hmm,' his father said thoughtfully. 'As it happens, we found them under the driver's seat in the Jaguar you drove to the marina.'

'There you are then. It must have been the chauffeur who stole them.'

'Collins shot him dead so we can't ask him, and anyway, who said anything about them being stolen?'

Jim hesitated for a second. 'Dexter. Al Dexter said they'd been stolen from him, and he thought I'd got them.'

'Hmm,' said Sir Joseph, looking over the rim of his glasses. 'Brooke is trying to track down which bank and deposit box the keys fit.'

'Mike did well, didn't he?' said Jim, changing the subject.

'Yes, he did. He must either be a resourceful or lucky man. Look, I've got to ring the office,' announced Sir Joseph, slipping his Hunter watch back into his waistcoat pocket. 'If you check with security in the arrivals area, they'll direct you to a holding room where you can wait for your friends. I'll join you later.'

'When are they due in?'

'BA068 is due to land at 17.05. See you both later,' said Sir Joseph, and left them to finish their drinks.

The long flight from Nairobi eventually came to an end. The 747 landed with a bump and the tyres sent out clouds of spray. A dull, grey evening, spitting with rain, greeted Mike and his party at London's Heathrow Airport.

Security men met them and escorted them to a room where Jim and Grace were waiting, along with a doctor and a nurse.

'Jim!' said Mike, rushing over and shaking his hand so hard Jim thought it might drop off. 'You're okay. Am I glad to see you!

I heard you were taken hostage.'

'Oh, I soon put my Tramer tuition to good use and escaped. But what on earth happened to your wrists and face?'

'I'll tell you about it later,' he said, dismissively. 'I'm really pleased that you're okay. You had me worried for a while.'

'No need to. It was just a temporary glitch until I sussed out the situation. The Dexters made the mistake of underestimating the comprehensive teaching I'd gone through at the training school,' he asserted.

Mike smiled, somewhat embarrassed before saying, 'Good for you.'

The doctor checked Mrs Charlie, and the nurse cleaned and dressed her wound. He also checked Mike's wrists and confirmed that the blisters on his face would soon heal and should leave no scars.

'Come and meet my friends,' Mike insisted to Jim.

There were smiles and handshakes all round with the introductions. Suzie was every bit as lovely as Jim had imagined her to be, even after such a long flight. She looked stunning and was charming, but exuded an underlying determination of grit and strong will that impressed him in the same way it did others.

He was equally taken with Jenny's beauty. She was just as attractive, but in a quieter way that hid her strengths and resolve. She took a fancy to him; they sparked, and hit it off straight away.

The doctor approached Mike, after seeing to Mrs Charlie. 'The wound is nasty, but not serious. The bandages should be changed in a couple of days and the wound cleaned again.'

'Right Doc, thanks,' Mike said, slapping him on the shoulder. 'I'll see that it's done.'

Sir Joseph Sterling entered the room with Detective Inspector Colin Brooke. Mike and Suzie greeted them warmly when introduced.

'It seems that we owe you a vote of thanks, Sir Joseph,' Mike said, with genuine appreciation.

'I'm pleased I could help. I didn't like The General much anyway. Perhaps with him gone, the country might stabilise and eventually become democratic. Though I fear there may be more self-appointed "generals" before then, who still think that they can rule the country with a gun.'

'In our line of work, that's probably just as well, or we'd both be out of a job pretty soon,' Mike stated.

'Quite so,' said Sir Joseph, not wishing to pursue the tricky subject at that moment. 'And I've just been informed that troops have recaptured Camp West – or rather, what's left of it. It seems the rebels had a spot of bother. Apparently they kept ammunition in a wooden hut after their jungle store was blown up, and somebody set light to it. It blew a ruddy great hole in the ground and torched most of the rest of the camp. Something to do with your escape, I understand?'

'What makes you think that?' Mike asked, in all innocence.

'About a dozen government troops were helped to get away and made it back to base...'

'Ah well! Yes... maybe we did have a hand in starting things – but the camp was still in one piece when we drove through the gates.'

'That's right,' confirmed Suzie.

'Mmm, well, anyway, I'd like you all to come to my office at eleven tomorrow morning so I can get a full account of what happened,' said Sir Joseph. It was an order that was delivered in such a way that it came across as an invitation.

Everyone agreed to be there.

Sir Joseph turned to Jim. 'I spoke to your Detective Inspector Parker in St Helier Hospital. He's doing fine. The operation to remove the bullet was straightforward and he's off the critical list.'

'That's good. Thanks, Dad.'

'He says if you're ever in Jersey, be sure to give him a miss. But I'm sure he was only joking.'

Everyone had a laugh at the remark, and it helped to ease the tension.

Mike gave Jim a brief account of how he met Mr and Mrs Charlie when he introduced them, and said that they would need somewhere to stay while sorting out visas and permits.

'Charlie's a good cook. His broth takes some beating,' remarked Mike, winking at him.

Charlie's smile broke into a grin when Jim said that he was happy to let them stay with him. If they wanted to remain in

England, they would need a job, and Jim could do with a cook and was still looking for a regular housekeeper. It also looked like the job of chauffeur was going to remain vacant for the moment...

Sir Joseph held up two battered watches to Jim. 'These aren't any good to me. Brooke tells me that the keys are newly cut and unmarked. It's impossible to tell which bank they came from, let alone which box,' he said, dropping them into Jim's hands. He slapped Jim on the shoulder. 'You keep them.'

Jim winced at the pain.

His father gave him a quizzical look, and he explained, 'I'm still a bit sore from the fight last night.'

'Oh, yes,' he said. 'Well done. I'll see you all tomorrow.' And with that, he and Colin Brooke left.

Jenny leapt to Jim's side. 'If you've some aches and pains, have you thought about having a massage to smooth them away?'

'Err, no. I haven't as a matter of fact,' Jim replied uncertainly.

Jenny locked her arm through his. 'I'm a qualified masseuse. Would you like to give it a try?'

'Umm, sure. Why not?'

'You be careful how you go,' joked Mike.

'I can take care of myself,' Jim smiled, taking an envelope from his pocket. 'This is for you,' he said, handing it to Mike. He walked through the doorway, arm in arm with Jenny, followed by Mr Charlie supporting his hobbling wife.

Mike opened the envelope to find two original keys and a note with a deposit box account number.

He looked at Suzie with a big grin on his face. 'The boy's coming along nicely,' he exclaimed.

'*Didn't* he do well?' said Suzie delightedly.

'How would you like another holiday? Without Martin this time. I fancy buying a yacht and taking a cruise.'

'Sounds great,' said Suzie, grabbing his arm. 'But later. Right now, how about those several dozen silk shirts you promised to dress me in... Randy?'

The End... or is it?